D0952736

THE HEART AND THE WILL

THE HEART AND THE WILL

SUSAN EVANS McCLOUD

Bookcraft
Salt Lake City, Utah

Library of Congress Catalog Card Number: 84-72388
ISBN 0-88494-551-0

First Printing, 1984

Lithographed in the United States of America
PUBLISHERS PRESS
Salt Lake City, Utah

To Jean Dunn

a Scottish lass
with the heart of an angel
who has loved me
believed in me
nurtured me
and blessed my life

Preface

Since the publication of *Where the Heart Leads* in October of 1979, I have received numerous requests for a sequel. Although my four succeeding novels, a children's book, and a biographical work have been introduced into the LDS market since then, this is the first opportunity I have had to meet those requests of my persistent and patient readers. I thank them for their loyalty and interest.

It has been a delight and a challenge to take up the threads of the Buchanan story, sort them, reweave them, reentangle them, reshape them again. Although this book continues their story, this book can stand squarely on its feet as a tale of its own, a tale whose substance and development are in no way dependent upon the original story. In this novel the characters take on new life, new depth, new dimension; but they are true to themselves in every way, and behave as they ought to behave, in accordance with the impact of personalities and circumstances upon them.

I would like to extend my thanks to those who have assisted me in this effort: Dr. Fred Buchanan and Betty MacRae for their information on Scottish facts and customs; Greg Seal for his continuing counsel on legal matters; Dr. Jack Johnson for his medical advice; Dan Briggs, gunsmith, for his recommendations and guidance concerning weapons; and Brian Patch, goldsmith, for his sensitive expertise.

1

Led on by heaven—
And crown'd with joy at last.
PERICLES

The skies, though a weak sun was shining, were filling with snow. Swirls of small brittle flakes danced against the tall, leaded-glass windows. Andrew leaned close and placed his hand lightly on Hannah's shoulder. "Snow falling on your wedding day means happiness," he whispered. "You're promised a dollar for every flake that lights on you." There was laughter in his voice and his blue eyes sparkled.

This is a fairy-tale wedding, Hannah thought. *Not like anything I'd ever anticipated; not like the pictures I used to draw for myself.* She could hear from the long adjoining room the sound of the pipes, a sweet high wail that swirled through the air. "She's wooed and married and a'," the piper was playing. Nan smiled at the quaint, foreign phrase. "Wooed and married—" so she was, and it all had been dreamlike, though at times overcast with a tinge of nightmare. And now, after all that had passed, she was really here in Scotland with Andrew beside her, living in a great house that was more like a castle, that fit into her fanciful girlhood dreams more than it seemed to fit into the world of the 1980s.

She was happy for these few quiet moments alone with Andrew to savor the event that had just taken place. They could not have been married in the large Church of Scotland kirk, though the banns had been called and properly posted. And since they were not yet baptized Mormons, the temple sealing would have to wait. The LDS bishop had suggested that the ceremony be performed at home, at Bieldmor. What more beautiful or romantic place? So Hannah Martin, twenty-one years old, of Nauvoo, Illinois, had stood in the great hall of her own new home while a Mormon bishop pronounced the words that made her belong to Andrew, and Andrew to her, words that opened to them a new world of promise and untried possibility.

Bieldmor House was the ancestral home built by the original Andrew Buchanan, whose skills and determination had carved a fortune. His pride and tenacity, his love for his lost son, the strange will he had concocted to keep the search for his son's seed alive, had all reached through time and distance to lift Hannah out of one life into another. Lined with tall oak trees, massive and gray and forbidding-looking, Bieldmor stood a gaunt sentinel in the sheltered valley, almost a mar on the landscape, not really in keeping with the pleasant, peaceful greens of meadow and trees and gardens. The house had been built as a symbol, a statement by a man who had grappled with life hand to hand and emerged the victor. It was not the gentle, white-columned home of men whom life had pampered for generations. And yet—Nan glanced over at Andrew. He surely was pampered, cushioned, and eased by the wealth that was his.

Will I ever be accepted as mistress of this house? Nan wondered. Andrew assured her she would, though his mother, Jessie, ruled here now. In time she must learn from Jessie how to run such a house.

Nan smiled up at Andrew and took his extended hand. Her thin satin slippers made no sound as they crossed cool marble floors, thin polished wood planks, and passed through the open doorway back into the Great Hall, which was flanked now with food and flowers—roses, lady's fingers, golden gorse, and white heather—and bright with the tartans of many clans.

The hours flew by merrily. There were healths to be drunk, with the bottle passed "deasil" or sunwise, and dancing to the strains of piano, pipes, and fiddle, with Nan and Andrew leading off the first reel. Nan had carefully learned the country dances, which *appeared* to be simple, but often required quite fancy footwork. Though uncertain and a little awkward, she loved the dancing as the throb of the bagpipes ran through her veins. Each time she came around the circle and saw Andrew waiting she was struck anew by how handsome he was, how masculine he looked in his hose and tartan with lace at his throat and a plaid at his shoulder and the small skean dhu or dagger tucked into his sock.

There was much friendly laughing and jesting when the tall, red-haired piper came to claim his honor—a piece of the bride's garter to be tied about his pipes as a trophy! Nan loved the soft Scots speech and the gentle way the men treated her. How gallant the gentlemen were! Half a dozen escorted her to the table, refilled her glass with ginger ale, brought second helpings of breads and salads and steak pie, entertained her with boastful tales of their own clan's prowess. She loved their manner and the poignant tales they told her; it was with difficulty that Andrew pried her away.

"Those lads have too many stars in their eyes," he said. The press of his hand on her waist was warm and intimate and she loved it. She had not failed to notice the many girls who flirted with Andrew and cast him sidelong glances. But she would not mention the fact. How could she blame them? Many must have entertained hopes that he would choose them. Now the strange, foreign girl had spoiled their dreams.

But tonight Nan felt neither strange nor foreign, nor awkward and shy, as she sometimes did. Today was her day and not one thing marred it. At one point Jessie glided near, squeezed her hand, and whispered, "You're holding up beautifully, lass." That was all. But coming from Jessie, it was impressive. This slender, regal woman who was Andrew's mother overawed Nan, even frightened her. She had heard of the woman's explosive nature, her jealousies, her frosty pride. And Nan had come from that hated place across the ocean to claim Jessie's only son. She must tread with care. She wanted to win this woman's approval—if not her love, at least her respect. And tonight, with the warmth, the lights and music, with kind faces around her and Andrew at her side, she felt she could overcome all, achieve anything she desired.

It was nearing midnight, but the crowd was still spirited. It was not just a wedding celebration they had come to. It was December thirty-first—New Year's Eve—a more important holiday in Scotland than Christmas. Andrew had returned from America in November; Nan had followed him a few weeks later. The holidays seemed a perfect time to marry. *When December's snows fall fast, marry and true love will last.* So ran the superstitious rhyme. And why not New Year's Eve for a wedding, when the whole world celebrated with you? Such was a popular practice in Scotland, Andrew had explained. For the new couple would awaken the following morning having been happily married for a year, and the day would bring in the double New Year of time and of wedded life.

Now they cut the wedding cake together, Andrew's hand placed over Nan's. Even this was different—not the frothy white cake Nan remembered from weddings at home, but a dark, heavy cake made with nuts and fruit and marzipan, spread with a hard glaze called royal icing. The small top tier Andrew set carefully to one side. "You must keep that for the christening cake of your first child," Jessie told them.

Nan smiled. "Our first child . . ." She had a fleeting vision of a little boy who looked like Andrew, dashing about in a miniature kilt and calling her "mither" in the lovely, lilting accent of Andrew's speech.

While the guests ate wedding cake Nan stood with Andrew's arms about her, sleepy and content. The last minutes ticked away rapidly. This year that was ending had brought her many surprises. It was incredible to think how the hands of time had reached backward and forward and wound their two lives together. Probability had little to do with life, Nan decided. Destiny breaks all the rules and will not be thwarted. And she, who had had little faith in her own tomorrows, now stood surrounded in dreams come true.

Many voices counted out the last fleeting seconds. The hour struck; Andrew sought her lips and whispered words for her only to hear.

"Should auld acquaintance be forgot . . ." How musical, how soft Burns's song sounded here! All over the world people were singing these very same words to welcome in the New Year. Her own family, sitting at Grandma's long table, would be singing as she was singing now:

"For auld lang syne, my dear, for auld lang syne . . ."

Nan closed her eyes. There was too much for her to take in here, too many crowded feelings she couldn't identify. But laced through all was this warm contentment, this bright assurance of Andrew's love.

The fiddle began to play, people paused to listen, quieting their laughter and speech, tapping feet to the contagious rhythm.

Step we gaily, on we go, heel for heel and toe for toe,
Arm in arm and row on row, all for Mairi's wedding . . .

Half a dozen voices began to sing and then others joined them. What gaity sang through the music! Nan strained to listen, to catch the unfamiliar words.

Red her cheeks as rowans are,
Bright her eye as any star,
Fairest of them all by far—

Many eyes turned with the words in her direction, to smile or wink mischievously. Nan felt a great tenderness for these people who seemed so willing to accept her as one of them.

"It's true," Andrew whispered. "There's no lass more lovely than my nut-brown maiden, Nan." He kissed the curve of her neck; his arms tightened around her. She touched his hand gently with light, tentative fingers. The music seemed to rise and swell— Nan wanted to dance with the music, skip and swirl and laugh out loud in sheer pleasure.

Plenty herring, plenty meal,
Plenty peat to fill her creel,
Plenty bonnie bairns as weel,
That's our toast—

With a shriek of discord the violin skidded, then halted. The voices stopped in midair as the great doors, flung suddenly open, banged against the far walls and reverberated with echo after echo of deep sound.

The figure that appeared in the open doorway seemed to bring the cold breath of the night with him. His hair was dark and tousled and wild. He remained framed in the doorway one breathless moment, then strode forward until he stood facing the bridegroom and bride. His blue eyes burned. Nan gazed into them, unable to turn her own away.

"What's this cousin—brother? Reveling—and myself not invited?"

The voice, the aspect, the air were so much like Andrew. Nan drew in her breath with remembered pain.

"Sticky business to include Edwin on such a day." A bitter smile pulled one side of the thin mouth upward. The voice was hard with sarcasm, cold with disdain.

"Were you afraid Edwin might cause a disturbance, cousin? Or worse—disgrace both himself and you." Edwin brought forth a bottle from under his coat and took a long swallow.

He's less drunk than he's acting, Andrew thought as he watched him. *It's the same old Edwin—the dashing act, the grandiose gesture. He wants to be seen in this light. It's his only cover.*

Edwin moved a few steps closer and his voice, when he spoke, was lower. Those nearest leaned forward and strained to hear.

" 'Tis I should be standing beside you, Andrew, and you know it. Not MacGregor, that fop. He's nothing to you." He flung back his head and flashed a look at the silent watchers. "Don't gawk at me. 'Tis first-footing, I am. Is it not luck for a dark-haired man to first cross the threshold? Good luck to the house for another year."

He moved swiftly; before Nan knew it his arm was about her, yanking her abruptly from Andrew's hold. "Aye, some bring luck, fair lass, and others disaster. Your happiness brings the destruction of me."

Perhaps he's more drunk than I thought. Andrew took a step forward. Edwin held up his hand as if to stop him.

"Just one kiss from the bonnie bride, a harmless gesture." He drew Nan close and his lips upon hers were firm and demanding.

She pulled back, but not away—his arm still held her, as did his eyes, in which she could now read more pain than hate.

"I impose." He held Nan at arm's length but did not release her. "The banished have no choice but to impose." The bitter mouth twisted into the crooked, pathetic mockery of a smile. He cocked his head and his burning eyes never left Andrew's face. "I have come—heaven knows why, Andrew. There is no help for me here, no home."

Across the room Jessie stirred and the uncertain group stirred with her, with a sound like the restless rustling of winter leaves.

"No word for me, cousin? Well, I shall leave you." His hand slid down Nan's arm until only their fingers were touching. "But trust, Andrew, you are not yet rid of me. You may play your pompous games—you may banish me, cousin. But you shall yet live to rue the day. You can never destroy me utterly."

His hand moved and drew his dark coat closer about him. His words, a grandly flung challenge, seemed more a cry to Nan, who stood close enough to feel them, to watch the tight lips tremble as he spoke, to see the spots of moisture stand out on his forehead.

He turned. His movements were swift and graceful. Looking neither right nor left, in a moment he had disappeared as quickly as he had come. For an instant his presence hung in the air around them. Then, with a long sigh, the party unburdened itself. There were shufflings and stirrings and low whispers. Nan, watching Andrew, tried to read his eyes. She could not. He, too, was good at disguises. She looked up to find Jessie at her side, surprised to see tears in the woman's eyes.

"Stay with her, Mother." Andrew turned. He had guests to attend to. He moved confidently among the crowd. With a touch, a look, a swift word he dispelled the shadow that one man had cast upon them all.

Nan didn't mean to speak; the words came unbidden. "You love him, don't you? Edwin, I mean."

Jessie's beautiful eyes studied Nan's face carefully before she answered. "Like a son," she replied, "like another son."

Nan reached for her hand, surprised when Jessie gave it.

"Did he frighten you?" Jessie asked softly.

Nan struggled to form a careful reply. "Yes, he is good at frightening me," she answered. "But something about him made me want to cry. Something sad and lost and little-boyish about him."

There was a gentle pressure of the slender fingers against her own, then both women lapsed into a heavy silence while the people in the great room, with their wits back about them, ventured to laugh and clown and make merry again, forgetting the turbulent moment, the awkward disturbance. Hannah marked the troubled look in her mother-in-law's eyes, and knew that for Jessie there would be no forgetting.

2

We, Great in our hope, lay
our best love and credence
Upon thy promising fortune.
ALL'S WELL THAT ENDS WELL

You think it will be that easy? Get serious, Bradley. Such things don't happen in real life.''

Brad stared at his younger brother, feeling cross and weary. It was true, James had met Andrew when he was here. But he didn't *know* Andrew as Brad felt he knew him. James had no testimony of the thing.

''When are you scheduled to leave?'' Sheila asked. Brad looked at his brother and sister and tried to smile.

''Next Friday. A morning flight.''

''And does Jennie go with you?''

Brad shook his head. ''There's no way Jennie can go. We can't leave the children—we've no one to leave them with, anyway. And we can't afford for both of us to fly there.''

James rose and paced a few steps, then stood facing his brother. ''I just don't see the sense in it, Brad. If it's real—if by some cockeyed miracle this fortune materializes—well, can't you wait till then to go over to Scotland?''

Brad ran tight fingers through his short, sandy hair. ''You don't understand. It's not really me, it's Andrew. For some reason of his own he wants me there.''

With an impatient gesture James returned to his chair, folding his arms in an unconscious gesture of disapproval.

"You've got to try to see it from his side for a minute. Andrew's the one who spent three months of his life in a foreign country, searching for a needle in a haystack—a search imposed upon him, you remember." Brad had to somehow try to explain, though it still sounded crazy—a crazy, incredible thing. "Then suddenly the unexpected, the miracle happened."

"Why does it matter so much to Andrew?" Sheila injected. "Didn't his finding you cause all kinds of family trouble?"

"Apparently. I'm not sure—I don't know the facts. Andrew doesn't think any of that should concern us. To us it's the money—to him it's the fascination of finding relatives, lost blood—discovering something that had been hidden for generations."

A slight smile teased at the corners of Sheila's mouth. "Do you ever let yourself think about the money?"

Brad didn't answer; James coughed and looked down.

"I don't," she continued, not waiting for their reply. "I can't. It would drive me crazy, you know. I just can't imagine—enough money to make us all wealthy, just like that."

Brad smiled slightly. None of them was rich now, that was certain: himself a schoolteacher just eking out a living, Sheila married to a teacher herself, James an electrician. Their other sister, Mary Ann, lived in California where her husband ran a computer consulting firm. He made five times what he could in Utah, but expenses in California were high. They might be comfortable. But rich—wealthy? Brad had to admit that it didn't seem real to him, either. Yet he was the one who had prayed and believed, who had wanted so desperately to know who he was, to uncover the knowledge of his true blood ancestry. He was the eldest son—the one with the ring.

"Do you trust him? Do you really trust him, Brad?"

Brad laughed out loud, almost with relief. "Heavens, yes. I've no doubts about Andrew, no doubts at all." If the truth were known, it was himself he doubted. Could he be everything Andrew wished him to be? Could he handle whatever challenges were coming?

"So what's the format, what's the plan? You go to Scotland. Then what?" James sounded less hostile, a little more resigned.

"I think Andrew wants me there to expedite things, whatever happens. And he wants to, well . . . introduce me, show me around."

"He's really taken with this long-lost relative business?"

Brad frowned. "Well, for heaven's sake, James, I can understand that. And there's the Church besides."

"Is he really converted? Is he . . . well, you know . . . sincere?" Sheila leaned forward a little.

"Look here, you guys. I *know* Andrew. Let's cut out this third-degree business, all right? Anyway, I don't have all the answers." Brad rubbed his eyes; he sounded as tired as he felt. Sheila leaned over and put her hand on his arm.

"I'm sorry, Brad. It's so crazy, that's all." She paused. "Besides, I do think about the money. At night when I can't get to sleep." She giggled abashedly. "You guys know how it is with women. I spend it over and over again. First for the bills and clothes for the kids, and then a new bedroom set, a microwave, a piano . . ." Her voice trailed, a little apologetically.

"Maybe it's best that you go over there. Get it all settled. We'll help take care of Jennie and the kids."

"Thanks, James." Brad felt as if a burden had been lifted. With support, however tentative, he could make it. Without it, on his own, how hard it would be!

He looked down at the heavy ring on his finger. He wore it all the time now. In a manner of speaking the ring was taking him home—or at least he was taking the ring back where it had come from, completing some kind of a circle, replacing a chink that had been lost for four long generations. He twisted the gold band thoughtfully. A diamond flanked by two smaller rubies. He was one of those rubies. He belonged. This was what he had prayed for; he couldn't turn from it. In some world, so different from his world, something was waiting—a piece of the future with his name written on it. That future was meant to be his; he would not deny it.

3

To seal love's bonds new-made . . .

MEASURE FOR MEASURE

It was a strange honeymoon at first, but Hannah loved it. Andrew took her on tour of all the family holdings, introducing her in place after place with a boyish pride. Most of the mills were just down the road in Paisley, but there were also the water works further up the Clyde, the banks and other companies the family held stock in, and the land outside Glasgow Andrew hoped soon to develop. It was too much for Nan to grasp. She couldn't imagine herself being part of this. Such wealth she had only heard of in stories and movies. She held her breath in fear that it might all melt away.

Most of the workers Nan met were sincerely friendly, despite the fact that she was so obviously an outsider. Once or twice she felt a coldness, a holding back. One young man in particular, as Andrew introduced her, stood with his feet planted far apart, arms folded over his chest, and surveyed her darkly.

"Seems like unco trouble to me, going all the way to America for a wife." He spoke to Andrew, but his eyes never left Nan's face. "Was it worth it to you, Andrew? Was it, now?"

The harshness in his voice made Hannah shudder. She was surprised to see Andrew smile at the disgruntled fellow and clap his shoulder in a friendly manner. "Aye, Davie. It was muckle worth it. Hannah's worth everything I own and ten times over."

Nan thought his reply a little exaggerated. Davie slowly dropped his eyes, shrugged his shoulders, and turned. For the first time he looked directly at Andrew. "Well, you've power to suit yourself, mon, that's for sure."

He walked off then, with his back to them. Andrew took Nan's arm and steered her out into the light.

"Please don't call me Hannah when you introduce me to people, Andrew," she whispered. "It sounds so staid! I see a picture of some dour pioneer woman with hair pulled back in a bun and a face full of wrinkles."

Andrew laughed. "That's not what the men see, I can assure you."

She dropped her eyes at that, a little embarrassed. When they were back in the car and driving away from the building she ventured to ask the question in her mind. "That young man, the last one you introduced me to. Why did he act so strange, Andrew?"

She watched Andrew's dark brow crease and his eyes grow troubled.

"Davie Ross? That's easy enough to explain. He's an old boyhood chum of Edwin's. He's bound to hold some rancor against me now."

"Why does he continue to work for you, then, if he doesn't like you?"

Andrew gave her a searching, but tender glance. "Jobs aren't that easy to find around here. Besides, he's worked in the mill since he was a lad. Davie and his father, and his father before him."

She nodded, feeling a little subdued. A lump grew in her throat as she thought of what she wanted to say next. They had talked very little of Edwin since that night—their wedding night, when he made his strange appearance.

"Andrew, how is Edwin? I mean—is he all right? Do you worry about him sometimes . . ." Nan held her breath. It seemed to take so long for Andrew to answer.

"All right? Edwin's always 'all right' and he's never 'all right.' "

"What does that mean?"

Andrew sighed. "It means, Nan, that Edwin has an uncanny ability to land on his feet no matter how hard he falls. But he's never had his life quite, well, quite in order. I don't think he's ever been really happy—you know—"

"I know." She took his hand. He seemed sad and quiet. She didn't want to upset him, and yet she felt compelled to go on.

"Do you ever wish—do you ever regret—" She couldn't quite say it. Andrew's frown was growing darker but his voice sounded tired rather than angry.

"I don't want to talk about Edwin, Nan. It's no cut-and-dried thing—not all black or all white—I know that. He did what he felt he had to do, and so did I. It's what he chose to do, what he was willing to stoop to! But not much can be done about any of it now."

Nan wasn't sure she agreed, but she didn't push it. She knew that the two men, who looked so alike physically—with the same lean, athletic frames, the deep-set blue eyes, the thick black hair—were really quite different in nature. She knew Edwin had hurt Andrew deeply, betrayed his trust. Yet beneath all this, *before* all this, they had been like brothers. Would it be impossible to ever find a way back?

When the tour of approval was completed Nan breathed a sigh of relief and was happy to drive to Prestwick Airport and catch an early morning flight to London. When she had first come, scant weeks before her wedding, she had flown directly to Scotland. Her father had taught her an early love of the English poets, but she had never been to London before. She could hardly wait; she had always wanted to go there.

The following days began a spell of enchantment for Hannah. She saw with her own eyes the romantic scenes of song and story. She and Andrew walked the Mall through St. James Park and gazed upon Buckingham Palace, shopped and ate at Picadilly Circus, walked the paths of Hyde Park and Kensington Gardens, where grew the delicate hawthorne trees Andrew loved. They visited Trafalgar Square and saw Nelson's Column, took a boat down the Thames to view the Houses of Parliament and Westminster Abbey.

Nan observed it all through new eyes, her gaze enhanced by the rosy perception of love.

They attended the theatre: Agatha Christie's *Mouse Trap; Evita,* the magical mistress of Argentina; *Amadeus,* the moving, tragic story of Mozart. In the National Gallery Nan stood and gazed at the startling portrait of Lady Jane Grey at the time of her execution, guileless in an exquisite white dress, her arms stretched out in silent entreaty. The spirit of the past, how real it seemed here! Nan felt her own spirit respond, almost painfully.

Most impressive of all was their visit to the Tower of London, the gray fortress encircled with high gray walls, housing so many dark, mute towers and buildings. Where the Thames licks the feet of the Tower stood Traitor's Gate, dank and almost moaning with old sorrows. Nan stood before the house where young Anne Boleyn had waited for death so courageously, and the cobblestone square on the peaceful green where the old chopping block stood harmlessly under the sun.

"William Wallace died here, Nan. Remember?"

Nan nodded. She remembered all too well the stories Andrew had told of the Scottish hero who in the late 1200s had suffered great personal loss for his country and defeated the English at Stirling Bridge, preparing the way for King Robert the Bruce to follow, only to be betrayed and captured—then drawn and quartered and beheaded here. How personal it seemed, how real his suffering!

"It matters, doesn't it, Andrew?" she murmured softly. "What one man does—how he lives his life." It was hard to put into words the vague, trembling feelings. "You and I—it will someday matter what we do. In ways we can never dream of now."

Andrew took her hand and they walked together, the fat ravens cawing raucously close above.

"Do you know the superstition about the ravens?"

"No, tell me, please," Nan urged.

"If the ravens ever leave the Tower, England will fall; she will crumble and cease to be."

Nan felt a sudden shudder pass through her. She smiled, but the smile felt stiff. "I hope they stay here—lovely and eerie and heavy with the past. There's something vital about preserving our past, Andrew."

One man came to her mind more strongly than ever: Andrew Buchanan, mill boy, weaver at the age of thirteen, who scrimped and sacrificed to establish his own mill, married well, grew step by step to position and power, who wouldn't let go of life even after he died, but dictated to his sons and their sons to follow.

"Charles didn't know, when he left Scotland, when he chose his own divergent path, how many lives would be changed and influenced by his choice, even long after he was dead."

"That's strange, I was thinking of Charles myself, Nan. Would he do the same thing over again? If he could see us, would he be satisfied?"

There were no answers. The questions hung and hovered till the ravens swooped them up on long silken wings and carried them over the Thames and away.

Germany. That was one place Nan had never dreamed of. They flew to Berlin, a city Andrew promised her she would love, and here Nan discovered a different world altogether. This city of over two million Germans was an exciting metropolis and more; it was a wonderland of rivers, lakes, and forests.

They toured the Olympic Stadium designed by Albert Speer and built by Hitler in 1936, and the Tiergarten, a large park where the embassies used to stand, still scattered with old statues, though Andrew explained that most of them had been ruined during the war. Nan liked best Winged Victory atop the Victory Tower, built at the end of the Franco-Prussian War when the German states were united. They walked the steep, narrow stairs to the top of the tower, Nan clinging to Andrew most of the way. *How narrow my own life has always been,* she thought as she struggled upward.

They ate and shopped at the Europa Center, laughed at the rare panda bears in the Zoologischer Garten. It was a rainy January, deeply chilly, but not bitter cold. Well-bundled they rode the ferry to Pfaueninsel or Peacock Island, Nan grateful for Andrew's German, however scanty. Here they roamed narrow walks through the quiet forest and ate a picnic lunch they had brought. Then a boat carried them further up the Havel to Tegel and they spent a charming evening at Alt Tegal, a re-created village of old shops and buildings, where no twentieth century cars were allowed. The street cafes still had a scattered attendance, but they sat inside where the lights were warm, eating varieties of Balkan sausage and rice and talking together.

Nan watched Andrew as she did so often, amazed still to think that he really was hers. These days of intimate living together had done nothing to spoil her trust and regard. Andrew was warm-hearted and easy to live with. She was the more emotional of the two. The thought teased at her as it did so often: *I made a much better bargain than Andrew did.*

She was quiet as they rode the subway from Tegel Station, switched at Leopoldplatz, and finally reached der Kurfuerstendamm and their own hotel.

"You're pensive tonight, Nan—or only tired?"

"I'm missing my family some," she admitted. "Father would love to see all I've seen. He'd condense it into rich capsules for his students." She laughed, but her voice sounded small in the clear night air. "And Mother—what would it be like . . ."

Andrew pulled her to him, aware of how painfully her own marriage had turned her thoughts toward her mother. "Nan, I feel powerless at such times to help you. I wish I had known your mother; I wish she could share in our life and our happiness."

She pillowed her head for a moment against his warm shoulder. Her mother had been dead since she was a child. Why did she still feel the loss so keenly? What a baby she was! Andrew had given her the world—wasn't that sufficient?

"Ich liebe dich," he whispered, and he kissed her. And in the kiss her world was restored. She clung to him, full of joy and longing.

The capstone, the grand finale of all their wandering was Rothenburg ob der Tauber, the storybook city that had stood unmolested one thousand years. The narrow cobblestone streets were flanked with picturesque shops to entice every whim. They entered the establishment of *Ernst Geissendorfer,* specializing in hand engravings on silk. Nan noted the sign: *Seit 1078.*

"Is that serious?" she whispered to Andrew.

He smiled. "That's right. Since 1078."

"That's impossible. Nothing's that old and still standing." She laughed softly as a thought struck her. "Whatever did you think of us at Nauvoo? Proudly showing off our ancient relics—all of one hundred and fifty years old!"

Andrew didn't laugh in return as Nan had expected. "What's the matter with that? They were old to you. And they have a firm claim of their own, don't you think, as far as historical interest is concerned."

He held the door for her and they walked out into the bright sunlight that reflected off the red-orange roofs, seeming to borrow a richer warmth from their color. He could sense that something was bothering her.

"Nan, you can't expect me to criticize Nauvoo. I came there a weary, homesick traveler. I found kindness and hope—I found love and you."

"You can be so eloquent, Andrew," she said, and she meant it. "I'm the writer—the one who's supposed to be able to talk like that."

"*Write* like that. Talking and writing don't always have much to do with each other."

They were approaching the Marktplatz fountain. Nan sat on the rim, and looked up at the tall, dark man beside her. "I love you so much, Andrew," she said. "But I feel so meager, so inadequate."

He sat down slowly beside her. "You mustn't, Hannah. I meant to please you with all this—" he spread out his hands—"this display. I didn't mean for it to overwhelm you."

"It's not just all this—it's you and your world. I don't fit in, I'm not prepared—what can I contribute?"

He cupped her chin in his hand and forced her to meet his eyes. "We'd better stop this before it gets well started. Contributing, fitting in—that's nonsense, Hannah." He paused. How could he explain this to her? Her eyes gazed wide and innocent, waiting his words.

"You're the woman I love. I married *you,* Hannah. Just be yourself and I'll be well satisfied."

"I'm not sure what you mean."

"Well, neither am I, but you'll find a way. Your fears could spoil anything you try to do, and you know it."

Nan nodded slowly. "You're right, I know. I'd just hate to fail you, to ever disappoint you."

She spoke softly, with her eyes averted. Andrew smiled to himself. She was still just a child in so many ways. Not much older than his sister, Janet, inexperienced—and these past months had been filled with change. Perhaps it had been too much all at once. He'd be gentle with her. It was easy to be gentle with Nan.

He drew her away from the Marktplatz and they walked together, discussing their immediate plans. First on the agenda would be the arrival of Brad Richards. Andrew seemed in a fever to have the whole business of the trusts and the will settled. And he was eager to share his world with Brad. Nan listened while he explored his ideas with her. *I will never tire of the sound of his voice,* she thought. It was that which had first attracted her to him, which had first, incongruously, drawn them together.

That night a heavy snow fell and the fairy-tale city, blanketed now, seemed to settle under it with a pleased sigh. Andrew fell asleep easily, as he always did. Nan lay awake, feeling drowsy, but contented. Carefully she left the bed and went to the window. She could taste the cold, clean air that seeped in through the cracks in the casement. She looked out. The orange roofs were gone; a broad field of white, cut by startling angles, shone pale in the moonlight. The bare, outstretched arms of the trees were now hung with cottony clumps of snow. The meandering path of stone walls was outlined with snow. Everywhere Nan looked was an image of beauty. She shivered, but remained there, unwilling to turn away, to break the spell of peace and perfection the night scene wove.

Andrew stirred in his sleep and she glanced toward him, feeling suddenly tender, remembering those ecstatic, painful, early emotions. When she had met him, when she had showed him the city that first day, she could never have dreamed the events the next months held for her: lost ancestors, missing gravestones, ominous strangers, her own great-great-grandfather's journal that held the key, and a gift bought for her when she was a child by a woman now dead—a gift that had waited nine years for her to receive it, a gift that had helped to change her life. Love and disappointment and treachery—hope and dreams come true—it had all been there. If she'd known that first day, would she have been frightened? Undoubtedly so—but she wouldn't have run away.

With some reluctance she drew back from the window, crossed noiselessly to stand beside the bed. She bent over the sleeping form of her young husband, brushed the stray hairs from his forehead, and kissed his cheek.

I must not run away now. No one knows his tomorrows. No one sees more than one step at a time. She walked around the bed and climbed in on her own side, curling up against the warmth of the man who slept there. *I'll be content,* she promised herself, *with one day at a time. I won't conjure up fears, I won't try to see ahead. As long as I have Andrew beside me . . . Andrew beside me . . .*

She fell asleep with his name on her lips and a youthful determination in her heart.

4

What kin are you to me?
What countryman? what name?
what parentage?
TWELFTH NIGHT

It was a big plane, the DC-10, bigger than Brad had ever been on before—not that he'd actually traveled by plane much. He'd served a stateside mission in the South, flown from Salt Lake to New Orleans and back again. And once as a boy he had flown to San Francisco to visit a cousin who lived there. Scant experience for a man of thirty-four who was flying across the ocean to claim a fortune.

The thought sent a chill along his spine. That was what he was doing, wasn't it? Boarding this plane and traveling to a country he'd never seen, a country he knew very little about, to arrive on the doorstep of people who were strangers. What was he to do? Just stand there, his arms stretched out, and expect Andrew to fill them with mythical treasure?

He felt a touch on his arm and turned. It was Jennie. He looked into her eyes and smiled. "I'm going to miss you."

Her smile was slow and more thoughtful. "Perhaps at first, but you'll be busy . . . so many new things."

He put his arm around her shoulder and drew her to him. "Oh, Jennie, this seems a preposterous thing to do."

Her smile grew wider and warmer. "I know, Brad. Remember that day when Nan and Andrew came?"

He nodded. He could still see them, a lovely young couple, framed in his doorway. "I'm Andrew Buchanan—I called you earlier. May I come in?" It had been more than the Scottish accent, Brad remembered, that gave Andrew's voice a lilting sound. He had been fairly bubbling over with pleasure.

Brad had glanced at Jennie, wondering why. He had been mystified since the call came for him at school and the soft, accented voice on the line had said, "I'm Andrew Buchanan from Lanarkshire, Scotland. I'm distantly connected to you, Mr. Richards. I have some news I know you'll be interested in. Good news of your ancestors—your family line." A simple statement, but it sent a shock through his system. *News of his ancestors, his family line*—the miracle he had been praying for!

Jennie shook him a little. "Brad, don't worry. Things will be all right. They'll love you, I know they will."

"Jennie, how can you figure me out so well?"

"I've had some practice." She shrugged, but her eyes showed her pleasure. She and Brad sat silently then, lost in their own thoughts. When the moment came it was difficult saying good-bye. Since being married they had never been separated for longer than a day or two. Jennie clung to him a little, but she didn't cry, at least not while Brad could see. Once he turned away he didn't pause or look back to wave. He couldn't. It was all he could do to keep walking ahead.

"Don't expect me to be kind, Andrew. He's a usurper! I don't feel the way you do about the whole thing. I don't think it's fair for you to expect me—"

"All right, Janet, all right. I know how you feel—"

"Oh no, you don't. And what's more, I don't think you want to." Janet's voice was angry and tight; she was close to tears.

"Keep your voice down or Mother will hear you."

"Oh, really, Andrew! Is it Mother you're worried about, or Nan?"

Andrew wasn't an easy man to anger. But he glared at his sister. "Come with me," he demanded. He took her by the arm and marched her outside, past the drive, down the flagstone path that led to the gardens. The brisk walk cooled his anger a little. He slowed his steps and released her.

"We'd best settle this, Janet."

"It can't be settled." She stood with her feet firmly planted, her head thrown back.

"Whatever do you mean? It's got to be settled."

Janet laughed. "That's right, Andrew. Everything your way—everything neatly cubbyholed into its place. Edwin's right. You've taken a liking to playing God."

"Don't bring Edwin into this—"

"For heaven's sake, Andrew, Edwin's the issue! You've cast him aside for this passion of yours, this American you've set up to take his place—"

"For the last time, Janet, *I* didn't do it! The man existed, the will existed—"

"But you were the one who brought them together, who pushed and pulled and turned everything topsy turvy. You're proud of yourself and you're happy, Andrew. And you don't care a bit about Edwin!"

Andrew turned—instinctively—not wanting his sister to see his expression. She was hurting him more than she knew. How could he protest love for Edwin when everything she said was true? For months he had worked to discover the man who was meant to inherit the lost son's fortune—unwittingly, not knowing the clause his grandfather had added that, if the missing descendants were not found within the specified year, the accumulated portion would divert to the issue of Sarah Bain.

Sarah Bain—his grandfather's sister, mother of Robert Bain, Edwin's father, who had died a failure and left one son—one bitter son with no legacy. Edwin—who always wished he was a Buchanan, who could spend his way through ten fortunes and not blink an eye, had discovered that he stood on the brink of his heart's desire and—never one to stand back for fate—had twisted events to his own liking, disregarding both morals and legalities. And Andrew, in a moment of shock and revelation, had banished his cousin biblically—yes, self-righteously, he supposed, as Janet accused. But the intricacies of events and emotions—Janet had no understanding of these.

"Don't try to make me feel sorry for you, Andrew. You're

brooding like you did when you were a boy. Well, I'm not Mother—it won't work with me."

Andrew turned and caught her hand, gently this time. "What's happened, Janet? It used to be you and me together. In everything, through all this mess—Father's death, my going away to America, your investigation of the Mormon church—"

"That was before Nan and before your American, Andrew. *You've* changed everything, Andrew, *you've* changed." Janet pulled her hand away. Her blue eyes trembled with unshed tears.

"Nan? Has Nan come between us, Janet?" Andrew's voice was soft and confused, and sad.

"Of course she has—not purposely, maybe." She conceded that, seeing the pain in Andrew's eyes. He moved toward her, but she stepped backward. How could a man his age be so simple, so naive! She could see tenderness and concern in his eyes as he watched her. And she knew him—she knew the next thing he might say: "I love you, we love each other, why can't we be happy?" Things just weren't that simple. Why couldn't he see?

"We were a family—you and me and Mother and Edwin—"

She had given him a small opening and he took it. "Ah, come now, Janet. Some family we were—"

"That doesn't matter. So we weren't always happy—so none of us is perfect. It doesn't matter! We were part of each other, Andrew, and you spoiled it. *How could you?*"

Her words were a childlike cry that sent a wave of compassion through him. He had always been her big brother, always been there to soothe away her tears, to comfort and hold her.

"Edwin's been more your brother than your cousin since you were boys. He looked up to you, he always tried to be like you—he loved you! And now you've destroyed him, Andrew!"

"He's destroyed himself," Andrew blurted, but Janet swept on.

"Now you're setting a stranger, a foreigner in his place. I can't understand that!"

He moved then, but she moved more quickly away. She ran lightly through the manicured gardens to the line of trees that could swallow and hide her. He watched after her a moment; he didn't follow. Her last words had been like blows. He felt worn and exhausted. He stood a moment, awkward and undecided, then turned and walked silently back to the house.

So this is Scotland, Brad thought to himself. The Scotland Charles Buchanan left behind when he boarded a vessel that sailed to New Orleans, then took passage up the river to Nauvoo, City of the Saints, nestling in a graceful curve of the Mississippi. Nauvoo, where Charles, planning a bright future, had found love and happiness, and an early death.

Both Nan and Andrew had met Brad at Prestwick Airport—Nan smiling, a little shy, Andrew warm and hearty. It was only about twenty miles from the airport to Bieldmor House and, once they drew away from the heavy congestion, Brad found himself leaning forward, searching the landscape, trying to catch all the sights Andrew pointed out.

"You give Brad no time to look at one thing before you're insisting he look at another," Nan chided, with laughter in her voice.

"It's hard to take everything in," Brad admitted, "but I love it. It's different from anything I've ever seen."

"I know," Nan agreed, "there's a different feeling. Nothing you can quite put your finger on."

Andrew sighed. For the moment he felt content. He had always been a man of action. These past weeks he had felt suspended. Now Brad was here, and things could shift into motion again.

The driveway into Bieldmor House was lined by tall rows of oak trees, barren now, tracing delicate patterns against the pale sky. *Bieldmor,* Andrew had told him, meant *great shelter* in Gaelic, and the house itself looked sheltered where it sat, the snug center of a secluded valley, concealed by the winding drive and the ancient trees. Brad had seen such houses only in movies or magazines.

"When was this house built, did you say?" He asked the question to cover his amazement. It looked more like a small castle than a house: dark and graceful, elegant and imposing, molded of some kind of stone, with four tall columns that eased its lines and a massive, recessed, fine-carved door.

"Begun in 1842, completed in '46, that is, the main building. A few years later the original Andrew added the west wing. The rest was tacked on by his son, my great-great-grandfather. Not much has been done to the place since then.'' He looked over his shoulder to where Brad sat, stiff and quiet. ''Don't let it overpower you, lad. You've as much right to be here as I have.''

''Hardly,'' Brad protested under his breath. The car stopped smoothly and Andrew cut the engine. It seemed they could hear one another breathe. Andrew opened his door and walked around the car to help Nan, taking long strides, exuberant still. He opened the door to the back seat as well. ''Come on, man, we all need to stretch our legs. There will be someone round to collect the luggage.''

Nan smiled encouragingly at their guest. ''If you must walk before you come in, Andrew, then take Brad with you. I'll go in and let your mother know we've arrived.''

The two exchanged a quick look of understanding. Brad felt relieved as he followed Andrew across the drive, over a stretch of grass to where a large pond and gardens beckoned. He wasn't ready to face the inside of that place yet.

Nan, watching them walk off together, smiled. It was like Andrew to do all he could to ease Brad's reception. He knew it would help, too, if Nan faced his mother first. She turned, surprised at her own calm. She liked Jessie. That didn't mean she wasn't duly impressed, subdued by the woman's imposing competence and self-possession. But she wasn't truly afraid of Jessie. She sensed a certain sympathy there, a warmth that the woman kept purposefully hidden.

She pushed her long hair back and behind her ear. It wasn't Jessie she was worried about today. She may prove a little distant, but she would be friendly—graciously polite, as the well-bred are. It was Janet, Andrew's sister, who posed the question. Janet, whom Andrew had painted in glowing colors as a gentle, warm, and loving girl, had seemed to change character before their eyes. She had never sincerely welcomed Nan, neither before nor after the wedding. She seemed pensive and withdrawn, and at times resentful. Would she be openly hostile to Brad? Nan hoped not.

She pushed the heavy door open and stepped inside. *Strange,* she thought, *before I came here, it was Jessie I was terrified of. I thought I could handle a younger sister.* She smiled to herself, though the smile was a little grim. *People never fit into the tidy slots we make for them. I suppose that keeps life interesting.*

She walked through the large, paneled entrance salon and up the stairway, unaware that she already moved with smooth confidence here, unaware that her presence had made a difference in the solemn, austere atmosphere of the house.

Jessie had already had enough of the stranger. She had presided at dinner, as was her duty. She had smiled and asked polite questions and listened serenely, containing her true emotions inside. The man wasn't really that bad; he wasn't offensive. He seemed well-mannered, he seemed to know his place—which surely wasn't here at Bieldmor! She wondered if even Andrew harbored regrets at the impetuosity of his actions. Watching the two men together she doubted it. Her dear, naive, idealistic Andrew.

Excusing herself she went up to her rooms, disturbed less by current events than old memories. That country—that rude, sprawling monster across the sea—kept intruding into her private existence. It had robbed her of peace, it had robbed her of her infant daughter—it had nearly taken her husband and son. Now it brought change into her life that she didn't desire. She drew back her curtain and looked out into the night. There would be snow before morning. She shivered a little. Change—always change and uncertainty. She sat down and picked up a book, but her mind wandered and she fought the unpleasant thoughts that intruded.

Janet had chosen, perhaps wisely, to be absent. And dinner had been a pleasant affair. *Brad can hold his own,* Andrew had thought as he watched him. His mother was not unimpressed, though she would never admit it. They had retired now to the gentleman's parlor where a crackling fire burned in the grate, spreading lazy warmth to the chairs where they sat.

"Would you like to retire now?" Andrew asked. "We've a big day tomorrow."

Brad nodded. He really was tired; he could hardly keep his eyes open. But he felt less tense, less awkward than he had expected.

Something about this place seemed right, seemed to stir a deep excitement within him. He fought a growing sense of anticipation; he hadn't expected this kind of response.

Nan came into the room to confer with Andrew. Brad excused himself and wandered off to find the Great Hall and the family portraits. Andrew had shown him the picture of Charles Buchanan this afternoon, but the moment had been too brief. He sought the portrait now, standing back so he had a good, clear view of the features.

Charles had the long, fine Buchanan nose, the jutting forehead, the sensitive brow. His eyes were the startling blue of Andrew's, but his hair was a lighter, warmer shade. The expression in his eyes—Brad couldn't define it. How he wished he knew more about this man! Then he smiled at his own ungrateful greed. Mere weeks ago he was still in darkness, praying for a miracle. Now he stood gazing upon the reality.

The adopted infant, baptized a Richards, had been the son of a woman named Rachel and this man—this Scottish gentleman, Charles Buchanan, who embraced a religion unpopular in his time and chose to cast his fortunes upon strange waters. And now his own had come back again. Tears stung in Brad's throat; he swallowed against them. How many times since he was a boy had he prayed and agonized over his beginnings? His being here proved one thing to him, if nothing else. It proved that his Heavenly Father was mindful of him, knew him, cared for him personally. He had that to give—he must remember. He had that to give these gracious people who had taken him into their home and their hearts and given him the knowledge he had desired, unlocking his past, unfolding a new future.

Charles Buchanan . . . he spoke the name out loud. *I hope you are not displeased with me. You sacrificed everything for what you believed in. And I am the result of that sacrifice, that belief, the living proof and justification.* He smiled at the man who gazed enigmatically down. *We'll take the future together, Charles. Together for the first time.*

"You're going and that's it, Janet. Don't try to defy me in this, too." Janet's fair blue eyes looked clouded and gray. "Don't scowl at me, Janet, you know it disarms me." That drew a slight smile from the pouting lips. "Come, you must face him sooner or later."

She sighed; she knew her resistance was vain. "All right, but only for you, Andrew."

She turned away. It was hard to displease Andrew, no matter how strong her own feelings were. She didn't want him to see how far he had won her. But as far as Andrew's American was concerned—that was another matter altogether!

It was the Sabbath and they were all going to church together. She supposed it was better having something they all could do. But she hadn't been to the LDS services for some time now. She didn't know exactly why. Something had jarred and become disjointed. It wasn't that her convictions had changed—just, perhaps, been intruded upon. She walked out into the paneled front salon and saw the American there. She hesitated, but he had already seen her.

"Hello, there. You must be Janet. I've been anxious to meet you." She could feel Andrew walk up behind her. She tried to smile. The American paused, looked more closely at her. "Andrew told me about your interest in the Church, how eager you were to be baptized."

Janet cringed. *How could Andrew have shared that with him?* There it was—the intrusion again. Brad moved closer. He had nice eyes, she noticed. His eyes were smiling, in a soft, crinkled-up-at-the-corners way.

"I admire you," he said, looking straight at her. "You found the truth all on your own, under difficult circumstances. I wonder if I'd have your courage, put to that test."

She didn't know what to reply. Andrew squeezed her elbow, steering her forward, rescuing her.

"She's spunkier than she looks." He winked at Brad. "Come on, Nan's already waiting at the car."

Despite herself, Janet enjoyed the meetings. She had a vague feeling of coming home, a pleasant memory of the warmth that had once engulfed her and drawn her here in her time of need.

Nan had attended less Mormon meetings than Janet. Each one was a new experience for her. She knew many of the hymns, thanks to Grant Morgan. She wished Grant could be here with her now. He had always been there for her to turn to, ever since she was a little girl. But she was far away and Grant was old now.

Brad loved the spirit of the people he met. The Scots had a gentle way about them. They were easy to talk to, easy to like. Sitting in sacrament meeting he missed Jennie sorely. It didn't seem right to be here alone. He felt dissevered, only half-alive without his family. He would write a long letter this afternoon and share with them everything that had happened.

Andrew watched the men and boys at the sacrament table and the leaders who sat at the pulpit. They all held the priesthood. It was Joseph Smith and the restored priesthood that had first drawn him toward this way of life. There was something in the faces of these men: something peaceful, something powerful—something he wanted. The old desires stirred. He had set them aside, busy as he had been with the business of living. They stirred, with a dull and persistent ache.

The Sabbath passed slowly but pleasantly. Janet brought Mary Cameron home with her. It was Mary who had introduced her to the Church when she and her family were taking the missionary discussions. It eased things, having the two girls to chatter together. Jessie was quiet and asked no questions about their day. She had resigned herself to her son's connection, but was secretly glad that he had not yet been baptized. Mormonism was an *American* religion. She resented that more than anything else about it. She didn't understand it, and she didn't want to. She tried to content herself with the fact that Andrew was home, safely returned to her in spite of her fears. She had submitted to the idea of an American daughter-in-law long before she met her. And Nan—Nan was pleasantly more than Jessie had hoped for.

She watched her now, serving tea to the others—hot cider, actually, with shortbread and scones. She was a graceful girl and, though she was quiet, Nan had a way of drawing people to her, making those around her feel comfortable. She approached Janet and her friend and smiled gently.

"I saved two of the nicest scones for Mary and you. And here's some warm raspberry honey."

Mary reached for the tray with a smile, but Janet pushed it away. "You shouldn't have bothered. No, thank you." Her tone was icy. The uncomfortable thought flashed through Jessie's mind: *That's how I often sound. But for Janet to take such liberties!*

She glided forward and stood beside her daughter. "You *must* try these, Janet. They're tricky to do, as you know, and Nan made them herself. I've never tasted better."

Janet glared at her mother, but she took the scones. Jessie had smoothed over the awkward moment, but she wondered what was the matter with her daughter, what caused her intense resentment of Andrew's wife. She had never been able to fathom Janet. There was not a warm, intimate feeling between the two. Some inner constraint kept the tenderness at bay, that tenderness which flowed so easily toward Andrew.

As soon as possible Janet excused herself, leaving even Mary staring hopelessly after her. She went to her room and locked her door. But the tears that had burned in her throat and made her head ache wouldn't come now to relieve her. She walked the floor, poor outlet for the emotions that churned inside. Perhaps she was growing up after all. A few months ago she would have dissolved in tears. But then, a few months ago Andrew would have come up to find her, coaxed her to open the door and let him in. Andrew could make anything right again. Just like Father.

Janet closed her eyes against the memory. She mustn't think of her father now. He was dead—he would never come back, he would never hold her again. He would never say, "Come here, Janet, my gentle lassie," with that sparkle in his eye that meant some promised pleasure. He was gone from her—Andrew was gone from her, too. Could she face life all alone?

With a sudden shudder she threw herself on the bed, but she bit back the tears. They were coming now, but she wouldn't have them. She wouldn't cry; only foolish girls cried. Tears were weak, and she mustn't give in to weakness. But the tears slid out of their own accord, and she buried her head in the pillow to silence the sound, and cried—wishing someone was there to hear.

5

You always end with a jade's trick;
I know you of old . . .
MUCH ADO ABOUT NOTHING

Andrew and Brad left for Glasgow early the following morning. Andrew was anxious to see his solicitor, sign papers, make necessary arrangements. But the day was mild and sunny and Andrew tarried, for the city was coming to life with a busy stir, and there are many fine sights to be seen in Glasgow.

"This is the largest city in Scotland," he told Brad, "second only to London in all of Great Britain."

"It's so clean, in spite of its size. How long has it been here?"

Andrew grinned at the innocent question. "You don't want to know. Its origins can be traced back to a church built here in the sixth century A.D."

"You can't be serious! Nothing can be traced back to the year 500."

"Well, it didn't become a population center until the 1100s." Andrew stopped the blue Healey along the curb and pointed upward. "See the cathedral there? It dates back to the same time, 1100."

Brad shook his head. "I can't comprehend it. I can't imagine living surrounded by things that old."

"It's all here. You can *feel* the history. Sometimes it crowds you." Andrew's voice was low and tender, almost loving. "No

Scotsman goes clad without his history, you know. It's like an outer skin he wears under his clothing—a fortification, an ancient strength."

Brad had been listening closely. "I can understand that. The Mormons feel the same way about their history."

"Yes, I know." Andrew's response was eager. "I could feel that in Nauvoo, and again in Salt Lake. They wear it like a badge; they're never unmindful of it. Every event in their lives seems related back to their beginnings."

"I suppose it has something to do with being different. The early Saints paid their way at a terrible price. Their kind of sacrifice —well, it's easy to sanctify that."

Andrew nodded. They drove to the University of Glasgow and walked the parklike grounds, then had a lunch of fresh trout and Scots-fried tatties on the crowded wharf. Brad was intrigued by the teeming activity around them, all so foreign in nature to him.

"A saltwater lake enclosed by desert is far removed from this ocean traffic. I'm fascinated," he frankly admitted.

"The old saying here is: 'The Clyde made Glasgow and Glasgow made the Clyde.' If you haven't seen the Clyde you haven't seen Glasgow. But we'd best save that for when we have leisure to take our time. Right now it's to Crombie and Stewart we're heading. We've the little matter of a will to take care of, lad."

Brad smiled, but he could feel his stomach muscles tighten—with apprehension, or just plain excitement? A few minutes later, seated across the desk from the thin, moustached, middle-aged Mr. Crombie, he wondered if his reaction had been some kind of premonition. As soon as he met the man's eyes he knew something was wrong.

"Nasty business, this, I'll admit I didn't expect it. Not even from Edwin."

The name sounded like a death knell. Andrew leaned forward. His gaze had grown deep and troubled. "What business, John? I know nothing of Edwin's doings."

John Crombie rubbed his narrow chin and looked straight into the eyes of his friend and client, though it cost him some effort.

"Legal notices of court action pending administration and probate of your family will and trusts were sent to all interested parties. Customary procedure, Andrew. Your cousin has filed an objection with the court."

Andrew made a sound under his breath, but John Crombie continued.

"He has every legal right to do so. A petition to determine heirship." He glanced somewhat apologetically in Brad's direction. "It involves some defensive action on our part, but we can manage that, Andrew."

"What does this mean in terms of litigation? Spell out, please, what this will mean to us."

"Of course, this is partly a stalling measure. It will involve a trial—a hearing before a judge, where evidence may be presented by any involved party."

"What can Edwin hope to gain?"

Mr. Crombie cleared his throat. "This throws the burden of proof upon us, Andrew. And, of course, we must face the possibility that the court could rule in Edwin's favor."

There was silence in the room for a long moment. Too long. Mr. Crombie pushed back his chair.

"We can handle this, Andrew. We mustn't panic. There are several courses we can pursue. We have an excellent case; you know that." He drew out a fat, dog-eared folder from his file. "If you've time, we'd best go over some of this now."

He paused. Andrew looked up and nodded slowly. Mr. Crombie sat down and opened the file. He shuffled through the thick stack of papers. This was going to take some time—and some doing, though he would not reveal that to Andrew. The matter was just a little too delicate for comfort. He looked up at the two solemn, expectant faces, cleared his throat, and began, in his most dry, professional, practiced manner.

"So I say, more power to him, Andrew."

"For heaven's sake, Janet, keep your voice down." Brad had retired to his room, but the last thing Andrew wanted was for him to hear Janet champion his foe.

"What did you expect Edwin to do? What would you have done?" Janet relentlessly demanded.

"Well, I would never have acted as he did—right from the beginning he made choices I would never have even considered."

"Andrew, how can you say that? You've never been in circumstances anything like his. You judge him more harshly than I think you'd like to be judged."

It was a good line for an exit and Janet used it, for Nan had just walked into the room.

"Where are you going?" Andrew demanded.

Janet answered him without turning around. "For a walk with the collie, if it's any of your business."

Andrew made a move forward, but Nan laid her hand on his arm to restrain him. "Let her go. You'll only make things worse. Let her sort things out for herself, Andrew."

"I don't understand . . ."

"No one ever understands what another person goes through. She's faced too many changes, ever since your father's death. At first you were here to help her, then Edwin. Now I've entered the picture, and you've taken Edwin out. More than anything else, I think she's frightened, Andrew."

Andrew ran his fingers through his hair—a tired, helpless gesture. "It doesn't come across that way," he objected.

Nan smiled. "She's young. Young people react in extremes."

"And you're ancient enough yourself to look back and know that?"

Nan's smile widened. "You're teasing me now." She kissed him lightly. "Sleep on it, Andrew. It won't seem so bad in the morning," she promised.

Brad had been the first to retire, but he was awake still. There was only one place he knew to turn at a time like this. He knelt beside his bed and poured out his heart there. "Have you brought me here for nothing?" he asked. He thought of the portrait downstairs of Charles Buchanan. He had arrived without a conviction; he had one now. He felt a destiny working here. But things had been thrown suddenly into chaos, and he feared—for the first time he feared what events might come.

He was placed in a singularly awkward position. If he fought this thing, how would that make him look? Like the greedy outsider, anxious to get his hands on another man's money. If he didn't fight, that was suspect, too, as though he put himself above it, disdainfully waiting for others to deliver the prize into his hands. No light came. He prayed long into the darkness, tired and frightened and terribly lonely.

Edwin, alone in his Glasgow flat, chafing at his confinement, paced the floor. Andrew would know by now of the step he had taken. He took grim pleasure in the thought of Andrew's anger; he savored it, as he savored the whiskey he sipped. Andrew had never been good at games; he was too straightforward. *You should not play games with me, cousin.* He said the words out loud, with a wry chuckle. *I do not play prettily, Andrew, you ought to know that. And this is one game I intend to win.*

The telephone rang with a discordant jangle that startled his fantasy. Edwin jumped at the sound, then set his drink down carefully and picked up the receiver.

"Edwin, that you? This is Jamie, lad."

Edwin let out his breath with an audible sigh. "Jamie. It's good to hear your voice, man. You got anything cooking up Portree way?"

"Matter o' fact, we do, that's why I rang you. We've got a little deal going—we thought you might like to throw in."

"I don't think so."

"Well, that was a hasty answer." Jamie paused and lowered his tone. "Let me tell you about it. It would be of special interest to you."

Edwin missed the import of the tone; he was already speaking, protesting with a friendly laugh. "Listen, I've got to keep my nose clean. I've a little scheme of my own going and I must keep strictly this side of the law. It's important, and it's personal, Jamie. Besides, you blokes are a little too big time for me, a little heavy into—"

"Och, Edwin, that's nonsense."

"Be that as it may, I must pass this time. Besides, I've a mind to flit for a season."

"If you flit, it will be to the States, I wager. Good gad, mon, there's nothing to take your fancy there." Jamie's voice sounded slurred and somewhat surly.

"I'm not certain of that. And besides, Jamie, I never was good at the waiting game. I'll go mad if I don't keep busy at something."

"Exactly. Now this little matter of ours—"

"No, lad, I don't want to hear anything of it. My mind's made up; I know what I'm doing."

"Well, suit yourself. Best o' luck to ye."

"Thanks, Jamie. I'll send you a postcard, how's that?"

They bantered back and forth a few minutes, and when Edwin hung up the phone he felt much better. He had grown sour dwelling upon his own morbid thoughts. Yes, what he needed was action, and the sooner the better. His plans were only half-formed and vague. But he remembered one of his grandmother's sayings: "There's more than one way to skin a cat."

There was a little matter of paying debts, of keeping one's word, though rashly given. The best way to get at Andrew was through Nan. And he had a good, though indirect, method in mind. He finished off his whiskey and poured himself another. *You shall rue the day, cousin, rue the day.* He felt better; yes, he was eager to move now, keen-edged and ready for battle again.

The following morning Andrew and Brad left early. "There's nothing for it but to go on as we'd planned," Andrew urged his guest. "I've been itching to show you the 'hame country.' I shan't let Edwin cheat me of that."

They followed the north bank of the Clyde from Glasgow to Dumbarton. The early morning sun, skipping over the river, glinted off the steep sides of the Rock of Dumbarton where it sat, securely moored in the river's depths.

"This is one of the most picturesque rocks in all of Scotland," Andrew explained. "It was from here, in 1548, that Mary, just a girl of six, boarded a French vessel and set sail for France."

"France? Then how did she get to be queen of Scotland?"

"When her young husband, the French prince, died, she returned here."

Brad nodded; he knew so little of Scottish history. The sleek Healey hummed through the rolling Kilpatrick Hills toward the lower end of Loch Lomond where the clusters of houseboats and rowing boats huddled, silent and moored. The winter hills, still half-shrouded in mists, faded into gray distance. Rowans and slender birch trees hugged the lakeside, their graceful trunks almost in the water. The lake appeared smooth and unruffled, as still as ice. For twenty-four miles it stretched before them, interspersed with wild, beautiful islands, set like green jewels in its midst.

"The bonnie, bonnie banks of Loch Lomond . . . that's one Scottish song I've known since I was a boy. But I've never imagined anything quite this lovely." Brad spoke the words very softly. The morning wind seemed to answer him with a murmur as sweet as song. Small waves broke against the brown stones at their feet. *This is part of me,* Brad thought. *These were my beginnings. The past I've longed for all my life.*

"Are you in the mood for a little exploring?" Andrew asked. "We can climb Ben Lomond and see clear across Scotland for miles and miles. From Inchmurrin we can gaze right into the highlands through a mighty cleft in the hills, like an open gate."

Something in Brad seemed to stir into action. "Lead on." He felt he could hardly wait, as though something momentous was waiting to happen.

Janet pulled her car into the narrow drive leading to the MacGregor estate. It was dark and the winter trees seemed to hold in the darkness, not even allowing the shadows to escape, but to hang in her pathway, trembling when she sped through them. She was happy to round the curve and see the house lights and the knot of familiar cars parked helter skelter. She swung the PA Midget to a tidy stop and cut the engine. The sleek sides of the car that shone forest green in the day gleamed black against the night's dimness. She ran toward the door and a friendly hand opened it to her before she could knock.

"Janet! It is you, then. We had bets you wouldn't show. You've missed two months now."

"Are you going to yank my membership, Gordie?" She moved past the young man and inside. But she cast him a gleaming smile in passing.

"No one'd think of such a thing—you're a popular member."

Janet laughed at the exaggeration in his tone. "It's not me but my car that's the popular member, I'm thinking."

She followed young Gordon MacGregor toward the game room where she could already hear snatches of voices raised in companionable conversation. How she enjoyed this company! There were few women here, and those were the wives or girlfriends of members. She was the only woman who held her own membership card. She smiled to herself. That had been her own little triumph. With Andrew's return, then Nan's arrival, and then the wedding, there had been too many demands upon her at home. She should never have allowed them to rob her of this.

As she entered the room several men looked up and smiled or spoke in greeting. Janet moved easily from group to group. These were mostly old friends; she felt safe and familiar here.

"Did you drive the green beast tonight, Janet?" Willie Stewart called from across the room. Janet nodded. "How's she runnin'?" Willie sipped from his steaming cup and regarded her with a laconic gaze.

"Like a top. Even one of the Cream Crackers couldn't take her."

There was an appreciative murmur, then Willie chirped back. "With mysel' behind the wheel, perhaps. But you, lass?"

"Any time you want a trial run, Willie, I'm ready."

"I'd back the lass any day," Dave MacKenzie spoke up. Willie threw his cap across the room at him; Dave caught it neatly. Janet smiled; she loved this affectionate banter. She sat down and reached for a mug of hot cider, curling her fingers around the smooth warmth. The talk went on. They were planning the first spring rally. Janet listened, adding a word now and then, letting her eyes roam over the fresh, eager faces.

"Do you hold the old Reliability Trials here still?"

Janet looked at the boy; he spoke with a foreign accent. He seemed to feel her eyes on him and moved his own to return her glance. He was a stranger, though he looked somehow vaguely familiar.

"Those bashes!" Willie laughed out loud. "You'll be jokin', I hope, lad. Those archaic, self-torture sessions went out with the war."

"We're more civilized now," Dave added, and they laughed off the matter.

Neil Sheffield, who had ventured the naive question, leaned back against the warm bricks of the fireplace wall and looked on for a while. These were a great bunch of guys and he was grateful for their ready acceptance of him. He tried not to stare too obviously at the girl. He didn't think she remembered who he was. But he had remembered, had recognized her as soon as she entered the room. He waited until the conversation deteriorated into small pockets of general hubbub and made his way toward the sofa where she sat. She looked up and smiled as he approached her. She had lovely eyes—a light, summer-sky blue, very soft and inviting.

"I didn't realize you were a member." He sat down beside her, casually, on the sofa arm. "It's a bit unusual, isn't it? A girl being a member of a sports car club?"

Her gaze seemed to take in everything about him. He was uncertain for a moment if she would reply. Then she seemed to make up her mind and the wary look in the blue eyes faded.

"Not so unusual, really. I was raised on sports cars. My father was an MG enthusiast. He and Willie's father organized this club. He knew John Thornley for many years. The PA Midget I drive was actually his car—before . . ." She paused, and he hurried to fill the gap.

"PA Midget—that's pretty rare, even over here, isn't it?"

"That's right. This one dates back to '34."

"What did you mean when you referred a while back to a Cream Cracker?"

Janet paused and Neil grinned. "Well, I've got to learn somehow."

"The PA Midgets followed the J2s," she explained, "but they had better features, such as their stronger crankshaft, which made them superb in competitions. Though manufacturers weren't supposed to enter company teams, MG backed three Midget drivers to the hilt. Their cars were painted MG brown and cream, so someone called them the Cream Crackers. It stuck. They were legends in their day."

Neil liked the sound of her voice; he wished he could keep her talking. "I'd like to see yours sometime, in daylight."

Janet smiled and nodded. "What do you drive?"

Neil squirmed a little and flashed her his boyish grin. "A little A."

"What year?" she asked.

"Sixty-two. It's a 1600 Mark II Deluxe. I was thrilled to get it. I always wanted one when I was a boy. But they're not so easy to find where I come from."

"America. Surely somewhere in the States."

"Do I catch a note of disdain?" He made a face and raised his eyebrows. "You don't remember meeting me, do you?"

Janet shook her head—slowly, for a vague impression was coming to her.

"That's all right. There were lots of new faces for you. But, of course, it was easy for me to remember."

She looked down, away from his steady gaze. "You have me at a disadvantage . . ."

"I'm sorry. My name's Neil Sheffield. I met you Sunday. At church—at sacrament meeting."

This time her response was quick in coming. "I don't believe it. What are you doing here?"

The question startled him. "Well, the same thing as you, I suppose . . ."

"Where are you from?"

"Salt Lake City."

"I knew it. A Utah Mormon."

"You make it sound like some kind of disease."

Janet didn't smile. He watched her expression, surprised and fascinated.

"As far as I'm concerned, it is. I apologize if that's rude—"

"No, no," he protested. "*I* apologize. I was under the mistaken impression that you were . . ."

"A member, myself? Interested?" She knit her brow as though struggling with some inner confusion. "That's neither here nor there, really. I must be honest. If you're a Utah Mormon, you're suspect; it's that simple."

"Condemned before I have a chance to defend myself—to even know the charges?" Neil still half-wondered if this was serious; he wasn't sure.

"That's right. They've caused me enough trouble already—Andrew's Americans—Andrew's Utah Mormons."

Stunned, Neil was silent a moment too long. Janet moved, unfolded her long legs, and stood, leaving him on his perch, alone and awkward.

He watched her walk away. *Good heavens,* he wondered, *what's going on here?* She intrigued him. He sat for the rest of the meeting trying to figure out what his next move would be.

When Janet arrived home nearly two hours later the lights in the front sitting room were still burning. She walked quietly, trying to reach the broad staircase before she was noticed. But Andrew called out to her. She walked to the doorway, but didn't enter.

"How was the meeting?"

Neil Sheffield's features flickered briefly before her eyes. "Fine, fine," she replied. "It was good to be back." She turned.

"Would you like to join us?" The voice was Andrew's American's. Janet froze. Andrew rose and walked over beside her. She could feel his concern.

"Brad's giving us the missionary discussions," he explained. "Nan and I never had the official lessons, only Grant Morgan's version." He smiled, as he thought about the old man.

"I've had all the discussions, remember?" Janet's tone was dull and unfriendly.

"I remember. We thought you might like to sit in . . ."

"I'd rather not. I'm tired. I'll see you tomorrow."

She turned and sought the safe haven of the stairs. The room she left behind was strained and silent. Andrew searched Nan's eyes; they were troubled like his own. Brad avoided their gaze. He had caused this problem. He knew it, but what was he to do? He ought to go home. He was nearly out of money, living on Andrew's kindness. He ought to be with his family where he was needed. Yet why did he feel as though something was unresolved, unfinished? It wasn't the will; it was nothing that simple. He knew Andrew had arranged these lessons partly for his sake—to make him feel useful, as though he were paying his way. Andrew's desire to have him here was sincere, he knew that. Was he pompous enough to feel he could do some good, make some kind of real difference with these people?

They continued, but things were not quite as they had been before. Janet had struck a discordant note that each felt in his own way; none could restore the undisturbed harmony again.

6

Do I entice you? do I speak you fair?
A MIDSUMMER NIGHT'S DREAM

Edwin had taken this route once before: the long, airborne journey, arriving a tired stranger in a crowded, impersonal airport, eating a lonely meal, arranging car rental. It had been easier before; he had been more driven. This time he was conscious of the strain, though in some ways he had more on the line this time, really. He had sold his interest in the Portree shop to finance this venture and others—to float him until the trial. If the case should go against him—well, he refused to allow himself to think about that, at least not now.

He drove from Chicago southwest, through the bare, brown prairie: a long drive—he could nearly cross Scotland in the time. He avoided Warsaw; he had no desire to return there, to the old hotel where he'd stayed before, where Andrew had found him and confronted him, and then banished him for his sins. He pulled into the small, sleepy town itself and secured a room at the Hotel Nauvoo, the stately gray pioneer building whose old-fashioned accommodations felt comfortably like home, though they were a bit shabby. He unpacked, placing things in a careful order. Edwin was somewhat fastidious by nature. It was necessary for him to have order, to merge some part of himself with this place if he was to feel at ease here. He showered and dressed with care, his sense of excitement mounting.

He looked at his watch: seven-thirty Chicago time. Though early March was considered spring, a cold darkness had settled and a wind blew from off the river with ice in its breath. He knew the way to Nan's house, but he didn't go there directly. He drove through the old restored sections and along the river, then back through the shuttered, unfriendly main street of the town. A small knot of girls stood on a street corner, talking and laughing. He slowed the car; they looked up as he passed. One waved her small gloved hand and giggled. *I might not recognize the girl if I saw her,* Edwin admitted.

He drove directly to the house. It was just as he had remembered, though barren now of flowers and green, with the cushions taken up from the old porch swing, which stood gaunt and awkward and uninviting. But a light shone over the porch, and inside lights as well. Someone was home. He walked up the pathway, stood on the cold porch, and rang the bell.

Julie, home alone, half-heartedly doing her school studies, welcomed the interruption and came to the door with a smile on her face—but the smile froze there. The man who stood framed in the doorway, his dark hair blowing, regarding her with beautiful deep blue eyes, could have been Andrew—at first she had thought he was Andrew, and had almost cried out delightedly, looking past him, expecting to see Nan there. But that was only the first blinking instant. The image adjusted. This man was different from Andrew, his face more lean, his body more thin and sinewy, and his eyes—his eyes were burning and intense, yet strangely cold. She shuddered. She, too, had her memories.

She's younger than I remembered, Edwin thought as he watched her. *And nothing at all like her sister. But . . . fair in her own way.*

He regarded her a moment longer, aware of her growing discomfort.

"May I come in? I don't know about you, but I'm half-frozen. We can stare at each other in there where it's warm as well as out here."

Julie moved away from the door so he could enter. *She is pretty self-contained, considering,* Edwin thought. He liked that. He hated a girl to stutter and giggle. As casually as he could he glanced about him. "Is your father at home?" The girl shook her head. "That little brother of yours?"

"No, no one. I'm here alone."

Edwin smiled, and his smile was boyish and charming. "Good. We're in luck, then." He chose the nicest chair in the room and sat down.

Julie didn't move. "What do you want? What are you doing here?"

Edwin leaned forward, his hands on his knees. His eyes had grown merry. There was warmth in his voice that was hard to resist. "I've been bouncing from place to place on business. Wretched country, America—indecently big. I've been hungry for someone to talk to, someone familiar—" He paused and his blue eyes searched her face. "When I hit Chicago, I thought of you."

"So you came all this way just to say hello to me?" Julie's voice didn't sound as responsive as Edwin wanted.

"Well, of course. I knew Nan would be thrilled to have news of her little sister." He hadn't meant that to sound patronizing, but it did. Instinctively he repaired the mistake. "Don't you suppose a man can get lonely, Julie?"

It was the first time he had spoken her name. She liked how he made it sound, the mere suggestion of some hidden warmth and intimacy. She almost believed him—she wanted to, but something held her. Her mistrust was deeply rooted; it stopped her now. Her own inherent insight came to her rescue.

"That's nonsense. Do you really expect me to believe you?"

His glance wavered and she caught it.

"I *don't* believe you, you know." She was trembling, amazed at herself, but she'd said the words. She felt fiercely glad that she had; she felt strangely elated.

There's more to be dealt with here than shows on the surface. Edwin paused. The silence was stronger than a reply. He was mentally going over his hand, fingering his cards, deciding his play. He rose and walked over to stand beside her.

"You're quite a girl in your own right," he said. "You're correct; I misjudged you." He could feel now that she was trembling. Unconsciously his charm became tender, tinged with a touch of sincerity.

"You deserve the truth, lass, and so I'll tell you. I'm here to see you and nothing else." He saw the surprise register on her face. "That's right," he continued. "I've been lonely and wretched and at loose ends. Andrew and Nan hold all the aces, have all the answers. So I've come to do my own thing."

"But why here? Why me? We don't know each other. I've only seen you from a distance, I only know—"

"You only know what Andrew was pleased to tell you."

"I know what I saw with my own eyes! I know how you frightened Nan—"

"Good grief, girl! What would you have done if you were me? That money was meant to be mine!" Edwin moved a step closer. Unconsciously Julie drew in her breath. "Andrew was so besotted with that milktoast American Mormon of his."

He paused and cocked his head at a rakish angle. "Be honest, Julie. I think you can. Do you really believe that dullard deserves a fortune? Money is like precious jewels, fine art—or beautiful women. It needs someone who appreciates it to handle it gently, artfully . . . lovingly . . ."

His voice, like sweet music, reached out to caress her. She trembled beneath the touch, as he knew she would.

"But your reason for coming here isn't me, it's Andrew." She spoke softly, as though she was thinking out loud. There was hesitancy in her voice; he could feel her groping. "You hardly knew I existed before. There's nothing to draw you back here except . . . revenge."

Julie spoke the word in a whisper. It hung between them. Edwin looked into the young, innocent eyes and a sharp twinge of conscience broke through his armor.

"I suppose that's true." His own words were measured. "That's not always an unworthy motivation, revenge. And there's nothing evil or harmful afoot here. I've been painfully honest with you.'' He took a breath, appealing to her sympathies with his eyes. ''There's much I could teach you, Julie, much I could give you—a whole world I could open up for you. You've as much right to your own chances as Nan, lass. What say you?''

Julie struggled beneath his gaze. Her mind was a boat that rocked and dipped and swirled on the waves of her indecision. He was so crazily handsome, so hard to resist. She and Nan were not really compatible as sisters. What he said might be true—perhaps he *was* her chance for romance and excitement, for something better in life than Nauvoo could give.

''All right. I don't see what it would hurt.''

''You'll see me, then? Tomorrow night?''

Julie nodded. ''Tomorrow's Saturday. You could pick me up at noon. There's a swimming meet at the college in Peoria I'd like to go to. It's a large city, we could find something to do after that.''

Edwin could feel the excitement, the elation of victory pound through his veins like intoxication. ''That's much better. I'll be here promptly.'' He took her hand. ''Nothing of this to Nan. Is that agreed, now?'' The ground rules had to be carefully laid, explicitly understood.

His touch, his simple touch had an influence on her. She was young and vivacious and eager for life. She smiled for the first time; the blue eyes smiled back. ''What Nan doesn't know won't hurt her. You have my word.''

He smoothed the small, soft hand with his fingers. ''Till tomorrow, then.'' He turned, casting one last, longing glance behind him.

She stood a long time where he'd left her, vaguely aware that here was a man, not a boy. She was playing with fire—she was taking a hearty leap, not a little step. But she was stubborn and this was what she wanted. Oh yes, she was very sure of that. She could still feel the press of his warm fingers and the caress of those magnificent eyes.

Once outside, Edwin took long, triumphant strides. He had won the first victory. He was intoxicated with himself and life, the challenging fascination, the twists and turnings, the terrible, wonderful risk of it all. She had thrown him a few surprises, proved more difficult than he had expected, and he loved it. But now he was right where he wanted to be. She was a woman, and she was young. She'd be easy to handle, easy to work any way he chose. He drove back to his hotel. He'd pour a tall whiskey. Maybe two. This was something to celebrate.

It felt good to be writing again. Nan licked the stamp and applied it carefully in the corner of the fat envelope. This was going home, back to the *Warsaw Signal.* Her own byline now carried a subtitle: *Foreign correspondent.* There was so much history crammed into this little space: great battles fought, prominent men who lived here. Loch Lomond country was especially rich in the history surrounding the hero, William Wallace, and not far away rose the magnificent castle of Inverary with its tumultuous tales of the Campbell clan. She felt more a part of things when she could write about them. And there was another benefit she had not foreseen. In her wanderings she was coming to know some of the local people. She liked that; she liked being hailed in a kindly way by someone she recognized, stopping to chat, discussing family and local news. The people in the LDS ward they attended were also friendly. She and Andrew had joined a study group some of the young couples had organized. And Nan met with the Relief Society women, not only in meetings but also at their homes, and learned to knit and tat and tie quilts. She loved it. In many small ways Scotland and Bieldmor were becoming home.

She looked up at the clock. Soon Andrew and Brad would be arriving. She'd hurry and post this, then see if Jessie needed her help with the meal. There were servants here, but Nan was learning one secret. A good mistress oversees every detail. Otherwise workers will soon become careless and sloppy. Nan marveled at how Jessie handled her people—her authority, tinged with an air of condescension. Nan didn't think she could ever manage that. She still felt awkward when people served her, and girlishly grateful. For the time being she was terribly glad that Jessie was here. Bieldmor House was a big place, so she and Andrew enjoyed all the privacy they wanted. She appreciated the time, the gradual easing this provided for her to grow into her responsibilities. All she really wanted now was to be with Andrew. She was glad that so little else was required of her.

"It's called the Central Clydeside Conurbation, a commercial sprawl that extends from Clydesbank to Motherwell and from Paisley to Airdrie, crossed over and fed and sustained, of course, by the Clyde." Andrew's voice held that tender note Brad had come to recognize whenever he spoke of his lands and holding. *This kind of pride is richly embedded,* Brad thought, *and runs deep.* It sometimes gave him a twinge of envy to listen to Andrew, to sense the scope of commitment, the vision, the breadth of action a man like Andrew could command.

"Textiles and textile fibres still make up nearly 40 percent of Scotland's exports," Andrew continued. He grinned across the table at his young plant manager, Scott Lindsay. "Thanks to men like Lindsay here we've conformed and adapted. It's no longer silk threads and fine lawn, is it? But woollen carpets and good, practical cotton cloth."

Lindsay grinned back. "It's a good enough way to make a living. One third of all Britain's carpets are manufactured here in the Glasgow area."

Andrew nodded. "It's near quitting time, isn't it? Let's just have a quick look at those figures, then Brad and I will get out of here and you can go home."

Lindsay dragged out the heavy, black, leather-bound books and Brad had an unsettled moment until Andrew smiled and said, "There's just a thing or two I want to show you. Promise I won't get carried away."

He had his hand on the cover but it poised there, froze, never opened before the high, piercing keen of an alarm sounded. He met Lindsay's eyes; nothing could be more horrible than a fire. In an instant they both were moving, Lindsay bent over a large steel safe working the numbers as casually as he might have ten minutes before. Andrew gathered up papers and volumes and ledgers, with a quick glance deciding which ones he might dare to discard. Brad watched the process, fascinated. When all was safely locked away the two men turned.

"Take the north staircase, Scott; that will bring you down quickly. Check the main rooms as you pass them, will you? And take Mr. Richards with you."

Lindsay didn't move. "Come with us, sir. The alarm's been sounding five minutes. The place'll be cleared. It's end o' the shift—half the place was empty, I'll wager, before the alarm sounded."

"Thank heaven for that. I'll just have a quick look 'round. Go on, now."

Lindsay no longer hesitated. He knew that to stand and argue would only endanger Andrew's life. "Follow me," he said to Brad, and as soon as the two turned, Andrew slipped through the opposite door and was gone.

He worked his way carefully along the long, narrow corridor, straining his ears to hear even the slightest of sounds. He knew circumstances were not wholly in his favor. He was glad the skeleton night crew had not yet arrived, that the timing of the fire made the risk to life minimal. But this was the largest of the Paisley mills and also the oldest, a full five stories high. The structure would prove easy prey to a fire, as would the cloth fibres and the chemicals used for printing and dying. How long would it take a fire crew to get here?

He hurried through room after room where the massive looms sat quiet, where knitting machines, rows of canned slivers, and long spinning frames in half-shadow seemed to crouch ominously. As he entered the large dyeing room he saw several people all fleeing from him, like shadows along a wall. He followed them through room after room. There was no sound here. He couldn't discern where the fire was until he entered the main weaving room and a wall of smoke caught him, like a blow against his chest, acrid and thick, swirling black around him. Here there were voices and people moving and he could see flames. Suddenly Lindsay was there pulling at his arm.

"The crew's arrived," Linday shouted. "You'd best give them instructions."

Andrew stared at him a moment, blinking and dazed. "I saw hardly a soul as I came through. Do you think the men are all out and safe now?"

Lindsay nodded. "They'll have men to check that. Come, the engines are at the north door, they'll be needing instructions."

Andrew took one last look around. The smoke burned in his nostrils, his skin felt tight and on fire. In the dim, eerie light, with his eyes streaming, he couldn't see to the opposite end of the room. The massive expanse seemed to stretch on and on. There at the end of the expanse, though he couldn't see him, he could imagine Andrew Buchanan standing—*the* Andrew who had built the mill, the man who had stared down upon him all his life, eagle-visaged, unsmiling, and stern—the young weaver who had grown up to build a fortune, who with his wit had contrived to control that fortune, though he'd been dead and buried now for a hundred years.

There was another tug at his arm. "Come on, Mr. Buchanan. You'll do no one any good standing here." Andrew sighed and followed Scott Lindsay out of the building.

"I should have torn this place down long ago." Andrew said the words out loud as they walked, but no one heard him. All the other buildings had been replaced or modernized. He had hung onto this one because he had something in mind for it, some crazy idea of building a museum, a monument to men like his great-great-grandfather and the wonders they had achieved in their time.

He walked through the door and the cold evening air stung him. Now at last he could see the burning building. Inside had been only dark nightmare and doubt. Here the blaze leaped with long orange tongues, licking and greedy, along the brick line, inside the black windows—everywhere went the flame, like an ugly red wound that was angry and bleeding. Andrew felt anger as red as the flame leap up within him. He felt impotent, betrayed, and outraged at the inane, inadequate means at his disposal to battle his raging enemy. He stood back and took another deep breath of the biting air, seemed to shake himself, then with long strides hurried forward, while the shadows of the burning dream flickered over his heart.

For the first few minutes after he was outside the building and safe, Brad stood off to one side, feeling slightly stunned and awkward. Lindsay had disappeared from his view; he didn't think Andrew had come out yet. It was early, no help had arrived. The low current of talk and activity held a strong note of fear in it. Brad stood chewing on his lip and watching, painfully aware of his own lack of involvement and competency.

Then he saw him: The man burst out of the far end of the building. A line of fire, like a bright orange stripe, ran along his back. Brad broke into a run; no one else seemed yet to have noticed. The man was stumbling aimlessly—staggering really—moaning, with his hands spread over his face.

Brad reached him and tried to tug him down onto the ground, but the man resisted. Suddenly one of the workers, a big, hefty man, appeared at Brad's side. "I'll give 'ee a hand," he offered matter-of-factly. Together they moved the hurt man, rolled him in the dirt, and smothered the flames. Brad pulled off his own light jacket and placed it around the man's shoulders, then tore strips from his shirt to wrap the man's face and hands. At last he looked up, aware for the first time of people around him, simply dressed men with simple, open faces. Several women were interspersed among them, middle-aged, solid, and motherly.

"You're hurt, lad," one of them said. Brad blinked stupidly at her. He looked down and realized for the first time that his hands had been burned. They were blistering in a place or two along his knuckles and on his palms.

"You'd best sit down with the rest," the woman urged, "till the men arrive to take you to hospital."

"Heavens, no," Brad protested. "I'm fine. Really."

He glanced over at a small knot of people, six or seven, some sitting, some lying on the ground, then walked closer to check out the situation. Though the injured had been covered with coats and blankets, they shivered in the moist cold of the night air. Brad turned to the women who had followed him and stood planted silently near him. "Do you live near here? Does anyone live near here?"

"In those houses up yonder," a woman acknowledged, indicating the place with a wave of her hand.

"We could use more blankets and Thermoses of hot drink. Could you help me?"

She turned, seeming grateful for something to do. "Mol and Mary," she bellowed, "you come with me."

Brad dismissed them and turned his mind to the others. "Is there a phone near here?" A man emerged from the crowd and in a thick burr answered. "I can get to one quickly. What do you need?"

"Call Bieldmor House and ask for Mrs. Buchanan—Mrs. Hannah Buchanan. Tell her what happened. Tell her we need food for the workers. Sandwiches and something to drink."

Without a word the man turned and disappeared. Brad took a breath and looked around him again. Several fire trucks had at last arrived to fight the blaze, along with an official-looking car or two. He caught sight of Andrew moving back and forth between them, instructing, conferring, answering questions. Brad bent and spoke to several of the injured men encouragingly, but was relieved to see the women trudge back into view. He looked around again at the men. "Must be something we can do, don't you think?" He walked along the building until he found one of the firemen. "There are men here, workers from the mill. Is there something they can do to help?"

The man hesitated a moment, then looked at Brad more closely. It was a bad fire, this one. They never had enough hands for a blaze of this kind. "See there?" He pointed to one burned-out corner of the building. "All that muck and debris has got to be cleared away. Reckon if they were supervised they could do it."

"Could I take responsibility for that?"

"Fire's out cold there. If you watch 'em I suppose they'll be all right, lad." He cupped his hands and shouted something to one of the others, then turned back to Brad. "Now, laddie, here's what I want you to do."

Nan wasn't alarmed when Andrew and Brad were late in arriving. They could have easily become sidetracked and forgotten the time, especially if Andrew was involved in his precious business. It pleased her to see the intense, almost boyish delight Andrew took in his work; it gave Nan a secure feeling, and a sense of pride in Andrew's integrity.

She and Jessie put everything on warm and held dinner. After a while they let the dinner go and decided that when the men came, if they hadn't already eaten, they would have to be content with fruit and cold cuts. Nan didn't eat; she didn't feel hungry. After a haphazard meal Janet left for a walk with her collie. Nan watched her disappear down the path with the dog trailing at her heels. She envied the girl's naive freedom. She wished she, too, could walk off into the woods, free of this terrible knot that was forming inside her stomach.

When the call came through with Brad's message she was fiercely relieved, and flung herself gratefully into action. Jessie joined her; they worked quickly and well together. A persistent thought kept coming to Nan as she watched Andrew's mother: *She loves him as much as I do, perhaps more. She was frightened to death that she might have lost him.*

They stayed at the mill site most of the night. Finally Nan talked Andrew into a few hours' rest. The loss had been devastating, as he had feared. He knew he'd have weighty decisions to make the next day. That alone convinced him to take the sleep he needed.

The following morning he and Brad drove to the mill together. They didn't say much, but there was an empathy between them. When they arrived there was already a line of people waiting. Andrew was drawn into interviews with insurance men and investigators, export agents wondering how this would affect the flow and availability of their product.

Brad, left to himself, wandered here and there looking over the damage. He began to recognize familiar faces around him, men he had worked with the night before. An idea began in his mind; he struggled to grasp it, form it into solidarity. Would he dare? Of course he would dare—that was what they were here for, these men whose lives moved around the mill, who were involved perhaps more personally than Andrew, who depended on each day's work for their bread and butter, to whom idleness posed a real threat. He looked around him.

"Jock," he called, "do you think you could help me?"

A man dislodged himself from the group and ambled forward. He had a mane of red hair with graying sideburns, a round face that was pink and mottled and small, squinty eyes that looked birdlike and honest.

"What can I do for you, governor?"

"Come with me. I thought we could assess the loss and see what we might salvage. Maybe we can put some of these people to work. What do you say?"

There were some shufflings and mumbled responses from the men who heard him. Jock rubbed his stubbled chin. "All right then, fine. Where's Jimmy?"

A young man came forward. The three of them started out together. They poked from room to room, examining supplies and equipment, moving and hauling and rearranging things. It was all Greek to Brad; he knew nothing of it. But in less than an hour the men had a fair idea of what might be salvaged and put into immediate use. They rounded up a dozen others Jock called out by name and set each to a task. Roller printers, creels, spinning frames, gray goods and rovings—they meant nothing to Brad. He did little more than encourage the men, talk with them, do small, mundane tasks they felt he could handle, keep some order in what each was doing and which ones were called. When he felt someone tap him on the shoulder and turned to find Andrew beside him, he was shocked to read the hands on his watch. One-thirty. Impossible. Where had the time gone? Tired, somewhat grimy, but happy, the men put their work aside, stood and stretched, began talking together.

"Mrs. Buchanan's back with more food, lads; follow me." They trailed out into the bright winter sunlight that flooded the yard where long tables were stretched, laden with sausage rolls, fruits, and fresh hot scones.

"Have you any idea what you've done in there?" Andrew asked.

Brad shook his head and reached for a hot stuffed roll. "Heavens, Andrew, it wasn't me, it was the men. I know nothing of what's going on, I just helped a little. I actually felt darned out of place."

Andrew stared at him until Brad felt a sense of discomfort. "You initiated and they followed."

Brad returned the gaze, still uncomprehending. "I made a few suggestions, Andrew, that's all, encouraged them some . . ."

Andrew's eyes were sparkling. "Those men are old, crusty, hardbitten Scotsmen. They don't take to foreigners telling them what to do. They don't *follow* just anybody. Do you know what I'm saying?" Slowly Brad shook his head. Andrew continued. "You've a marvelous way with people, Brad, can't you see that? You've worked wonders with those men—I know them. I know somehow you won their respect before you got them to do what they're doing."

"That's how you want to see it," Brad replied. Andrew blinked back at him. Brad was glad when some fellows came up and diverted Andrew and drew him away. He reached for another sausage roll, struggling suddenly with a warm feeling inside, a feeling that surprised and disarmed him. He was glad Andrew wasn't there to read the emotion in his eyes.

7

O fairest beauty, do not
fear nor fly!
HENRY VI, PART I

It was Friday evening, nearly a week after the fire. Jessie had retired early to her own rooms. Janet had announced that she was driving to meet Mary and a group of girls in Paisley. Andrew was closeted with Brad. They were often together, discussing deep, weighty things of no interest to Nan. He had promised to break up the session early and take her out for the evening. She planned to hold him to it. She used the interim to finish the letter she was writing Grant Morgan. She missed the old man terribly. He had been her first contact with the Mormon church, her first and dearest example of what a Latter-day Saint person can be. It helped a little to share the events of her new life with him, to imagine the pleasure he felt in reading her words.

But Nan missed more than his company—she missed his counsel. Bieldmor House was so large that sometimes she was tempted to invite Grant here to stay for a while. It would be delightful showing him the things she loved, and the local people would like him, she knew. Sometimes she indulged in a daydream or two about it. Strange, but she missed Grant more than she missed her family. Her father never wrote letters; Julie wasn't much better. When she did write her letters were short, full of surface news, as though she had dashed them off in a hurry, having more important things she wanted to get to. That was like Julie; they had never been close to each other. As the older sister she supposed that was largely her fault, though not wholly; they were at core so different. Grandma wrote faithfully twice a month, kind, cozy letters, so much like her. But Nan's life for years had been different from theirs. Andrew and Scotland had seemed to cut the last tie between them, so they were bound now by an old, thin tendril, not strongly nourished. Nan knew time and distance would further weaken even that.

While Nan wrote and thought, Janet drove the old road to Paisley. It was mid-March and the weather was damp and rainy. It did nothing to lift her spirits. She pushed on the gas, skidding a little when the tires hit patches of mud on the pavement. An evening with the girls wasn't something she relished. She usually had no trouble getting a date. This weekend she had turned down three different offers. She didn't feel like being bright and pleasant—chit-chatting, making good company. At least with the girls she could be herself, quiet and even moody if she felt like it.

She drove the old black Magnetta; she wouldn't take her own car out on a night like this. She wasn't watching the road very closely and just past the bridge where the road curved gently she was forced to turn wide, her tires skirting the brush along the roadside. Before she was back on the pavement she heard it: a sharp crack, then the wheel lurched drunkenly. She was going a little too fast; she let off the gas pedal and, recovering herself slightly, steered into the swerve, coaxing the car back under contol. She slowed and pulled off the road, the split tire thumping. A flat tire, alone—on a night like this! She sat for a moment with her elbows propped on the wheel, disgusted and angry, loathe to face the weather and the job before her. At last, with a sigh, she buttoned her coat up snugly and stepped out into the chill, lonely night.

It took a while to fit her key into the lock and open the boot where the jack was stored. She stared at the ugly black thing. How could she do this? It would ruin her clothes to squat down in the mud. She wasn't certain she knew quite how to work it. Andrew had shown her once or twice, but not until now had she ever had need of the knowledge, opportunity to put what he'd told her to use.

Gingerly she lifted out the apparatus. She was glad no MG Club members could see her now. Her father had taught her to drive and she drove with a passion. But maintenance was another thing.

She remembered uncomfortably Andrew's recurring teasing: "A real sports car enthusiast knows his car, backward and forward, like the inside of his hand. He'd as soon tinker with it as drive it. Otherwise, how could he bear the cantankerous thing?"

She stooped and felt along the edge of the mud-caked wings for a place of attachment. She didn't hear the car's approach till it left the pavement and crunched over the stones and loose gravel near where she stood. She straightened up, her heart thumping wildly inside her. Should she hurry back into the car and lock the doors? Nonsense, she ought to know most of the people who passed here. She needed help. She'd just have to take her chances.

Neil had recognized the Magnetta immediately. His own heart had started beating when he saw it. Could it be Andrew needing some help—or was he in luck? He was out of his own car almost before he had stopped it. It was a girl, all right—Janet or Nan? He sought her face: long, delicate nose, eyes lost in the darkness, fair hair that shone golden beneath the moon.

"Hello there. Lucky chance that I happened upon you. What's the problem?"

Janet hesitated. She knew that voice, but it took her a moment or two to place it. Then the features and voice together sparked recognition. His own hair, tawny and long, feathered over his forehead. He had a habit of pushing it back with thin fingers every now and then as he talked—a small, nervous habit. He pushed it back now as he smiled at the girl. Janet's smile was only tentative, a concession.

"Just a flat tire. I can handle it," she answered, wondering as she spoke what madness compelled her, what stubborn feminine pride.

"That's silly," he said, his voice even and pleasant. "As long as I'm here I may as well do it for you."

She stood with her hands in her pockets and watched him. His movements were deft and efficient; she liked how he moved. Though he was thin of build he had broad shoulders. She liked the shape of his hands and the shape of his head and the thick sleekness of his hair against his collar. He stood up and she gave him a towel to wipe his hands on.

"Thank you," she said, feeling unexpectedly awkward.

"My pleasure. What's this car called—a Magnetta?"

Janet nodded. "A Magnetta Saloon, 1960. A small, practical English family car."

"Not for the size families they grow where I come from! And hardly 'practical' if it's an MG."

Janet smiled, this time a little more openly. "That's what Andrew claims. It's madness, I know." She glanced over to where his car sat, slim and pale in the dim light. "Are you enjoying your own bit of madness?"

"You bet I am. Wouldn't trade it for a Corvette if I could. Listen, it's cold—" He rubbed his hands together. They would be cold, Janet thought, working the jack as he had with no gloves. "There's a little place I know of not far from here. We could run over for a mug of hot cider and something to eat. That is, unless . . . well, I suppose you were heading somewhere . . ."

The seconds it took her to answer seemed long and strained. Neil was aware that the wind had risen and lifted her hair in long tendrils of golden gauze about her face. Janet considered her choice; she knew the girls wouldn't miss her. It would be intriguing spending the evening with him. Suddenly the challenge, the unknown and uncertain, appealed to her.

"I'd have to make one phone call, but that won't be difficult. Yes, I could come."

His smile was slow; it crept over his features like a warm promise. "Good. I'm glad. Could we pull the Magnetta off down that side road, lock 'er up, and you ride along with me?"

"I think so, yes."

It was hard to control his elation. "Follow me. It's just a few yards from here."

He climbed into the low white car, turned the key, and pushed the starter button. The engine hummed into life with the low, sweet throb he was coming to love. He pulled out, keeping an eye on the black car in his side mirror. He didn't want to lose sight of the girl behind him for even one minute.

"I must have scared you off—you haven't been 'round to examine the Midget." There was laughter in Janet's eyes as she spoke the words. Neil wasn't certain how much ridicule was laced in with the laughter. He had always been simple and forthright in his manners, not subtle or complicated, or given to moods. He twirled the half-empty mug in his hands.

"I'm afraid you did just that. I hadn't yet worked out a way around it. You're very convincing, you know, when you want to be."

"I come by it honestly, believe me," she answered, and he thought he perceived a slight bitterness in her tone.

"Be assured. I shall avoid like the plague any negative differences between us."

"Don't you think we'll be hard-pressed to find something to talk about, then?"

He regarded her with kindly gray eyes. "I don't think so. We've MGs to start with. That should keep us awhile. We're not as different as you might think. I've Scots blood in my own veins."

She lifted her eyebrows slightly. "A drop or two?"

"Oh, a little more than that. My great-grandmother came from Scotland as a girl, only thirteen, fourteen years old, crossed the plains with a handcart, then married a young man from Scotland when she reached Utah."

"Pure blood on one side—that's encouraging."

The slow smile spread over his features, friendly and guileless. It was refreshing to find such sincerity in a man. "Well, I'm wandering off into dangerous waters talking of Utah. Just wanted you to be aware of the connection."

She inclined her head slightly as though in acknowledgment.

"What about you? What do you like besides MGs? Let me guess—" He drummed his fingers along the thick table. "I would say you like Beethoven better than Bach, wind better than sun, long wild drives in the moonlight. And poetry. Yes, I would guess you like poetry."

"That's pretty good. You've given us something to start on."

The waiter came with their order. An hour later, after returning two or three times to refill their mugs, he brought hot mince pie, but they hardly touched it. They were involved in a very intense process, a tentative, high-risk, absorbing discovery.

"I wish you'd consider it. You know it's a serious offer." Andrew stood leaning against the low mantlepiece in Brad's room. "I've explained to you, Brad, I've real need of you here. It's not only the mills; I have other schemes hatching."

"I know. The developmental communities."

"That's right. There'll be men to manage, and you could do it. I'd pay a high price for a man like you."

"I appreciate the confidence, you know I do. But I can't see uprooting my family and coming here, all on your good graces—"

"For heaven's sake, Brad!"

"There's something too easy about it, Andrew, that bothers me."

Andrew turned with a sigh. They'd gone through this how many times now? "You're as stubborn as any Scot—you're at home here that way."

"I suppose you're right." Brad stood, then walked over and took Andrew's hand. "I can't tell you what this visit has meant to me, Andrew, how deeply everything here has touched my life."

Andrew nodded. "We work well together, don't we? Get along well together—that's also a rare, vital factor."

Brad laughed. "You're incorrigible."

Andrew smiled. "Well, I won't give up, Brad. I'll let you know as soon as the court date's set. If we're lucky we'll get in sometime this summer. You can come back with your family then."

Brad's expression darkened.

"I know finances are a concern, Brad, but I can arrange that. It's the least I can do—"

Brad shook his head. "It's the money and more. It's the whole idea. I can see us arriving and settling in like a group of vultures: waiting, watching, licking our chops in anticipation."

"That's rather gruesome, but colorful. All right, Brad, relax and we'll see what happens. Fact is, lad, I'll miss you terribly."

Brad looked into the kind, handsome face of this man who was more like a brother than the one he had left at home. There was something between them. Was it partly the blood that ran through their veins? Could such ties, watered down by generations as they were, make an actual difference?

It was his last night at Bieldmor House. After Andrew left him he finished packing a few odds and ends, wrote in his journal, then organized and reorganized his things. He was too tense to settle down to sleep. Quietly he found his way through the darkened house to the portrait hall and Charles Buchanan. He switched on the light above the picture and it shone like a spotlight, so that Charles's eyes seemed to gaze at him, smouldering and alive. He gasped a little. It was a false trick image, nothing more. But it spoiled the simple purpose for which he had come: to gaze homagelike at the face and gain there some peace. There was no peace for Bradley Richards this night, and no answers. The features of the portrait seemed closed, indiscernible. The burning eyes could be expressing anger and disapproval as easily, perhaps more easily, than the compassion Brad sought there. It was a meaningless, rather superstitious thing to do, anyway. He switched off the light and groped his way back in shadow, struggling against the strong urge to turn around, feeling the gaze of the deep, piercing eyes still upon him.

8

I loved him, and will weep
my date of life out for
his sweet life's loss.
KING JOHN

It was nearly spring; Edwin kept reminding himself of that, though March in Illinois wasn't much better than in Scotland. He was growing restless—it seemed he'd been here far longer than three weeks. He'd downed too many bottles of whiskey and watched too much American television. The girl—thank heaven the girl had proved interesting. She was a canny little thing in spite of her age. He enjoyed her company and her conversation. He enjoyed the fact that other men, seeing her, usually turned around for another look. He enjoyed watching that certain expression come into her eyes, a gaze that was totally open and adoring. He had earned that look by careful cultivation. He did small, gentlemanly things for her. He learned her little quirks, her preferences, then worked to please her. It was an old formula, tried and true. And it worked splendidly with the young American schoolgirl.

He put on his jacket and walked out of the hotel and across the street to the drugstore, thinking to buy a newspaper or two to while away the hours until the evening, which he would spend with Julie. There were two or three people inside, but he paid them no attention. His purposes here didn't extend to camaraderie with the natives. There wasn't much about these small-town Americans he'd found to his liking. He was thumbing through the magazine rack when he realized someone had approached him.

"Excuse me." Edwin didn't look up, but the young man continued. "I understand you're going to be around for a while so I thought I'd better introduce myself."

"Really?" Edwin's eyebrows shot up in a high, tight arch and his voice was chilly. "Is there some reason why you and I ought to be acquainted?"

The young man with the thick sandy hair didn't ruffle easily. "Yes, I think so. My name is Tom Briggs. I used to date Nan quite a bit before Andrew showed up here. My kid brother and Nan's sister, Julie, are friends."

"Ah, I see, you're the self-styled local hero, sworn to protect the innocent. Very touching."

Tom Briggs didn't blink or recoil. "Call it what you want. Just be careful—be very careful where Julie's concerned."

Edwin was seething inside, but no sign of that showed in his haughty demeanor. He fixed Tom with a gaze that was both detached and disdainful. "Two rejections in one family. I understand that would be difficult to handle."

Tom moved a step closer, his head and his voice lowered. "Fred and Julie have never dated each other. That's not the point here. I don't think you understand me. There's just one thing at stake—your own two-bit hide if you step out of line."

Edwin didn't know whether to disdain to reply or to throw back a challenge. A challenge might come across as petty and childish if he wasn't careful. Far better to handle the chap with a pair of kid gloves.

"You've made your point, sir—crudely, but adequately. Now, if you'll excuse me." He walked superciliously past, keeping his manner deliberately slow and casual. He paid for his papers and then left the drugstore, content that he'd carried the final point, but furious that such an inferior individual should presume to treat him in such a rude manner.

Tom, with lowered brows, watched him leave the drugstore. "That one's no good," he mumbled under his breath. "He may look like Andrew, but the resemblance stops there.'' Tom was honest; he didn't know how to be anything else. He might resent, he might be jealous of Andrew. But he would admit that the man who had won Hannah's love was a gentleman.

''This Edwin is a rude, conceited fool,'' he said through clenched teeth. But saying it didn't make him feel any better. He grabbed his half-finished soft drink and went back to work.

That evening Julie noticed a difference in Edwin's mood. She had come to recognize when he was restless, but this was different, a smoldering kind of discontent. She could feel it, almost taste it, like the slightly scorched taste in ruined food. She did everything she could to dispel it; she could usually lift him out of his darker moods. But this one she couldn't touch. She lapsed into a kind of silence of her own until Edwin, rousing himself, took notice of her. He was kind; he was never unkind to her.

''I've made you miserable,'' he said, ''and I'm sorry, Julie. It's just something eating at me that you can't help.'' He asked her questions about her day, questions that would divert them. She tried as she always did to make herself interesting to him. They stopped by the only drive-in that was open in town and he ordered everything he could think of that was her favorite, laughing when she protested.

''It's a harmless indulgence; you need some meat on your bones,'' he told her. ''Take a bite of each one just for flavor and leave the rest.'' He watched her; she really was quite disarming. Fresh, with the bloom of youth on her skin and hair. She *was* thin, but shapely, with fine long legs, a more compact, athletic feel to her body than Nan had. Nan was old-fashioned femininity. Julie carried the warm, energetic appeal of American women: innocent, yet open, supple and unrestrained.

''Are you homesick as well as bored, Edwin?'' she asked him, then regretted the question when she saw the look it brought into his eyes.

''Aye, I'm very much a homebody, Julie. My heart's always in the Highlands, wherever I go . . .''

She smiled. "I know a verse like that. We read it in English class."

"Well, don't quote it, please."

"I won't. I'm not Nan."

That brought an awkward silence, a strain between them.

"I've too much of the reiver in me, Julie." He said it softly.

She leaned forward over the table. "The rover?"

"No, the reiver—the bold adventurer who takes lightly the laws that other men make, who thrives on danger and forbidden fruit." He wasn't smiling; he was watching her closely.

"I don't quite understand," she said, "but if I did, I think I'd agree. I think if I were a man I'd want to be something like that."

Just one corner of his mouth turned up in a smile. "I suppose you might, and if I were there to teach you I don't think you'd regret it one bit." He rose from the table. "Time to go home, princess."

They walked out into the chill night. The wind moaned about them, as restless and lonely as Edwin's eyes. They drove past a house with a large cardboard sign that announced Free Kittens. Edwin pulled up in front and they went inside.

"Which will you have?" he asked. Julie chose a white one, white and fluffy, a ball of soft silk with two sky-blue eyes. "She's fitting," Edwin announced. "She's like you. I'd have taken the sleek, thin, black one with black agate eyes."

Julie shivered under his gaze. For the remainder of the way to her house she sat close beside him, aware of his pulsing warmth where his arm touched her own. When he stopped the car he leaned over and kissed her, not once but several times, and his kisses were tender, so tender they made her ache inside.

The next afternoon when she came home from school there were presents waiting: a jeweled collar with a bell for the cat and a basket with a silken pillow for it to sleep on. For Julie there were a dozen white roses. The note read: *To the princess and her new kitten, With love, Edwin.* There was a letter tucked in with the roses which said, "I'm off to Chicago for a few days. Don't worry. Got to get out of here for a spell, or go mad. Miss me a little, Julie. —Edwin."

So he was disappearing again. He'd done it before. She had no idea what he did with his time in Chicago. Well, she did have some ideas, but she didn't like them. She didn't like to be so abruptly reminded of how boring, tame, and uninteresting she must appear. In Chicago he would go out with women—clever, sophisticated women, not high school girls.

She looked down at the kitten who sat curled on her toe biting her shoelace. "You were just a tidbit, something to salve his conscience," she said, but the kitten ignored her. *Miss me a little*—she laughed out loud. If she could do that, miss him a little, she'd be all right. It had gone far past that point and she knew it. She would be in misery, half-alive till she saw him again.

Bad luck comes in runs; tragedy strikes not once, like lightning, but two or three times at the same hapless spot before moving on. So it was with Nan that early spring, her first spring as a married woman, her first spring in Scotland. Perhaps the mill fire was really the presage, the actual beginning. But it seemed to start with the accident by the pool.

She had taken her great-grandfather's journal out into the sunlight. She wanted to read again Daniel Martin's own words, touch the core of the elusive thing they all struggled for, that had touched all their lives both for good and evil. It seemed strange to think of the handsome young Charles in the portrait living and breathing in the setting Daniel described, falling in love with the non-Mormon girl Daniel wished to marry, being strong enough of will to draw her away, win her love and devotion, change her allegiance. He had been born to riches and a life that promised success and ease. But he, too, had changed his allegiance and gone his own way, fired with youthful enthusiasm, sure he could add new honor to the Buchanan name. And all he had found was heartache and persecution, shame not of his own making, and early death.

Nan sat in the sun and read the journal, only vaguely aware of Janet's approach, vaguely aware of the yipping collie that pranced beside her. She sat on the low wall by the pond where the sun-soaked rocks gave back their store of heat, lusciously warm against hands and legs. As Janet came up to sit beside her Nan turned and Tybalt, the collie, jumped up in greeting, knocking the heavy journal from her hands. She gasped; the water was deep here. She couldn't jump in and retrieve it. The thick leather volume slid into the water, noiselessly disappearing from her sight. She stood staring stupidly at the spot.

"Janet, do something! Get Andrew. Do something quickly!"

Janet ran, afraid to argue, eager to leave the unhappy spot. When Andrew arrived he pulled Nan gently away. He poked into the pond with a long, pronged stick, searching for the journal. It was nearly an hour later when he came in carrying the sodden, unrecognizable mess. The ink had run, the thin, delicate pages had disintegrated. The water had destroyed what the long, silent years had so carefully guarded and preserved.

Something that precious could not be ruined so quickly, so cruelly, so irrevocably! She blamed herself more than she blamed the dog or mere circumstances, and fretted at the further barrier this might place between herself and Janet. She felt, for the first time since she was married, miserably disappointed and unhappy. She went to bed late, but she didn't sleep. She tossed and turned and half-dreamed, and awoke unrested.

It was April and she awoke to birds' song. Bright, brave birds, to believe in the promise of spring. She tried to think of other things, put the nightmare behind her. She had copied the vital pages from the book, so she hadn't lost the evidence they needed, evidence to prove Brad Richards the legal heir. She ought to be grateful for that, Andrew gently reminded. But it wasn't for evidence she had cherished the journal. What could she say, when she herself didn't understand? It had something to do with those long-lost people and their spirits, with the link between her life and theirs. She felt she had betrayed them somehow in destroying their record, and in a small, superstitious way she felt it an omen.

She went through the motions of the day, feeling dull and stupored. In midafternoon she heard the phone ring and Jessie call to her. She picked up the receiver, thinking to hear Andrew's voice. What she heard instead sent a cold wave through her.

"Nan, honey, this is your dad. I'm sorry to call you—" He paused. He was never one to make conversation. He had called for a reason; he thought he ought to get right to the point.

"Grant Morgan died last night. They found him this morning."

"Oh, Daddy, oh no."

"I'm sorry, Nan. I knew you'd want to know right away."

"Yes, thank you, Daddy." Nan moved the phone so that she could sit down. She felt weak all over.

"He died sitting up in his chair. He'd been reading. Didn't suffer much, I suppose."

"I'm glad for his sake. He deserved to die that way." She paused. "Do you know what book he was reading?"

She shouldn't have asked that. Her father's voice when he answered the question was guarded and rough. "Book of Mormon's what they told me. What else would it be?"

"Have the services been set?"

"Yes, I waited to call till I knew. They've been scheduled for Thursday. They want to give his children all time to arrive."

"Good. I'm going to try to come myself."

"You are?" There was anticipation in his voice.

"I'll have to talk to Andrew. I'll call you later."

"Good. Well, that will be fine. I hope you can come, Nan."

"So do I, Daddy—and not just because of Grant. I'll call as soon as I know. Give my love to Grandma."

She hung up before realizing that she hadn't mentioned her brother or sister. She hadn't thought of either Julie or Jonathan. She sat with her hands in her lap. Could he really be gone now? She had meant to have Grant come here for a visit. She had meant to have him help bless her first child. She had meant—with a sense of great sorrow it struck her—she had meant to have Grant baptize her into the Church!

It was her own fault. She had thought there was time; she had been too busy, too concerned about other, far less important things. Now time had reached out and snatched him away, and none of her anger or heartache could bring him back. She sat huddled in the chair feeling small and frightened, and terribly betrayed by life.

"Of course you must go. You should be there, Nan, as much as any of his children."

Nan smiled up at the kind, gentle eyes that were watching her.

"I'd go with you if this fire business was all taken care of. But, actually, even though it will be much harder, it will be good in some ways for you to go back alone."

She didn't disagree; the same thought had come to her. Andrew made arrangements for her to leave the following morning. She fought back the flood of misgivings she had. Every time she looked into Andrew's face she weakened. She remembered how painful their separations had been before. But they had not been apart for more than one day since their marriage. It was easy for her to fall into the habit of depending on Andrew for everything, letting him take care of all difficult or unpleasant details, or the little things she felt incapable of. Now she would no longer have his strength to rely on. She would have to handle each difficult challenge alone.

They spent the evening alone together. Nan hadn't seen Janet around all day. She would be leaving early the next morning. She didn't want to risk it and wait till then. So, late, very late, when she saw Janet's light on, she slipped through the hall and knocked resolutely at the closed door.

She waited. There was no response from within, so she knocked again. This time she heard shuffled movement, and the door slowly opened. Janet stood on the other side staring back at her.

"May I come in, please?" Nan asked. Janet merely nodded and stood back from the door so Nan could pass through.

"I hate to disturb you so late," Nan apologized. "But it's important for me to see you before I leave. Did you know I'm flying to Chicago tomorrow morning?"

Janet nodded again, nothing else. She was making it hard. Nan swallowed a lump in her throat and continued. "I just want to ask you to take special care of Andrew while I'm gone."

"I did that before you came."

"I know you did." Nan took a deep breath. This was going badly. "Look, I'm sorry things have changed. I can't help that, Janet. I haven't wanted to take him away from you. One love doesn't cancel out another. You're his sister—his love for me can't change that, can't lessen the bond between you two." She paused, aware that her voice was tense with emotion. Consciously she struggled to calm herself.

"For a long time I've known how deeply he loves you, how important you are to him." Nan smiled just slightly. "I was a little jealous of that at first. I always wished I had an older brother, someone to turn to after my mother died. And I guess I failed with my own little sister. I could never seem to build the kind of relationship you and Andrew had." She stirred uneasily while the silent girl watched her. "In fact, I'm frightened to go back and face Julie again. I don't want anything to go wrong. . . . Well, anyway . . ."

The blue eyes watching her face were very disarming. "What I mostly wanted to say was, I understand. I know you and Andrew shared a lot of life together before I came into the picture. I respect that. And I respect the pain you went through when you lost your father—" Her voice began to waver. She panicked at the thought of crying before those eyes. "At least you had Andrew to help you then. When my mother died I had no one to really turn to."

She moved to the open door and grasped the handle, grateful to feel its cool hardness against her hand. "I'm sorry. I'm not very good at this sort of thing. Thank you for letting me talk to you, Janet. I—"

She wanted to say more, but she really couldn't. She turned and made a hasty, ungraceful escape, feeling blundering, foolish, and awkward, as she did so often around the girl. The blue eyes that had stared so relentlessly at her softened, and filled slowly with unwanted tears.

9

Muffle your false love . . .
Comfort my sister, cheer her:
When were you wont to use my
sister thus?

THE COMEDY OF ERRORS

It was good to be back. Even the hustle and bustle of O'Hare felt like home, and the pleasant, even, mid-Western voices with no kind of accent at all sounded like sweet, familiar music to Nan's ear.

She wasn't sure just who would be coming to meet her. Probably her grandmother and Julie. Her father never took a day away from his classroom if he could help it. She was sure she had told them the proper flight number. She couldn't imagine they wouldn't arrange to be here on time.

She walked to the end of the seating area and looked one way, then the other, but found no familiar faces among the crowds. She stood, perplexed and indecisive. She felt a pressure, a touch on her arm, and turned. He had come up from behind; he stood close beside her. She gasped at her first reaction to the dear, loved face and constrained an impulse to reach out and touch him. She said nothing, but stood before him, trembling.

"My, but suffering becomes you, Hannah. You look breathless and wounded, and elegant, my dear."

"I am breathless and wounded, and you ought to be thrashed, Edwin. What kind of a trick is this! What are you doing here?" She nearly shouted the last words at him, and stomped her foot in sudden anger. "How dare you come here? Now? You knew I would think you were Andrew. You're cruel—"

While she scolded he led her away. "We'll have plenty of time to talk. Let's collect the baggage. First things first, my dear."

Nan stopped cold, jerking his hand, and he turned around with a quizzical look to face her.

"First things first. That's right. The first thing is an explanation. The second a phone call to Nauvoo. I have no intention of going anywhere with you, Edwin."

He seemed to slump; his eyes became dark and uneasy. "I've made a mess of things this time, haven't I?"

"Yes, you have. Your cruel little joke backfired. You thought it would be great fun to meet me here—great fun for who, Edwin?"

The distress in Nan's voice struck a chord in Edwin. He paused. He had no blithe answer this time.

"I didn't think it through," he confessed. Then, interjecting a melodramatic note, "that's so like me, Hannah. Juvenile, inane—yes cruel, even cruel, for I know that's what you think me."

Nan sighed at his play acting. "Don't whine so, Edwin, it's unbecoming. Besides, it isn't true. You thought it through and liked the idea of taking your chances."

"I'm sorry enough for it now." Nan couldn't help laughing. He was such a picture of contrite sincerity.

"You blowhard, you phony. All right," she conceded, "I'm stuck with you for the duration. Let's get my bags. I've questions enough to keep you talking from here to Nauvoo."

When it came she took his explanation quite calmly. She seemed able to read between the lines where he was concerned. She remembered the wild pain she had seen in his eyes on her wedding night. She believed it was with him still, that pain, covered over with layers of seeming indifference and vanity that he hoped would conceal it. She could understand many things, but not all.

"So you're here to dally away your time and Julie's the plaything. Why choose Julie for a victim?"

He shrugged slightly, unconcernedly. "Why not? She's young and innocent, eager prey—"

"Stop it, Edwin. This is more than a clever exchange of words. What's the matter with you?"

"I shall take that question as rhetorical," he replied, "and not hazard an answer." They were approaching a lighted area off from the highway, a cluster of restaurants and gas stations. He turned toward it, slowed the car, then pulled off at the side of the road.

"Listen, Nan, when I heard you were coming my first impulse was to get the blazes out of here. Julie never would have told—"

"Oh, she's that duped, is she?" He was surprised at the bitter bite in Nan's voice. "Surely there were other people who have seen you, Edwin, who could give you away. Anyway, you like hand-to-hand combat, don't you? Facing the enemy eye to eye. It's the danger that's your intoxicant, win or lose."

"Astute, my dear, astute." He raised an eyebrow as though in sudden distress or pain.

"So you remained to fight it out. How noble."

"Sarcasm doesn't become *you,* Nan." His tone was so soft and sincere that it stopped her. She stared at him, long and deep, till his gaze nearly fell, nearly dropped before hers. At last she released him.

"You're right. Does revenge become you, Edwin?"

It was a startling left hook; it caught him off guard. The mask, so carefully crafted, seemed flimsy before her, frighteningly inadequate.

"I didn't make the rules, I just play the game."

She laughed softly at that. "Edwin! You may play the game, but certainly not by the rules."

"Clever, my dear, but the truth is it's a dirty game any way you play it, by any man's rules."

She shivered. His voice opened chasms within her. She said softly, "I've never looked upon life that way."

He touched her then. With his fingers he tilted her face till their eyes met. His own revealed more than he meant them to.

"That's all well and good for you, Nan. You've never had to. I pray heaven, believe me, lass, that you never will."

The incongruity of the moment struck her. She could not doubt his sincerity. But his actions belied his words. It was *he* who threatened, he who hacked at the roots of her own security. She sighed. There would be no way to tell him.

"Would you like a bite to eat?" he asked. She nodded her head.

He drove the car into a lighted parking lot and stopped it. He came around to her side to help her; she gave him her hand. There was nothing more she could do for the moment. But the confusion of all this burned inside her, like the hot pillar of Andrew's fire against the cold night, and with little pinpricks of pain the contradictions ate into her mind and would give her no rest.

"I don't have to talk about any of this, Nan, especially with you."

The two sisters sat together on the bed in Nan's old room. Julie's face looked pinched and white, her eyes defensive. *She's grown up a lot in the past few months,* Nan thought, looking at her.

"I'm concerned, Julie. I know how much he can hurt you."

"Concerned! That's very touching. Well, never mind."

"But, Julie, although he might like you, he's using you—"

"And what's new about that? Don't we all use each other? Why single him out? Just because he doesn't try to hide what he's doing?"

"All right, all right. I'm sorry, Julie." She dropped her eyes from before the intensity of her sister's gaze. She felt suddenly, overwhelmingly weary. "What about Daddy? How have you gotten around him?"

"Easily. I *told* him what I was doing, I didn't *ask* him. Then I ignored the whole issue and so has he."

Nan sighed and Julie snapped back in reaction. "He learned with you, Nan, that opposition would do him no good. First the Mormon church, then Andrew. I get the feeling that you think everything *you* did to defy him was justified. But, of course, what I do isn't."

Julie rose from the bed. "I'm tired, and I suppose you are, too. I'll see you in the morning." She turned to leave, then hesitated. "Look, Nan, I'm all right, really. I know what I'm doing." She walked to the door, then paused again. "I'm glad you're home, Nan," she said softly. "Good night."

Nan felt like crying as she watched the door close behind Julie. She wasn't sure why: she missed Andrew, she was lonely and tired; she hated Edwin, and she felt sorry for him; she was angry at Julie, and worried to death about her—too many dark shadows colliding clumsily inside her head.

Julie's words sound logical and brave, Nan thought to herself. *But she doesn't know what she's talking about. The hurt hasn't come yet, she hasn't felt it. She doesn't know how much pain could be waiting for her.*

Janet hated to admit it, but the house seemed different without Nan there. Certain little touches were missing: the fresh flowers she set in the rooms, the music she played, the American foods she had introduced into their menus. And her laughter. The house seemed so still without it. She tried to put their last conversation out of her mind. But three days after Nan had left, when Mrs. MacRae came over all excited about a tip for a story for Nan, Janet listened patiently, took down the information, and promised to have Nan call the old lady when she returned. A few weeks ago she wouldn't have listened, or would have thrown the information away. She'd done so before; what was stopping her now?

Andrew wasn't one to sulk; he could manage without Nan. But the same light wasn't in his eyes as when Nan was with him. Janet wrote out a small, formal invitation and set it on his bed. The following day she received a formal acceptance tucked in with a dozen roses. She was delighted. Nothing pleased her more than the prospect of an evening alone with Andrew. Or, at least, so she thought till the telephone rang.

When she heard the voice on the other end a warmth spread through her. "Neil, how kind of you to call," she said, slightly disturbed at her own reaction.

"Not kind at all. Motivated purely by self-interest. I was wondering, Janet, if you'd like to come out with me—"

"That depends," she interjected, somewhat saucily. "If you have a *Church* dance or party in mind, Neil, please spare me." She felt compelled to keep within the dimensions she had so carefully set.

"Slow I may be, Janet, but not foolhardy. No, there's a concert I'd like to take you to Thursday night. I have a couple of tickets—"

The silence set in before he had finished talking. *Oh no,* Janet thought, alarmed at her own distress. *That's my date with Andrew!*

"I can't, Neil, but I'd really like to. I'm sorry."

He was too disappointed to notice the warmth in her voice. "That's all right, I understand. I should have called earlier."

There was a pause, and then her laughter came over the line. "But it took this long to work up courage to call me, right?" He smarted a little, not sure of the girl's intentions.

Why am I doing this? Janet thought. "Listen, Neil," she said, "I've another date that night, and I simply can't break it."

What could he say to that? He stammered a little. "In fact," she added, "you'd have to go some distance to outclass him." There was laughter in her voice, but Neil was confused still.

"I'm sorry to tease you," she said, "I've a date with Andrew. But I'm free on Friday."

"I'll take it," he said. "We'll find something to do. Shall I come at seven?"

"That will be fine—"

They talked for a moment, then said good-bye. *What am I doing?* Janet thought in the silence that followed. But she wasn't afraid. She felt deeply excited, deeply alive. She needed someone, and she felt drawn to this young man. What she knew of him gave her no reason to mistrust her own instincts. All other dislikes or discrepancies she would put aside for now.

She sat alone, in a room full of silent strangers, yet she had never felt more at home, more at rest. She touched the folds of the handkerchief in her lap and smiled. Edwin had driven her to the Mormon chapel this morning. He had been quiet, but she had felt his sympathy.

"Do you have a handkerchief?" he had asked.

She shook her head. "Some Kleenexes."

"Those will never do. Here, take this," and he gave her his own. He had walked with her to the door. His eyes looked sad. He was a skillful actor, she knew, but the look in his eyes seemed to be real.

With her finger she traced the lettering stitched in the hanky. The initials *EB* with great flourishes: *Edwin Bain.* The same initials could stand for *Edwin Buchanan.* But they didn't—and nothing Edwin might do could change that fact.

The organ music died and Nan glanced around her. The services were about to begin. The bishop rose and stood before the congregation. The closed casket with Grant's body in it rested off to one side draped with a long spray of flowers, surrounded by flowers.

She had gone to the viewing the night before, waiting in line to file past—anxious, uncertain. She had never looked on a dead body before. When Grant's wife, Ellen, had died she was too young to attend the funeral; her father would never have granted permission for her to be there. When her mother had died it had been again forbidden. She was always considered too young, too impressionable. But now that she was grown-up, everyone assumed she could take it.

When she had stood beside the casket and lowered her eyes she had nearly gasped at how real Grant looked, how familiar the dear, gentle features were. She had bent and touched his hair, ever so gently, marveling at the peace the blank features held, longing to feel once more his strong arms around her, aware that the spirit, the man, was not here, but feeling him—feeling the warmth of his presence as though he stood beside her and held her hand.

She felt it again today. As the bishop was speaking, as others rose to pay tribute to their friend, she knew that somehow Grant was here and his presence took the bitterness out of the tears she shed. How selfishly she missed him and longed for his comfort! No one could bring heaven and earth closer to one another than Grant could. She remembered the many evenings they'd spent together when he had opened to her what he called "the simple beauties of eternity." She remembered the evening of her twenty-first birthday when Grant had presented her with a Book of Mormon, engraved with her name nine years before, kept lovingly for her through long, patient years. She remembered Monday night home evenings together when Grant had taught her the words and tunes to his Mormon hymns: "The Spirit of God," "O, Ye Mountains High," "O My Father." Without him, where would she be today? How empty her mind and heart would be!

At last the beautiful moments drew to a close. A soloist began to sing the beautiful hymn, "O My Father":

O my Father, thou that dwellest
In the high and glorious place,
When shall I regain thy presence,
And again behold thy face?

The words sang like a prayer breathed in harmony, sweet and unburdening:

When I leave this frail existence,
When I lay this mortal by,
Father, Mother, may I meet you
In your royal courts on high?

The tears ran shamelessly down Nan's cheeks and a thought came to her: *Grant's with Ellen now. He's happy. But I know Grant. He won't rest till he finds my mother.* She wondered what her mother was like. She wondered what she would think when Grant started talking. *Oh, Mother, please listen, please listen!* she begged in her heart.

"I'll drive you to the cemetery if you'd like," Edwin told her. "And I promise you can trust me. No quick disappearing act, no missing headstones."

She knew she ought to be offended, but she smiled gently. "No thanks, I'd rather go later, by myself. There are too many people there now."

"Then what is your pleasure?" Always the gallant, the polished cavalier. Nan stared at the features, only slightly distorted from those she loved so dearly. It sent a chill through her. "I think I'll just go home, if you don't mind."

"Why should I mind?" He turned the car, but his blue eyes frowned and the dullness was back in his voice.

Oh, Edwin, Nan thought, *how quickly you change! How hard it would be to keep you happy!*

He pulled up outside the house but he didn't move. Nan sat

silent, too, watching him—waiting. "You really loved the old fellow, didn't you?" he said. Nan swallowed and nodded. "I envy you that. I'm not sure I've ever really loved another person—that way."

"Your mother?"

"Not my mother! Jessie—Jessie would come the closest."

"She loves you, too."

"Why do you say that?" His voice had grown guarded now.

"I saw it in her eyes that night. And she told me; she told me she loves you like a son."

Edwin's hands were clenched on the wheel; his fine knuckles whitened. He made a small sound under his breath and opened the door, came around to help her out, not looking at her. Nan wished desperately she knew what to do.

"Do you want to come in? I know Julie would like to see you."

He still didn't look into her eyes. "I don't think so. I'm afraid I'd be very poor company. Give her my apologies, will you?"

He turned. Nan walked up the path. Upstairs a small white hand dropped the fold of drapery, blotting out the tall, dark man whose features had blurred with the tears that entered her eyes as she watched him. For two days now he had been constantly at Nan's side. She had hardly seen him, hardly spoken to him. There was something in his eyes when he looked at her sister that made Julie's blood run cold.

She closed her eyes. *Don't cry, you stupid fool, you knew this was coming. You know he doesn't really care about you.* She knew, so why wasn't she able to hate him? Why did that knowledge make her yearn for him even more?

Early morning by the river. How long since she'd been here! Nan spread her sweater and sat on the old log beside the willow. Tiny new buds of green shone like stars in the branches that drooped and draped so gracefully over her head. It was here she had stood that first day with Andrew and listened while he explained his strange mission to her: told of his father's death, of the ancient will and the search for the missing heir it had forced upon him. It was here on this spot where he first had kissed her, where he had said, "Take care of yourself, Hannah Martin, with me not here to look after you." And her heart had cried, in pain, *Oh, Andrew, will you ever be here to look after me again?*

She trembled at the remembered emotion, with a new appreciation for the fate that had unerringly brought their two lives together. What if—what if Andrew had never come? How could she have lived her life without him?

She rose and walked down to the water's edge. The shoreline was soft and muddy and strewn with debris that the spring floods had washed onto the land and discarded. The Mississippi went noisily about its business this morning. Nan stood listening to the old, loved sound, breathing in the dank, heavy scent of the river. She thought of that other river so far away whose many moods and landscapes she had come to love. The words Andrew had taught her to sing ran through her mind: "Oh, the river Clyde, the wonderful Clyde! The name of it thrills me and fills me with pride. And I'm satisfied, what e'er may betide, the sweetest of songs is the song of the Clyde."

The sweetest of songs . . . she mused. *Yes, the Clyde sings a sweet song to me. But before the Clyde came the Mississippi, ancient in its own place, mighty and proud. It was here, to the Yankee tune of the Father of Waters, that love first spoke to Andrew's heart and mine.* She wondered how many times Charles and Rachel Buchanan had walked here together, with the new city growing before their eyes and new dreams shining in their hearts.

Oh, river, she marveled, *how many old secrets you carry! Do they burden you, or do you harbor them joyfully? Or are you so busy with your own affairs that you scarcely notice the passing fears and hopes of the human heart?*

The sun was warm on her back when Nan left the spot and turned her face homeward. The song she hummed under her breath was not to the Clyde, but an old frontier ditty in praise of the Mississippi.

10

Be friends: an thou wilt not, why then, be enemies with me, too.

HENRY V

It's Nan." Janet held out the phone. Andrew took it quickly. Could anything be wrong? "Hello, darling, it's me."

Janet watched her brother's face as he listened. Whatever could Nan be talking about for so long, with no response from Andrew? But his features had brightened. When at last he spoke she was taken aback by his words.

"The first flight I can book! I'll be there, Hannah."

What could it be? "Bless you for thinking of it. I feel that it's right, Nan; yes, I do. I'll talk to the bishop and arrange for the necessary recommends—and a time for you to call him. I think he can interview you long-distance, knowing you as he does."

When he hung up the phone Janet had to bite her tongue to keep from asking. Would he tell her? She waited expectantly. "I'm flying to meet Nan—in Salt Lake," he said, in a tone so joyful that she felt a small shaft of envy.

"Salt Lake? Just like that. What for, Andrew?"

He paused and considered a moment. "It's time, Janet—past time." Suddenly she knew; as he said it, she knew. "We're going to be baptized."

The shaft of envy drove in deeper. She remembered with painful clarity how she had felt when she had approached Andrew last fall concerning her own baptism. *I'll wait until January,* she had said, *till I turn eighteen. I'll wait that long, but I won't wait any longer.*

She had worried about obtaining her mother's permission. Looking back on it, she seemed so innocent, so docile then. *January.* So much had happened before January; the discovery of Andrew's American heir, Edwin's banishment, Nan's coming, the wedding—her own petty angers and resentments. Now January had come and gone and she was eighteen, and unbaptized still.

"Janet?" Andrew was watching her closely.

She rose and walked to the window. "I think that's fine, I really do. If that's what you and Nan want, if you're sure. What about Mother?"

"Well, I'll just have to tell her. By this time I don't think anything else will surprise her." He grinned boyishly. "Will you help me, Janet? I've so much to do in so little time."

She was happy to help him, glad he had asked, relieved that the conversation had ended before the topic of baptism had somehow been turned in her own direction.

It was Nan's last day in Nauvoo; the time had passed far too quickly. She was tying up loose ends, an exhaustive process. She had already been to Grant's grave and his old home as well, where his daughter had graciously given her several mementoes.

"You knew him in some ways better than we did," she said, "and he loved you as well as any of us, I know."

That meant more to Nan than the gifts; those words were bright treasures that replenished her storehouse of faith and self-regard.

She found time to spend alone with her brother. "I need a new bagpipes record," he announced gravely. "My old one's worn through." She promised him another and fed him with stories of the castles and battle sites he would see when she brought him for a visit to Scotland. "When?" he pressed, but she held him off. "After all this mess is settled," she explained. "It will be worth waiting for," she promised him with a smile.

She didn't spend the time with her father that she wanted to. He seemed evasive, almost preoccupied. When she told him about her baptism he roused a little. "Well, the old man got what he wanted in the end, even if he didn't live to see it." There was no bitterness in his tone, just resignation. Nan looked more like her mother now than she ever had. He kept his distance for his own reasons, loath as he was to renew old pains.

"I'm sorry," Nan told him softly. "There's not much I can do to change things now. I never meant to cause you sorrow."

"I know that. Things happen. You find your own way, and you have to follow. I know—"

She felt with those words that he understood. She knew what even those few words had cost him.

So the hours slipped through her fingers like the fine spray that blew up from the Mississippi during a storm, touching her briefly, then dissolving into air. There was not much she could do where her grandmother was concerned. She was there, a solid part of her background: washing, cooking, sewing, caring for creature comforts, efficient in needs of the flesh, but little more. She had shut out the world of the spirit long ago, content to take life as it came and to ask no questions. Nan had struggled against that narrowness when she was a girl, but accepted it now with resigned patience, able to love her father's mother for what she was.

That left only one person: Julie. Since that first night, they had spoken very little together. And Edwin, except for helping her through the funeral, had made himself really quite scarce. She knew Julie was suffering. She had never seen her sister so silent and withdrawn; that was not Julie's way. How impotent Nan felt before life's forces, how helpless to change things, to do any good!

She was sitting alone in the front room brooding about it all when the doorbell rang. When she opened the door she was thoroughly surprised by the person she saw there. Tom stood smiling at her gently. "You're more beautiful than before," he told her bluntly. "I wouldn't believe it if I hadn't seen it with my own eyes."

"You're kind. You were always too kind. Come in, Tom." She stood back so that he could enter. He walked through the door, but remained standing close beside her, searching her face. "I hope it's all right that I came." A small smile played at the corners of his mouth. "I kept waiting to run into you, but I didn't. Julie said this was your last day . . ."

"Heavens, yes, I'm glad you're here, Tom, really. Sit down and catch me up on the local news."

It was easy to talk to Tom. He, too, had matured some. She enjoyed their conversation without the old strain, without the old sense of guilt that had plagued her.

"You like Scotland, then? It seems to agree with you." It was an earnest question, Nan knew, not a pleasantry. And it implied: *Do you like married life? Are you happy?* She knew if she answered *no* he'd get set for battle, suffer anything to protect her from pain.

"I'm very happy in Scotland, Tom. I have a wonderful life there." She smiled slightly, reminding him of her old, shy way. "It's very demanding on me at times, but it's warm and good there."

Tom nodded. *That's all I really wanted to know.* She could read the words in his eyes. "I'm glad, Nan." He paused and then drew a deep breath, as though taking a plunge. "I wish I could feel as secure about Julie's future."

Nan felt tempted to respond harshly. *What business is Julie's future to you?* But she understood his intentions, his way of thinking, his inborn protective nature. "You mean Edwin," she said.

"Exactly. I hoped you'd do something about him."

She sighed. "It isn't that simple, Tom. He isn't a disease, he's a person—and so is Julie, for that matter. She's a very strong-minded girl—"

"She's a child. She needs someone to look after her interests."

Nan smiled. "I'll do what I can," she said gently. "To tell the truth, I have more influence with Edwin than I have with her."

"That's not encouraging. I can't see anyone moving him."

She raised an eyebrow; she couldn't resist it. "Not even me?"

He grinned back. "Well, yes, maybe you . . ."

She turned the subject. "What about you, Tom? What have you been doing?"

"Working at Ives, of course. I run the place now."

"I know. I'd heard. I'm happy for you."

He shrugged his shoulders. "Well, it's a good beginning. My grandpa died last winter and left me some of his land and livestock. I've got plans—"

"Don't tell me," she said, "I remember. You want to purchase a John Deere dealership."

He beamed. "I didn't think you'd remember. I just may be able to swing it now. I've nearly got the capital they require—"

"Oh, I hope it works out for you, Tom." She nearly added, *If anyone deserves it, you do,* but caught herself just in time. He wouldn't like that. He had never believed he deserved her. Andrew's coming was a catalyst; he had told her that he didn't believe himself worthy of her love.

She walked him to the door. He lingered. "Thank you, Tom. I'm so glad you came. And thank you for watching out for Julie. I like just knowing that you're here."

He nodded. "I guess it will be a while till I see you again. Take care of yourself, Nan." He bent close and kissed her tenderly on the cheek. She stood quietly under his touch. "Good-bye, Tom."

She watched him walk with long strides down the walk, get into the Ives Garage truck, and drive away. Life seemed to her so capricious in its choices: this one for love and happiness—that one for loss; this one for pain and failure—that for success. Her own happiness seemed suddenly delicate and frail. She shivered and closed the door on the bright spring day.

Nan had to have one last walk by the river—at night, alone, when all was shadow and stillness. The water lapped like a lullaby at her feet and the night wind spun soft whispers among the high branches. He found her there. For a moment he watched her as he had that October night six months before. She moved with the same graceful loveliness, posing a picture whenever she chose to linger or pause. A lump rose in his throat. It seemed lately that he had more trouble with his emotions than ever before. That was something he needed to watch, a sign of weakness.

He moved out from among the shadows and approached her. At first she didn't notice him there. When she turned, when she saw his face, her eyes grew haunted and a tremor, like light wind across water, passed over her face.

"At first, for a moment or two, you were Andrew. You often are. I don't like that." Her voice was whisper soft. He drew closer.

"That's one advantage to myself I can't alter. But I'm sorry if it causes you distress." His voice sounded different somehow; she couldn't read it.

"Are you, Edwin? You haven't always been so. I seem to remember a time or two—quite distinctly—when you used that likeness to frighten me, even to cause me pain."

He seemed to wince; she felt it more than she saw it. "Those times might be excused if not forgiven. I knew less than I do now. I didn't know you. It was a struggle, you remember, for self-preservation."

"Isn't it still?" she asked, feeling a tightness in her throat, wondering what he would answer.

"Yes it is, but it's gotten sticky."

"How's that?"

One corner of Edwin's mouth lifted up as if in a smile—a sad, enigmatic expression. "The vague, impersonal chess pieces in the game, sweet lass, have turned into flesh-and-blood people. It's my fault, my error—my own false move."

This is getting morbid, Nan thought to herself. "Well, Edwin, you didn't come here to tell me that."

"No, I didn't."

"Why did you come?"

"I'm not certain." His voice held that same unreadable expression.

"To uncover whatever you could for your own self-interest." It was a statement; it came out flat, almost void of expression. Nan moved and sat down on the log, wrapped her arms around her knees, sitting huddled, protected. "Well, it's late and I'm tired, Edwin, so here's the scoop—no sparring, no deals to be made. It's just yours for the taking."

He made a small sound under his breath, but Nan went on.

"Andrew's meeting me tomorrow in Salt Lake City. We're going to be baptized into the Mormon church. We'll spend a few days there, I'm sure, then go home together. He'll go back to his business and I'll rattle about Bieldmor House with Jessie, trying to learn how to become a lady, writing articles on the side now and then.'' She took a deep breath, but it barely broke her stride. ''When the court date is set they'll inform us, as they will you. I suppose we'll catch glimpses of each other now and then, frosty smiles across the expanses, behind lawyers' backs—'' She paused. ''Does that cover things, Edwin?''

''No, not really. What about now—what's happened here?''

''Oh, yes.'' She deflated quickly; the brave, hard brightness was a thin pretense. She didn't even try to maintain it. ''That is the crux for you, isn't it, Edwin? I don't know—I haven't told Andrew yet.''

She could read the relief in his eyes, but also surprise. ''There was no reason to tell him long-distance. But when I see him again—'' She tilted her head, looking almost apologetic. ''I can't lie, Edwin: I've no wish to.''

He nodded, only so slightly. He was otherwise still, standing poised and unruffled and self-contained, with all the sticky emotions under safe cover.

''This is crazy,'' Nan said, ''we're enemies, Edwin. We're on opposite sides, remember? And there's one more little matter, isn't there?''

''Julie.'' He said the word softly, like a caress. It startled her; she sat up straighter, watching him.

''If I were her brother rather than her sister I could say, 'You do anything to hurt her and I'll take it out of your hide—' ''

''That's already been said.''

''What do you mean?''

''Some chap here.'' Nan couldn't tell if Edwin was annoyed or amused. ''Cornered me in the drugstore—obnoxious fellow.''

Nan laughed. ''Was he tall and quiet, with sandy hair?''

''That's him. He gave me his name. Tom something—''

''Tom! Of course, Tom. I should have known.''

Edwin was bristling a little now. ''So you know the fellow? He ought to be taught a lesson or two himself.''

"He has been, Edwin." Her voice was gentle. "He has been." He moved closer, intrigued, knowing something was coming. "He's been in love with me for years, since we were children. This is a small town, it was always assumed—well, you know. But I never really loved him the way he loved me. Then Andrew came."

"I see. You don't have to go on."

"But I do. Tom's a fine man, gentle and stable. I was everything to him, and when he lost me, he took the loss like a man—"

"Touché!"

"Edwin—" She gazed up at him, earnest, appealing. "Why can't you ever see things from anyone else's point of view? Always the narrow, how-does-this-affect-*me* reaction. Tom's not involved in your affairs; he's no threat to you. You wear blinders—you take what you want and move on. So often you leave the best behind."

"I don't think so. That's a pretty picture you draw, Nan, but unrealistic. People aren't the Pollyannas you make them to be. The only ones who get anything in life are the ones who take it."

"I don't believe that."

"Oh, but lass, yes you do."

She glanced up, startled. "Look at yourself," he continued. "You've taken what you want from life. A timid soul would never have defied her father, become involved with a stranger, a foreigner—taken the chances you did. You have a low profile, Nan, but you know the score. You go after what you want until you get it. You look after your own interests first."

She'd never looked at herself that way before. She sat stunned and silent, grappling with the unpleasant images his words brought forth.

"That's life, Nan. You've been too sheltered to know it. You're as much a part of the process as I am." He came close; he could see he had really upset her. "Don't take it so personally," he said a little more gently.

She glared back at him. "You may be right," she said, "but you don't have the whole truth. There's something deeper I can't put my finger on. You've lost your innocence and your faith, Edwin, and when that happens, it dulls everything you touch. You walk on the surface, you won't get involved, you won't get *committed!* All right—I admit that the hard realities are there. But there's love and beauty there, too, and you're missing it, Edwin, because you won't make room in your life for anyone else."

She had struck home with one perfect thrust; she had disarmed him. He moved back, away from the danger, instinctively.

"Pretty," he responded, "very pretty. But worthless where I'm concerned." The pain broke through. She heard it in the last few words; it stung her, as a wet wind off the river, with teeth of ice. There was silence. She could hear the soft hum of insects, the rhythmic slosh of the gentle water.

To the devil with women, Edwin thought. *Especially this one.*

"I'm sorry I've ruined your evening. I didn't intend to." His mouth twisted into a wry, crooked smile. "We've played this scene before, haven't we? Farewell, Nan. Forgive me a little, if you can."

He disappeared into the shadows. The night closed around her. She stared after him, but she could see nothing but the deep, empty dark.

11

Therefore take the present time,
With a hey and a ho, and a
hey nonino . . .
AS YOU LIKE IT

Andrew's plane arrived first. Heber Shumway met him. The old warmth returned with the first handshake. Heber had served as Andrew's genealogist, his first Mormon friend. It was he who had given Andrew a copy of the Book of Mormon. "Welcome back, Andrew," Heber said quietly. Then, with a twinkle in his eye he added, "I wasn't sure for a while that I'd see this day."

Andrew dropped his eyes. "I've no one to blame but myself," he admitted. "It took Grant Morgan's death, I'm afraid, to bring us to our senses."

When Nan searched the sea of airport faces and found Andrew's she wanted to cry. She felt the weight of the last few days slip from her shoulders, dissolve from her tired mind and lift from her heart. When he took her in his arms she leaned against him, feeling his strength and love flow over her like a balm. Just being with him restored her.

They drove together to Hotel Utah where Andrew had secured a room. He told her bits and snatches of news as they traveled, but she said very little until that night when they had dinner on the quiet terrace and she felt free to share with him some of her thoughts, put words to the feelings and experiences of the past week. He listened carefully, lovingly, watching her features, the play of light and shadow in her eyes, drinking in the intoxication of her nearness. He was too caught up in his pleasure, too lulled by her presence, to take note of her sense of hesitation, the troubled expression that sometimes crept into her eyes. She knew she would have to broach the dread subject, and would have no peace till she did.

Following dinner they took a long walk through the city. Andrew was oblivious to her uneasiness; he didn't want the bright evening to end. When at last they reached their room both were bone-weary and sleepy. Nan perched resolutely on the edge of the bed.

"There's one more thing, Andrew."

"I agree," he said warmly.

She laughed. "No, not that. This is serious. Will you let me talk to you, please?"

Something in her voice alerted him. He came closer. "Of course, Nan, of course. What is it, lass?"

He sat down beside her and took her hand. She squirmed a little. "Well, it's not earth-shattering. But you ought to know, I suppose. Edwin's in Nauvoo."

She held her breath. His eyes grew stormy; his hand on hers tensed. "The mongrel! Why didn't you tell me sooner?"

"Don't be angry."

"Good heavens, Nan. He's up to no good. What's he doing?" He moved impatiently. "Nauvoo!"

Nan took a deep breath. "He's been seeing Julie. He had some pathetic notion that he could hurt us that way."

Andrew muttered under his breath. "This time he'll be sorry. This time—"

She put her finger to his lips. "Andrew, please. You can't be bitter and angry. Not now. We're getting baptized in a few days, remember? What good will it do to get baptized with hate in your heart?"

He grimaced at her. "You would bring that up! All right, then. I'll take the first plane to Chicago and strangle the fool and be back in time for the baptism, with all my sins behind me. How's that?"

"Andrew, that isn't funny!"

"I'm sorry. But what a meddlesome wretch he is! What about your sister?"

Nan shook her head. "I'm not certain. I tried to talk to her, but she wouldn't listen."

"Did you see Edwin? Did you talk to him?"

"Oh, yes." Something in her tone made him take notice.

"What happened? Did he hurt you? Nan!"

She gazed at him. How could she tell what had happened? How could she explain things she didn't understand?

"Edwin isn't a simple person; you know that. At times he was very helpful and kind. Almost *sensitive,* Andrew, like you would be."

Andrew winced as an old image stirred inside him. He could see himself and Edwin as boys. He was an active boy; he liked sports, he liked people. It had been easy for him to achieve. *But Edwin.* Edwin had been vivacious and full of life. So eager to please, so eager to be like Andrew, to do everything Andrew did, and to do it better. He succeeded sometimes, too. But success would drive him—drive him more than failure. What was it? Edwin never seemed to get enough!

"Andrew?"

"I'm sorry, Nan. I was just remembering . . . when we were lads." Other pictures were coming, pictures long submerged. "He *was* a sensitive boy, you know. If ever Janet was hurt he was there before I was. When our dog was hit by a lorry it was Edwin who cried. I can still see him rubbing his fists against his eyes, angry that he was crying . . ."

"You see. It's not all black and white with Edwin."

"Maybe not. But, Nan, he's gone too far. He's betrayed himself too many times. He can't tell the difference any more between wrong and right. No matter what he chooses to do, he feels justified. That can be dangerous, Nan."

Reluctantly she nodded.

"He's a master actor, especially with women. Julie's too young and inexperienced to see through him."

Nan hesitated. Julie hadn't said so, but she would guess that her sister had seen through Edwin long ago, that she *knew.* And, if that was the case, then she really cared. That possibility made Nan shudder.

"Whatever disguise or deceit he chooses, it doesn't really matter. He's charming, Andrew. He'd be hard to resist."

"Surely Julie can't handle that. He'll hurt her—one way or another."

"I know. But what can I do? She's made her choice and she won't turn from it."

Andrew rubbed his eyes, with a tired, discouraged motion. "Maybe now, now that you've been there, it will all turn sour. Knowing Edwin, that could happen. The danger's gone, the element of surprise, of deception. The sooner he leaves, the better for Julie."

Nan sighed and stretched out on the bed. Her mind was tired, more tired than her body. She closed her eyes. She felt Andrew's arms close around her; she nestled against him. "Oh, Andrew, it's been so long. Will you hold me? Just hold me awhile?"

He nodded against her hair. She fell asleep in his arms and he waited until she was sleeping soundly to hazard a move. Then he drew the covers around her gently. She slept like a child, with an innocence on her face. He kissed her. "Sleep sweetly, darling," he whispered. "I'm here."

She hadn't seen him approach. All that day she had waited, wondering if he would come, and when. As evening fell and there was no sign of him, Julie grew tired of constantly running from window to window, retouching her hair, listening for the phone to ring. Her father had driven Nan to the airport early that morning. She had hoped that Edwin might come then. But now supper was past and night had settled, and her sharp anxiety had hardened into anger. She walked out into the backyard to give scraps to the cats. She didn't hear him until he was right beside her.

"Julie. I thought you would never come."

She jumped back. "What in the world are you doing here, Edwin?"

"I'm not quite certain. I wanted to see you, but when I arrived I realized I didn't want to see anyone else. I hadn't quite decided what to do when I heard you."

She could smell whiskey strong on his breath. But under the bright outside porch light she could see his eyes. They didn't appear glazed or bleary, but clear and watchful as ever.

"Why don't you come with me for a little ride?"

Julie shook her head. "I don't think so."

"You know you've missed me; why won't you admit it?"

Her hard anger broke into small pieces, sharp as flint. "You make me sick. As much as I know you, I can't believe this."

"What can't you believe, Julie? I'm listening, get it out of your system." He stood with his arms folded, casual, laconic, watching her with an almost bored expression.

"Since Nan came you've ignored me entirely," Julie began, "and made a fool of yourself hanging around her."

"I had my reasons."

"I'm sure you did. You think she's pretty, don't you?"

Edwin sighed. All women were like this, though he didn't know why. He must humor the girl; heaven knows he'd humored many much older than she.

"Of course I think she's pretty. I can see, can't I?"

"But it's more than that. Sometimes in your face—"

"Don't try to read me, Julie. Believe me, you won't even come close." His voice was sharp with disdain. She shivered.

"You think I'm too young and ignorant to know anything, don't you? I suppose you don't think I have feelings, either."

"I know you have feelings. I've catered to them these past weeks—and gladly. You must remember our initial bargain, Julie. You're overstepping your bounds, lass."

She took a deep breath. She knew he was right and she wanted suddenly to appear less the fool in his eyes. "So what now? Are you going back to Scotland?"

"If you mean right away, I haven't quite made that decision." He cocked his head and a tiny sparkle crept into his eyes. "If I go, will you miss me, Julie?"

"Of course, I'll miss you. You know I care about you, Edwin."

"And the hurt tone implies that I do not care about you? Rubbish!"

She stood stunned; she stared hard at him. "Listen, lass, be honest again, if you can. If I left what would you miss—me or the attention? The little gifts, or the giver? The glamour and prestige of having an older man, a foreigner court you? Come, Julie, let's call a spade a spade. Do you really care what happens to me—what I think, what I feel, what I suffer? I don't think so."

For the first time he moved, unfolded his arms, came closer until he was standing beside her.

"Very few people ever really care about someone else. I don't think you're in that category, not yet." He leaned forward and kissed her cheek, gently. "When you've figured it out for yourself, let me know. Sleep well. I'll see you tomorrow, Julie."

He left and she stood alone, grateful for the night to cover her newly exposed feelings. Instinctively she knew that what he had told her was true. But there was too much behind it for her to grasp. She wished Nan were here. Nan could explain it for her; Nan had always been able to think more deeply. Besides, she wished suddenly for someone to hold her, like Nan used to hold her when she was a little girl and cried for a mother she didn't remember. Nan had been able to help her then. Perhaps no one could really help her now.

Flow gently, sweet Afton, among thy green braes,
Flow gently, I'll sing thee a song in thy praise . . .

The soft sounds of the old song came over the phonograph. Neil, watching Janet, wondered. It was their fourth date, perhaps still too early. But he took the chance.

"There were words to that tune that the Scottish emigrants sang, written by John Murdoch in 1851."

"Really?" She turned to him, interested. He detected no hesitation, no shadow, no withdrawing. "Do you know them?"

"Some. It had several verses." He said a few lines for her softly, in time with the music.

Oh Scotland, my country, my dear native land,
Thou land of the brave and the theme of my song,
Oh why should I leave thee and cross the deep sea,
To a strange land, far distant lovely Scotland from thee.

Janet smiled. "Say more if you know them."

Oh Scotland, my country, the land of my birth,
In fondness I'll ever remember thy worth,
For wrapped in thy bosom my forefathers sleep,
Why then should I leave thee and cross the wild deep?

"They're better than I expected. Do you know more?"

He was getting a little nervous now. "I'll give you one more," he agreed.

But why should I linger or wish for to stay,
The voice of the Prophet is "haste, fly away,
Lest judgments o'ertake you and lay Scotland low"
To the prophets in Zion, Oh, then let me go!

"They really believed that, didn't they?" Janet said softly.

"Oh, yes. The Scots are loyal, you ought to know that. They'd been used to following their clan chiefs for generations. It was easy for them to make the transition and follow the voice of a prophet."

"I suppose so. They certainly suffered for it," she said.

He smiled. "I can't deny that." His own voice was soft and musing. "But they certainly did what they did with a will. You know, one of the very first branches was organized in Paisley as early as 1840. The Church was popular here. A large percentage of the early converts were textile workers."

She raised her eyebrows. "Andrew would like to know that. And did most of them go to Utah?"

Neil nodded. "Oh yes, they called it 'home to Zion.' My great-grandmother's baby sister when she was born was blessed that she might grow up in the faith and live to 'go home to Zion.' "

Janet shook her head. "How do you know so much about it?"

He shrugged his shoulders. "I've studied it some. I like history, and my grandfather gave me an interest in Scotland. He came back here as a missionary himself. He loved it. He told me story after story . . ." His eyes grew soft; she could see the love in his eyes. "I used to wonder when I was a boy," he confided, "what would have happened if my Scottish ancestors had stayed here, if I'd been a Scottish child."

"Did you like the idea?"

He smiled shyly. "Aye, lass, I had all sorts of fancies—boyish dreams, you know, of war and tragedy, saving the fair damsel, winning a hero's praise."

"I had no idea you were such a Scot in your heart."

Her words and the tone of her voice sent a great thrill through him. Those few moments between them colored the rest of the evening. When the hour grew late and he took her home they both lingered, spinning out their last moments together.

"Neil," she said, "Nan and Andrew will be back the middle of next week. We're having a dinner on Friday night. Would you like to come?"

He looked into her eyes to see what he might find there. "Are you sure?" He had to ask it.

"Oh yes," she said. "They'll talk on and on about Salt Lake, I'm certain, and they'll need a sympathetic ear."

He laughed at that. "If I can be useful—"

"Well, yes, you can. But that wasn't why I asked you."

"I'm glad to hear it." He nodded just slightly and pushed back his hair with that impatient, boyish gesture she'd come to love. He kept his eyes on hers; his soft gaze warmed her. He hadn't meant to, but he drew her into his arms, and when he found no resistance he drew her closer and kissed her. It was more than either one had anticipated. He released her very reluctantly. Somehow they said good night; somehow he left her. What was between them was in the open now. Both knew it—and both were frightened for their own reasons.

It was a sunny morning, but early, and the temple grounds were quiet. They held a peace that seemed to hover, not quite still—a murmuring sort of peace with old voices in it. And this morning there was promise in the air, as new and pure as the spring sunlight.

Nan and Andrew entered the baptistry together, then parted, Nan going to the women's dressing room with Lucille Shumway and Jennie Richards, Andrew following Heber and Brad. Once dressed in white baptismal clothing they met again and sat in the front row together before the font. Nan felt more wonder than she had on her wedding day. She kept taking steps that changed her life in some major way. There would be nothing left of her old self if she wasn't careful. It frightened her a little.

Andrew's eyes held a calm and peaceful assurance. He knew this thing they were doing was right—the conviction coursed through him. He glanced at Brad. When he had shown up at Brad's door and told him of their decision, tears had filled Brad's eyes. "If nothing comes of our association but this," he told Andrew, fixing him with a burning gaze, "then I, for one, shall be well satisfied."

They sang "The Spirit of God Like a Fire Is Burning." The song reminded Nan of Grant, and her last fears melted away with the music when his words came back to her mind: *Keep your heart in the right place, Nan, and try to be patient. The Lord will take care of you.* "Oh, Grant," she whispered, "he has, he has." She sensed, for perhaps the first time, the meaning of those old childhood words which Grant had used so often to soothe or instruct her. She began to see a pattern to her own life and to sense that her purpose, her own individual purpose, had never been known, had never been given place. This ordinance today was like the key to unlock the future that waited inside her.

Brad baptized Hannah and then Andrew. Andrew insisted that she go before him. "If I had not met you that first morning in Nauvoo," he said, "all this would have been lost to me. In all ways you represent my happiness and my future."

Nan thought small, peaceful thoughts as she dressed to rejoin the group. There was a spirit here; she could see it as well as feel it. It glowed in the people's faces and shone in their eyes. It was both sweet and strong, thrilling and subduing. It was the most glorious thing she had ever known.

Heber Shumway confirmed them both as members of the Church and pronounced upon their heads the gift of the Holy Ghost. Nan prayed inwardly for the power to receive it. She wanted to keep this spirit strong in her life, to know that help was there when she called upon it; she longed for that wisdom and strength that surpassed her own.

But the crowning moment for Andrew had not arrived yet. Solemnly the men placed their hands on his head and Brad conferred upon him the Aaronic Priesthood, bringing him into his priesthood line, as Andrew had drawn him into his blood line, and they found a twofold brotherhood together.

Andrew sat under their hands overcome with the knowledge that this authority would at last be his to share. He remembered his early impressions, his early conviction that Joseph Smith was, indeed, a remarkable man. Raised on heroes as he had been, he could see in the Prophet the hallmarks of a great man. Walking the places the Prophet had walked, seeing the things he had built, reading the words he had spoken, realizing that thousands of people lived their lives and prospered according to the principles this man taught gave him respect for the power of this great spirit who had been born with a special mission to perform, endowed with capabilities to see and understand things not understood by common men, endowed with capacity to perceive and suffer and sacrifice beyond the ability of others—and blessed with the greatness of heart to do so.

Now he was being granted opportunity to share in the Prophet's work, to join this magnificent fellowship of men who loved each other and labored together to serve a God they called Father, who was a real and powerful force in their lives. The realization surged with great joy through his being. He was taking this priesthood upon himself. It was a sacred responsibility and it was an honor, and Andrew had never been one to take either lightly.

A few moments later he and Nan stood alone together staring up at the gray granite spires of the temple.

"We could always be sealed in the London Temple," Nan mused. "But it wouldn't be quite the same. It all began for us here. . . ."

"Yes, it ought to be here," Andrew agreed. His tenderness for her was an ache within him. He felt an urgency that was hard to contain. He would not rest until Nan was his forever. One year—one year seemed so long to wait. So much could happen in a year. A small tremor ran through him, a slight depression of spirit, almost a fear.

But Nan, resting against his chest, felt a peaceful assurance. Grant's words had come back to her mind like a benediction: *Keep your heart in the right place, Nan, and try to be patient. The Lord will take care of you.*

She intended to do her part; she no longer doubted that the Lord, in his power and mercy, would accomplish his.

12

Tidings do I bring and lucky joys,
And golden times and happy news.
HENRY IV, PART 2

Edwin didn't mean to overhear the conversation. He was sitting in the greasy spoon restaurant alone. Tom, with his back to him, wasn't aware of his presence. Edwin had good ears and a long habit of pure concentration when necessary. Once he tuned into the exchange he turned his total attention upon it. The two men were, apparently, close friends. One was asking questions and Tom was replying—in a quiet voice, but distinct and slow.

"It's not capital, I've got what they normally require. It's backing; they want more security, what old man Turner called 'a sound footing, young man; just in case'—"

"Well, their 'just in case' won't happen, they know that. And they know you've got what it takes to succeed. It has to be a safe bet for them."

Tom shook his head. "They don't want a safe bet, they want a sound proposition. It's company management more than the bank. They think I'm too young. I have no real experience behind me. If I had a partner or some form of securities guaranteed . . ."

Edwin might not have thought of it; the idea might never have come without jogging. He had enough on his mind as it was right now. But Tom's friend did the trick inadvertently.

"Too bad Nan's not around still. She's got all that money—"

Tom stood, upsetting his glass; Edwin shrank into his corner. "Don't even hint at such an idea, Hansen. I'd beg in the streets before I'd take money from Nan."

"Settle down, Tom. You're so cockeyed where Nan's concerned. Finish your hamburger, will ya?"

Tom sunk slowly back into his seat. Edwin pressed the tips of his fingers together. His mind was racing, churning the prospects back and forth restively. *I could pull it off! For a shilling I ought to try it.* It was a game, and Edwin was in need of a game right now. *It would please Nan.* He liked that thought. This country bumpkin disdained Edwin, and that grated on him. *If he is forced to receive aid from a man he mistrusts and despises,* Edwin thought with relish, *what could be sweeter victory?*

He waited until some time after the two men had left together. He was carefully plotting his course, going over the fine details in his mind. The challenge of the situation appealed to him strongly, the idea of pitting himself—his wit, his nerve—against unknown odds. He rose, paid his bill, and left the restaurant, then strolled casually down the street to the bank on the corner. By that time the exhilaration had coursed through his system. He was ready; in fact, he was eager. He walked through the door, looked around a moment, assessing the layout, then sauntered back to where the private offices clustered. "Is Mr. Turner in?" he asked a secretary.

She looked up. When she saw him she smiled; Edwin *was* charming. "May I say who's calling?"

"Edwin Bain. But the name will mean nothing to him. Tell him it's in connection with the Tom Briggs application, if you'd be so kind."

The young girl was happy to be so kind. A few moments later Edwin sat across the desk from a middle-aged man who regarded him with a curious expression.

He crossed his legs, then folded his hands on his knee. "I apologize, Mr. Turner," he began, with a tight, polite smile. "I've had some unexpected delays, and I know both you and Tom are concerned."

Mr. Turner coughed and rubbed his finger along his moustache. Edwin's smile grew broader. He was loving every minute of this. He proceeded slowly, deliberately drawing out the process for the perplexed and uncomfortable Mr. Turner.

In less than an hour his business at the bank was concluded. He walked directly back to his hotel, and waited. If his bet was right, Mr. Turner would call Tom Briggs in and the two would confer. Edwin smiled at the prospect. Then Tom Briggs would head with dispatch here. He hoped the time frame wouldn't be off; he had plans for the evening. He rubbed his hands together and poured a drink. Just one to nurse until Tom came.

The knock on his door was the first indicator; it was sharp and insistent. He opened the door. "Come in, Tom," he said, "you're precisely on schedule."

Tom pushed past him and stood with his legs firmly planted, his arms akimbo, as though he was preparing for physical combat. Edwin's mouth twitched in anticipation. He knew that in the combat of words and ideas he had the decided advantage.

"All right, let's have it. Just what are you up to?"

Edwin's lopsided grin broke the fine, straight lines of his face. "Didn't Mr. Turner explain the arrangements to your satisfaction?"

"Cut out the baloney. What are you doing and what are your reasons?"

"Sit down, Mr. Briggs. Please." Reluctantly Tom sat. His perplexity was perhaps even greater than his anger. He knew he would have to let Edwin play out his hand, no matter how he might choose to do it.

Edwin stood with his hands clasped behind his back. "It has come to my attention—inadvertently—that you are, so to speak, up against a wall—that your enterprise, although otherwise secured, might falter for lack of one small matter: financial backing."

"And what's it to you? You go into my bank and my banker pulls out my personal papers for you. What was it he called you? My silent partner—my *benefactor!*"

Edwin inclined his head. "Ah, that would smart, wouldn't it? He did not speak falsely. Don't be so touchy, lad. I signed papers as well—"

"Yes, I know! For what earthly reason? I don't understand this!" Tom's dismay distorted his features.

Edwin raised a tentative eyebrow. "My reasons? They are several. First, I must admit to a dislike of pompous, boring, too often incompetent capitalists. You represent the underdog, and it has ever been my way to throw in my weight with the underdog."

He paused a moment, for effect. Tom watched him intently.

"My second reason? I had a little business of my own in the Highlands which grew flat and uninteresting. I sold out my share several months ago. The money's been merely gathering dust." Edwin shrugged. "I thought it might spice things up a bit to put the lot on the line for you."

"That makes no sense at all. You don't even know me."

Edwin held up a reprimanding finger. "Ah, but I do. Perhaps better than most others know you."

Tom was thoroughly overwhelmed and confused. "I may be capricious," Edwin resumed, "but I am not imprudent. I'm taking no risks with you, Tom Briggs, and I know it. You're as solid as the Rock of Gibraltar—isn't that what they say in this country?"

Tom nearly smiled. "Would you mind explaining? I still haven't the faintest idea—"

"But you have. I've given you two good explanations. The third, as you may have sensed, is the nucleus, however." He paced a few steps, then paused. "How can I put it? Let me merely say that you and I share an affection for a certain young lady—a sympathy, an interest—"

"What do you mean?" The words were a challenge; Edwin had probed his sore spot. Edwin sighed. Perhaps it was time to stop, to change tactics, at least.

"All right, lad, calm down. I'll be more direct. But you must stay where you are and hear me out, no matter how much you might wish to strike me."

Edwin pulled a chair close and sat on the edge, facing Tom. He leaned forward with the palms of his hands on his knees.

"You're in love with Nan—you always were and you always will be."

Tom made a sound under his breath. "That's none of your business."

"No, it isn't, but it's turned to advantage for you. You see, I care for the girl myself, in my own way."

"I don't believe that."

Edwin's mouth turned down at the corners and tightened. "Well, *that* is none of *your* business. And more to the point, I owe her. Not once, but several times. It's awkward being so much in a woman's debt." He ran his finger under his collar and cocked his head. "This will definitely even the score considerably."

"How could it? What difference would this make to Nan?"

"Your success? Your happiness? Don't underestimate her, man, that would be an insult. She cares for you still in her way, and you know it. It would bring her pleasure to see you prosper."

Tom turned away. The blue eyes that held his were too cunning, too probing.

"I can reject the offer, tear up the papers, if I already haven't."

"Yes, you could, but you won't. You're not that much of a fool."

Tom looked up again, elbows on his knees, with his chin in his hand. He stared hard into the cool blue eyes. "I don't like you, Edwin Bain, and I don't trust you."

Edwin didn't move a hair. "That's one thing in our favor. Good foundation for a partnership."

Tom slowly shook his head. "I don't know what to make of you."

"You don't need to make anything of me; that's neither here nor there. The legalities are taken care of. My percentage is small, but I expect in time I may gain considerably from it. I shall make no demands—" A smile played mischieviously across his face—"I trust you. Believe it or not, there may be ways I could help. I have experience setting up a business. But we'll see about that, play it by ear—"

He clapped his hands on his knees and rose. "Will you shake on it?" He put out his hand and grinned. He was enjoying the game immensely. Tom hesitated. Edwin was in no hurry. His blue eyes were friendly, his stance relaxed. Tom shook his head again and stood up slowly. Even as he grasped Edwin's hand he didn't know why. He didn't understand any of this yet, but he had a feeling, and his feelings had seldom led him astray. This was one of those crazy moments out of nowhere that you only had one crack at, and then it was gone. Tom wasn't the sort of man to take chances. But he shook the Scotsman's hand and trusted his feeling, even if he couldn't trust the Scotsman himself.

Things were different between them now and they both knew it. Julie made sincere efforts to please Edwin, to discover his likes and dislikes, to learn his opinions. He was aware of what she was doing, and yet he enjoyed it. He held back less than he was accustomed to. Consequently they conversed more when they were together. Edwin found himself enjoying Julie's company with an intensity he hadn't experienced before. He refused to analyze what he was doing. He would be leaving in a few weeks, and that would be that. Meanwhile he may as well enjoy himself.

For several days he heard no more from Tom Briggs. Then Saturday morning when he picked up Julie she casually remarked, "Tom called last night. He said to tell you that if we didn't have anything particular planned for the day we might stop over. He'd like to show you around the place."

Edwin grinned. "That's what he said, is it? What do you think, Julie?"

"I think he'd like to take you up on your offer to help. But he can't quite make himself come right out and ask."

Edwin nodded appreciatively. "Would you mind if we went? It won't be much fun for you."

"Not at all." She almost had added, *as long as I'm with you.* But she stopped herself with a smile. "Will I be in the way?"

"You could never be in the way, Julie. If nothing more, you'll be something lovely to look at."

Jessie was the first person Nan told, even before Andrew. Why, she wasn't certain. But once she knew, she felt compelled to share her joy with the older woman.

"I'm going to have a baby," she said.

"Are you sure?" Jessie asked her.

"Yes. I was sure before, but I've seen the doctor."

"All by yourself? Does Andrew know yet?"

Nan shook her head. "I believe he suspects it, but I haven't told him."

Jessie walked over and took her hand. "Nan, I'm happy for you," she said. "I'm very happy. A new generation—that's good. Won't Andrew be pleased?"

Nan smiled. "It doesn't seem real yet."

"How are you feeling?"

"All right so far. A little queasy now and then, and tired."

Jessie smiled. "We must take better care of you now. What date did the doctor give you?"

"Late December. Somewhere near the twentieth, he said."

Jessie nodded. "How nice that will be! A Christmas baby."

Nan was relieved. Their baptism had brought some strain. Jessie said little; she offered no overt criticism, but the difference made itself felt in little ways. Perhaps this baby would draw them all closer together, give them some reason to be united. Nan hoped so. Nothing could bridge a gap between two women as well as a baby.

Later that evening when they were alone she told Andrew the news. He stared at her. "Nan, that's wonderful! Are you certain?" She nodded. "Are you all right?"

She laughed softly. "Yes, Andrew. Can you believe it? A child of our own?"

He took her into his arms. "I have a feeling that we don't even know what happiness is yet. We think we have everything, but we're only beginning."

He kissed her. Her lips lingered softly on his. *Nothing,* she thought, *could be more wonderful than this.* And she savored it. Perhaps tomorrow *would* be better. But this one brief moment was perfect, and hers to keep.

Andrew had overextended himself a little and he knew it. But if any one of the half-dozen deals he had going came through he'd be amply compensated and justified. He'd purchased a large block of stock in British Leyland at Linwood and he didn't want to be forced to drop that. He had an opportunity to purchase additional bank stock, but he had poured alarming amounts of money into construction of the new mill, in spite of the insurance compensation.

The problems involved in these enterprises were staggering; the small, nagging details could overwhelm him at times. But Andrew felt confident in most of the areas in which he operated. He had experience in the business end; his major concern was the politicking, the touchiest aspect of all.

The same day Nan told him about the baby he had a slight run-in with the Scottish National Party. He had an appointment with Scott Lindsay to finalize some details concerning the new mill. When he arrived Scott said, "There's a Nationalist Party man waiting to see you. Shall I show him in? He's been here the best part of an hour."

Andrew frowned. "Put him off till another day."

"I've put him off three times already, sir. You'd best see him."

For years Andrew had resisted involvement in the popular Scottish movement for devolution. He supported the basic idea of home rule, but some of the party's interpretations, some of their methods, some of their objectives were not his own. He met with their representative, Mr. Menzies, and they talked around half a dozen issues. Menzies wanted a commitment of support on Andrew's part, or at least a financial pledge.

"We draw much support from your peers, Mr. Buchanan, in the New Towns and the central Glasgow region. We stand behind—"

"I know what you stand behind," Andrew had answered sharply. "We've gone over it several times now. I'm sorry, sir. I'm just not ready to throw in my weight with the party."

"That's exactly it, sir; the party needs people like you."

"There are still too many issues I disagree with. The means of dispersal of power to local authorities, for one thing, and cooperatively-owned industries for another—"

"That's the way of the future." Mr. Menzies spread his hands. "The way of progress." Andrew knit his brow and didn't respond directly.

"Self-government as it is currently headed deemphasizes production for export," Andrew continued. "It seems to be producing no goals I can perceive to cover the responsibility—nor organizations, especially for working-class education, that will prepare our people for the needs of the society you espouse."

Mr. Menzies coughed slightly. "We *are* wasting each other's time, Mr. Buchanan. I can see that now." He rose stiffly. Censure was strong in his attitude. Andrew was angry. With the same coldness he ushered the man out and tried to put the unpleasant encounter behind him. Politics! What a necessary evil they were! He was glad when other matters claimed his attention. And once confronted with Nan's happy news his sense of contentment dispelled all frustrations and disappointments from his mind. She was renewal, she was his refuge, his safe harbor. He knew that not all men lived with such fair advantage. He had been blessed in many ways, but his greatest blessing was this beautiful, sensitive woman he called his wife.

Janet had been reluctant to face Nan again. Their last encounter stood like an awkward barrier between them. Janet didn't wish it to be so. For some reason she found herself wanting to talk to Nan. She had no one to share her experiences with. She had long since stopped trying to go to her mother. She missed Edwin. Edwin would understand, listen carefully, have something clever to say. She didn't want Andrew to know of her feelings for the young Mormon. He would be too pleased, too hopeful, and that kind of pressure was something she wasn't interested in right now.

The night of the dinner when Neil came to join them Janet sat tense and watchful, scarcely having a good time till she realized everyone else was. Her mother was glowing, of course, because Andrew was back. Donald MacGregor, Andrew's boyhood friend who had stepped in as best man when Edwin was out of the running, was there with his brother, Gordon. There was talk of Salt Lake and the baptism, true, and how the Wasatch mountains compared to their own Grampians. But she and Neil and Gordie could talk MG's, and Donald and Andrew talked currency values, textile prices, and politics.

The evening was over too soon for Janet. Neil left along with the others, and she hadn't had him alone to herself at all. He had found a moment to come up beside her and ask softly, "May I see you tomorrow? Are you free?" She had smiled and nodded. "Will you wear your hair this same way tomorrow?" he had asked, touching it as he spoke, stroking it softly. "You've never looked more beautiful than you do tonight."

Why did his words send such a thrilling sensation through her? Why did it please her so much to know that he cared?

Alone in her room she gazed at her image in the mirror. Her skin was very fair, unfreckled, which was fortunate, considering her red hair. Though her hair, she mused, fingering it, was as much blonde as red. Her eyes were blue, but not brilliant like Andrew's—too light, as though half the color had washed away. She had never thought of herself as being beautiful—pleasing, yes, even pretty by most people's standards. She untied the pale blue ribbon and began to brush through the golden mass of curls. Neil thought she was beautiful. More than once he had said so. Why did she trust his sincerity more than she did that of other men? *Why,* she asked the image in the mirror, *do I feel beautiful because he thinks me so?*

The following morning when Janet came down for breakfast Nan was sitting alone at the table. Janet sat down uncomfortably, but Nan smiled brightly at her.

"Your mother has one of her club meetings this morning and Andrew left early for the mill," she said by way of explanation. "I'm going visiting teaching myself in a few minutes, and should be gone most of the afternoon on a newspaper interview." Janet nodded and bent over her food. Nan was nearly through eating; perhaps she would leave. Janet hoped so.

"Neil Sheffield is very nice. I'm glad you invited him, Janet. He has such a charming way about him, don't you think?"

Janet looked up, startled; Nan's brown eyes were sparkling. Janet conceded a little. "Yes, I think he does."

There was a moment or two of silence. Then Nan said—suddenly, as though she had made a decision—"I saw Edwin in Nauvoo."

Janet gasped.

"I didn't think you knew he was there," Nan continued, her small white forehead wrinkling in concern.

"Why didn't Andrew tell me?" Janet's voice held both disappointment and accusation.

Nan shook her head. "I'm not sure. He knew it might upset you—"

Janet's gaze grew hostile; she pushed back her chair. Nan laid a detaining hand on her arm. "Please, Janet. I thought you might like to know how he is."

"Of course I'd like to know how he is! Andrew should have told me!"

"Andrew didn't see him," Nan continued softly. "I did. And he gave me strict instructions to give you his love—and this."

She brought an envelope out from her lap and gave it to Janet. It was sealed with Edwin's signet and bore her name written in his precise hand.

"He gave *this* to *you?*" Janet's voice reflected confusion. "I thought you were enemies, or at least in opposite camps."

"That's exactly what I told him. But Edwin is persuasive—"

"Why would he bother to be persuasive with you?"

"Oh, that I think I can answer. For one, he was guilty. He'd been in Nauvoo romancing my sister—for obvious reasons."

"Your sister?" Janet was liking this story less and less.

"Remember, I told you I hadn't been too close to Julie. She was more than happy to go along with Edwin. And, as both you and I know, he *is* charming, extremely charming . . ."

"Well, what about you? Why did he concern himself with your opinion?"

Nan smiled, and the expression was so sweet and so gentle that Janet felt it, softer than the touch of Nan's hand on her arm.

"That's easiest of all to explain," she replied. "In spite of the fact that he may do hateful things, the last thing Edwin wants is to be hated. He considers all of his actions justified. And his motives—he looks on his motives as good, even pure. He hates to be disliked or rejected—" the smile grew softer yet—"especially by a woman. He must win every woman to him in his own way."

"Has he won *you* to him?" Janet's pulse was pounding. She was unable to sort out her feelings.

The blunt question forced Nan to pause and consider. "This makes no sense, but yes, in a manner he has. I no longer see him as a figure, an impersonal representation with a label across his chest stamped *evil* or *betrayer* or *liar*—do you know what I mean? He's a human being and there are good things about him, endearing things—" She paused and her eyes grew a little misty. "Because you love him, I'll say this, Janet, though I wouldn't say it to very many people. Edwin may be weak, but he's a sensitive man. He's suffering, I know he's suffering. I've seen it in his eyes."

Nan rose and walked over to stand behind the girl with her hands on her shoulders. "I'm so sorry, Janet, I didn't mean to make you cry." She touched the golden hair gently. "Try not to worry. Remember him in your prayers. I do."

She turned discreetly and went from the room, but she left behind her a touch of warmth that the girl clung to, the only comfort for the tears that her heart was crying.

13

What was your dream?
I long to hear you tell it . . .
RICHARD III

Edwin knew nothing about American farm equipment, but he was fascinated by the machines and their names: tractors from the 2750 turbo-charged 4-cylinder model to the 4250 model with 120 hp for high-clearance crops; Dyna-Carts, combines, heads, platforms, and windrowers. The sophistication, the specialization was beyond him. But he helped Tom set up his bookkeeping.

"I've got a brilliant little highlander," Edwin explained, "five foot two with a moustache as long as himself who can add up four figures in his head. He runs the little fishing business I had interest in in Portree—keeps inventory down to the last piece of fly bait, the last fishing hook. If anything's missing, if the records don't jive, it comes out of our pockets."

Life was serious business to Tom; in fact, one of his few faults was that he tended to make of life almost a drudgery. Nothing could be more important than the success or failure of this new business, and he had set forth with a will, with his jaw set and his teeth clenched. Edwin brought fresh air, life, even humor, and Tom's intensity couldn't stand up before the onslaught. He weakened. He softened; he even began to smile. Rather than blunting the edge of his powers, this assuagement increased them. Tom held his breath—appreciating, but disbelieving, growing to like and respect Edwin more as each day passed.

"I ought to put you on the payroll," he told Edwin, intending to compliment him. "You do more work around here than ten men." But Edwin was horrified.

"Work for wages!" He drew himself up with his old haughty demeanor. "I've never worked for wages in my life; heaven forbid it!"

Edwin was comical, he was ingenious, he was inventive; Tom was continuously impressed with new skills or perceptions Edwin casually brought forth.

"You have a natural head for business," Tom told him one evening, when they had worked ten long hours at a stretch together and enjoyed every minute. "You grasp things quickly, much more so than I do." Edwin shrugged and turned away, unimpressed, uninterested. "I'd like to see what you could accomplish if you ever really devoted yourself to something."

Edwin didn't reply and Tom was dismayed at his sudden silence. Later, after dinner, as they walked together, Julie noticed that he was brooding still.

"Did something go wrong today?" she asked.

"You might say that." He spoke the words slowly and the humorless smile played around his mouth.

"I'm sorry. It must have disturbed you. You're terribly quiet." *And sad,* she thought to herself.

Edwin inclined his head. "Yes, I do grow quiet when I'm disturbed. Do I bore you when I'm like this? Does it upset you?"

For some reason Julie reached out and took his hand. "You could never bore me, Edwin," she smiled. "But it does upset me to see you unhappy. You suffer with such . . . such . . ."

"Intensity." Edwin smiled at that and laughed a little. He squeezed the hand that he held in his. "Kiss me, Julie. There's nothing to make a man forget his woes like a woman's kiss."

She protested, but in the end she kissed him. *Her lips are so soft,* Edwin thought, *so terribly sweet.* Julie could feel the intensity in his arms, in his kiss. She trembled at the response it awakened. She could sense his vulnerability with a woman's instinctive perception. She stroked his hair, letting the lush ebony thickness run through her fingers.

Tom's innocent words had awakened a specter in Edwin's mind. They were nearly a perfect echo of Andrew's praises, given just as sincerely nine months before. "Spectacular performance," Andrew had called it—Edwin's running of the family business while he was away, chasing his elusive American heir. Edwin shuddered, remembering the painful emotions of that day.

"Confound it, Edwin," Andrew had said, "you've got a grasp on things it took father six months—a year—to hammer into me." But then came the rub, the thrust, the Achilles heel: "You've too much natural ability, Edwin, you don't have to push yourself. If you ever gave your best the world would sit up and take notice."

The words echoed with cruel mockery through his head. *How does a man give his best with his hands tied behind him?* His best! What was his best, anyway? A figment of imagination, a fleeting promise, too insubstantial to ever spark into reality.

There were too many hungers inside; he was hollow with hunger. He turned to the girl in his arms, transferring his needs into one passionate, anguished appeal for her affections.

It was dark and Andrew still wasn't home yet. He worked long, long hours in Glasgow these days. *I could use Brad—I could use ten Brads,* he often grumbled to himself. He felt like a juggler. If he missed one ball the whole batch would scatter. Perhaps he had too many balls going at once; perhaps he was greedy. But he didn't want to let even one slip through his fingers.

Jessie was in her rooms and Janet was out with her collie. Nan paced a little, ill at ease. It was dark; Janet ought to be back by now. Nan went to the window and saw a dark shape off in the distance. That must be Janet coming. She went to the door, pulled it open, and walked out a short way to meet her.

Janet saw her coming and called out. The tone of her voice drove sharp stabs of fear through Nan. She began running and as she drew nearer saw that Janet had the huge collie cradled in her arms; she was bent with the burden. She had placed her light sweater over him. Tybalt was whining and shaking terribly.

"Janet, what happened?"

"Nan, please, get Andrew!"

"He's not home yet!" a sensation of panic rose in her as she saw the deep alarm in Janet's eyes.

"It's not much farther now. Can I help you? Here—" Somehow, together they carried the animal up the wide stairs. Nan pushed the door open and ran for a blanket to lay him on. She could see in the light that he was hurt and bleeding. She felt helpless; she knew almost nothing about dogs. She wasn't an animal person, really. The cats of her childhood had self-sufficiently taken care of themselves. She had done little more than feed and pet them.

"I'll call Andrew," she said. "Should we call a vet?"

"Yes, we've got to get him to the vet."

"Can you tell me what happened?"

Janet looked up. "We were attacked by a rabid dog. Walking past Cumming Wood their little terrier came out of nowhere. He and Tybalt know each other, but he was wild. He lunged for me, but Tybalt stopped him." There were tears running down her cheeks now.

"Oh, Janet, don't try to go on. You stay with him, I'll hurry and call."

She tried the Paisley mill and two numbers in Glasgow. Nothing. *Where could Andrew be?* Half a dozen other places, she thought ruefully. Her mind considered only a moment, then she thumbed through the pages till she found the listing for Winston Sheffield. She knew Neil would be more than happy to help Janet. It was a natural excuse for getting the two together. She dialed the number. *Please let him be there,* she prayed.

"Hello."

"Hello, Neil?" Nan gasped. "It's you? I'm so grateful."

"What's the matter, Nan?" She could feel the concern in his voice.

"Janet's dog's been hurt and I can't find Andrew. Would you mind coming? We need to get him to a vet. She's quite upset, she's—"

"I'll be there in less than ten minutes."

He hung up before she could thank him, but her own panic subsided. Once Neil was here they would not only have the help they needed, but Janet would have his comfort as well.

Janet didn't question why he was there, but when she saw him she rose from her place beside the dog and went into his arms. She had never before known the comfort that she felt there, with her head against his shoulder, secure and warm. Neil thought he knew how much the dog meant to her, but he was surprised at how deeply upset she was.

"We'll take care of him, Janet, don't worry," he told her, but she didn't seem encouraged by his words.

They made a bed for him in the back of the Magnetta and drove the few miles to the veterinarian's office in the back rooms of his large Victorian home. Once they had the dog inside Neil felt greatly relieved. Here were lights and warmth and skill and knowledge. But the old doctor, talking to Janet, was shaking his head.

"Yes, that's right, the Cumming terrier is rabid. They called me only this morning. It took them several days to identify his condition, then they confined him and contacted me. Or at least they thought they had him confined. When they went back for him he had broken out and disappeared."

He turned to Neil. "Rabies is a viral disease," he explained, "that attacks the nervous system, eventually penetrating the spinal cord and brain. When it reaches the furious stage it's mere days till death comes. Tybalt here's been bitten several times . . ."

He turned back to Janet and put his arm around her.

"What can you do for him? How will you treat him?" Neil asked.

The doctor answered, and his tone was gentle. "There's no treatment, lad. There's nothing we can do but to put the poor beast to sleep."

Neil stared at the man numbly. "I had no idea—did you know this, Janet?" She nodded her head, and the tears spilled out of her eyes. Neil felt terribly foolish. A great tenderness for her welled up inside him. But he felt helpless and inept before her pain.

The old vet took him by the arm and they left the room together, softly closing the door behind them. "Sit down, lad," the man said kindly, and sat himself, pulling out a pipe and a pouch of tobacco.

"She needs to say good-bye to the dog alone." Neil nodded. The older man studied him over the rim of his pipe. "Her father gave her that dog six years—ah, it must have been eight years ago now." He shook his head and puffed out a long, thin stream of smoke. "It's a shame, a crying shame to lose him this way."

It seemed a long time the two men sat together, waiting. They didn't talk much. The doctor leaned back and sucked his pipe. Neil thought of the things Janet had told him about her father. He had no idea what she was going through. He had two kind, normal, attentive parents, and all the love and support he could use. He had never faced the awful, solitary darkness Janet had gone through.

The click of the door handle turning broke his reflection. Janet entered the room. Her eyes were dry. She gave him a look that warmed him, then knelt down beside the doctor.

"I'm leaving now. I know you'll be gentle with him—"

She put her head down on his lap and he stroked her hair. "Aye, lass; aye, lass. You come back tomorrow, you and the lad, and I'll have him ready. You can bury him down by the rowan tree."

She smiled faintly. Her eyes were still dry. She rose and walked over to stand beside Neil. "Will you take me home now?"

He walked to the car with his arm around her. They drove in silence until he made the first turn onto Buchanan property.

"Would you mind stopping here for a moment?" Janet asked.

"Of course not." Neil slowed the car and glanced at her face.

"Take the dirt road—off there to the right."

He obeyed her instructions. The road, little more than a path, wound through thick foliage, then ran itself out at the foot of a small meadow. Where the line of trees skirted the edge of the clearing a small stream, or burn, trickled through. Neil heard the faint music of the water when he stepped out of the car. They walked through the tall meadow grass, through splotches of shadow into patches of hard, bright moonlight. He held her hand. At the edge of the clearing, set slightly apart from the others, a large old rowan tree reared its head. He had seen many rowans since coming to Scotland, but none as grand as this.

''Is this the tree the old doctor spoke of?'' Neil asked, his voice as soft as a whisper.

''Yes. This one is hundreds of years old.'' She touched its bark gently, running her fingers along the indented lines. The moon's glow filtered in feathery sprays around them, touching her hair and face with faint golden sparkles of light.

''Some ancient person planted it here, firmly believing that it would grow to protect him from witches and evil spirits, that its berries would bring good fortune to his family.'' She smiled. ''Some would call the spot hallowed.''

''Would you?'' He bent close; her hair, trailing moonshadows, brushed his shoulder.

''I've come here since I was a child; it's my own private sanctuary. Of course, when Father died I spent hours here. Then last summer and autumn when I was deciding what to do about joining the Mormon church . . .''

Neil caught his breath. ''Is that when you took the lessons with Mary's family?''

Janet nodded. ''I believed easily, but then, I was helped along.'' A shadow, more of pain than anxiety, passed over her features.

''How were you helped, Janet? Can you tell me?''

She gazed up at his face a moment, then sighed. ''Shortly after Father's death I began having dreams. Each dream was exactly the same, in every detail. My father would stare out at me, his eyes so lonely, so filled with pain. He seemed to be always searching for something.'' She shivered. ''When I began to look into the Church, when I learned of its doctrines, when I read the Book of Mormon, when I prayed . . .'' She paused and drew a deep breath.

''Go on,'' Neil urged her.

''I don't know if I want to,'' she said.

''Janet, please. Please trust me.''

''When I did all those things I began to believe it. Then I came to a point where I knew it was true, where I decided to be baptized, no matter that happened. It was after that, one night when I had been reading about temple work and baptism for the dead, that I fell asleep and dreamed again—but this was a new dream. I saw Father standing outside a beautiful building. He was with a group of men, and they were all dressed in white. He turned and seemed to smile upon me. I could see that he held an open book in his hands, though I couldn't tell what it was. But I knew he was happy. He had found what he had been searching for. He smiled; I'll never forget that smile—"

She put her head down and her hair spilled golden over her shoulders. "I woke up, and I knew what the answer was. Father had been searching for the truth—for the gospel. Perhaps because of him I had found it, too."

She shifted uneasily and pushed her hair back from her forehead. "I had been reading about temple work, remember. I could see clearly what had to be done. Andrew and I must join the Church and do his work for him. I was sure of it—I was so sure . . ."

Her voice wound down with a weariness Neil could feel. She sighed again.

"Aren't you sure any longer?" Neil's voice was so kind that she lifted her eyes to meet his.

"I don't think I've lost it, I don't think I've changed— it's as though that knowledge has slipped into some dark hole in my mind. It's as though a fog is in my head and I can't work through it. I don't understand. Everything was so clear before."

"Are you afraid your father's angry or disappointed?"

"Not angry. He always was patient with me."

"Then be patient with yourself, Janet. He knows the things you've been going through. He can afford to wait a few days longer. He's proud of how far you've come alone."

"Don't say that. You have no right to say that! You're humoring me as if I were a child."

He took hold of her hand and pulled her gently against him. "I think too much of you to humor you, Janet. And I do have a right to say what I said. I love you for one, and that gives me the right."

She drew in her breath and her eyes grew wide.

"I love you!" he said again. His lips found hers. He kissed them once, then again. "Don't run away from me, Janet. Don't be afraid."

She put her face against his shoulder and he held her. For long moments she stood in his strong embrace while the moon rained silver arrows down from the branches and sent whispers trembling through the light leaves, and the rowan spread like a shelter above them while the healing fingers of love wove their delicate art.

14

Farewell: thou canst not teach
me to forget . . .
I know no cause why I should welcome
Such a guest as grief . . .
RICHARD III

Edwin had already taken his leave of Tom Briggs; that hadn't been easy.

"I'll be darned, but I'm going to miss you, Edwin," he said. They had worked out the business details to each one's satisfaction. "I'll be back," Edwin had said, but the words lacked conviction and he wondered, even as he said them, if they were true.

Now Julie. He didn't think about Julie. From the moment the letter had arrived he'd forbidden his mind to rest upon her at all. He had known this would happen, and so had she; it was the natural end to the beginning they both had accepted.

When he picked her up for the evening he drove to the river—not the same spot where he'd talked with Nan, but further around. He was having difficulty himself in facing the moment, so he drove out of the town and down the highway that wound from Nauvoo toward Carthage. He was quiet, and she didn't press him. He found a spot where the trees thinned and a wide point of water pushed into the land, green and black and ink blue in the evening shadows.

He stopped and they walked awhile. An errant sunbeam danced a farewell over the river, revealing the store of glistening emerald jewels, trailing across them so they bubbled and sparkled and leapt against the blue air. Julie dipped her hand in the glistening spray; it dripped from her fingers reluctantly, drop after jeweled drop. She turned to Edwin. "You're leaving. When are you leaving?"

He gazed at her. Was she more woman than he had supposed? What perception was this?

"A letter arrived from my solicitor Monday. A court date has been assigned: the first Thursday in August."

"That's nearly two months away."

"There's work to be done now."

"Something to run back to. I know." She turned from him again. "You've known since Monday. Why have you waited to tell me?"

"If I knew the answer to that," he said, "I'd be gone already."

She didn't respond. She was trembling inside. She had never felt more miserable, more unsure of herself, more helpless.

"I leave tomorrow morning," Edwin said, breaking the silence.

"Then it's over," she murmured, and her voice was no more than a breath on the air. "Will you let me know how you are? Will you write?"

"I make no promises," he replied in a hollow voice. "I refuse to look ahead one day from this point."

She turned so she was facing him. "Edwin, you are such a coward!"

She walked past him and back to the car. He stared after, aware even in his shock of the grace of her body, the soft movement of her hair with the lift of her walk. He followed slowly, he got into the car, but he didn't start it.

"Julie—"

"I don't want to talk to you, Edwin. Take me home." Her voice was soft; he couldn't discern her emotions.

"Do you really *want* to go home and brood? It's our last night together."

"Take all of you I can get, is that what you mean?" She looked into his eyes; there was much to read there. She wished she was more adept at the art. But some of what she saw frightened her deeply; she wasn't prepared for what she saw. *I must not let him kiss me,* she said to herself. *Not even touch me.*

He turned the car around and drove back to Nauvoo. He didn't want this. He had pictured something far different for this night. He pulled up by the park and tried once more.

"Come walk with me, Julie."

She turned to him. For the first time he saw pain in her eyes. "I've known you were selfish and cowardly, Edwin, but never cruel. What do you expect me to endure?" It was almost a cry; it pierced through him—he wished he had never heard it.

"Julie," he said, "I can't leave you like this."

"How would you leave me? What more do you want from me, Edwin?"

"You musn't care so much," he protested with sudden vehemence. "I'm not good for you, Julie, I'd spoil you, taint you. I warned you at the beginning not to care!" His words sunk into his own heart like pieces of lead.

"That's not as easy for other people as it is for you, Edwin. It's all right, it's my own concern, I'm not complaining. I'd rather care like I do and be hurt than to be like you!"

There were tears in her voice, but her eyes were dry still. She had never been more desirable to him, never. He ached to touch her, just once, one last time. But he was afraid. He started the car and drove to her house, and she left him. He went back to his room alone and the long night set in, and the friendly bottles of Dewars could not dispel it, nor loosen the terrible tightening on his heart.

Neil wasn't sure it was the right thing to do—not yet, maybe not ever. He didn't trust his natural impulses in such things. But the puppy won his heart the first time he saw him, and he was from the same bloodline, the very same original sire as Tybalt. So he purchased him, wincing a little at the price, then with some hesitancy drove out to Bieldmor.

It was early morning and Janet was there, and as luck would have it she was alone in the stable wing that was used as a garage. He sauntered in, leaving the puppy safe in a box on the floor of his MGA. He was still uncertain what to say, or how to approach her. But she smiled so warmly when she saw him that he felt encouraged.

"I've been doing some detail work on the Midget," she explained. "Here, will you hold this?"

She handed him a bottle of leather treatment, then continued rubbing out a portion of the leather seat surface. "I'll be through in a minute." Her golden hair clung in damp tendrils about her face. He restrained an urge to reach out and touch it. Instead he touched the satin-smooth wing of the old MG. "You take good care of her," he observed.

"It's a pleasure." She straightened up and arched her back. "There, that ought to do it. That's harder work than it appears." She took the bottle he had been holding and put it away.

"Would you like a cold drink?" she asked. Neil hesitated. He must broach the subject soon, somehow. She looked more closely at him. "Are you all right, Neil? Is something the matter?"

He rubbed his toe along the rough brick flooring. She walked out into the morning sunlight, shading her eyes with her hand. "You should have parked over here out of the sun," she told him. She glanced at the low MG. "Looks like you could use a little elbow grease here yourself. Where did all this mud come from?"

She walked up close to the car and the puppy heard her. He whined; then the whine increased to a pitiful wail. Janet stood still. "Do you have a dog in there, Neil?"

He stuck his hands in his pockets. "Why don't you open the door and see for yourself?"

She slid the side curtain back and reached inside to push down on the wire that would release the door catch. Noiselessly the door swung outward. The puppy wiggled and jumped at the sides of the box. She watched him a moment, then dropped to her knees and gently lifted him out. "He's a tri-color. Very good markings. Where did you get him?"

"A place called Murray's."

"That's the very best kennel around for miles. That's where —" She stopped suddenly and stood up to face him.

"I know, that's where Tybalt came from. I found the old man. Told him I needed the best he had. He remembered, said Tybalt would be 'verra harrd to match.' "

She ran her fingers through her hair and kept staring at him. He moved a step or two closer. "Don't be angry, Janet. I wanted to get him for you, but I was afraid—didn't want to do more harm than good. But I couldn't resist him—I didn't expect *that* to happen—"

He reached for her hand. "I don't mean for him to replace Tybalt, or to even do much about the pain. I hope you don't think it presumptuous of me—I don't mean to try to step into your father's place. But I did think it was fitting in one way. Both dogs were gifts from men who love you."

There were no tears in her eyes as she moved toward him. "I don't deserve this, Neil."

He didn't like to hear that. "Don't say such a thing; don't even think it. It's my pleasure . . . to bring you any happiness I can."

For Neil the statement was eloquent. Janet clung to it, savored it, tucked it away in her heart. She leaned forward to kiss his lips. "A down payment," she whispered against his ear, then kissed him again. He hadn't expected that. His arms closed around her, and for a time the dog was forgotten altogether.

Nan had no warning, no way to anticipate it. She went to bed feeling fine. When she woke the next morning she felt strange inside and her head was dizzy. Then the pains started in earnest and she called the doctor, who insisted that Jessie bring her to him at once. His orders were clear: she must go straight to bed if she wanted to keep the baby. She obeyed, but it made no difference. That same afternoon she checked into the hospital and by midnight she had miscarried a tiny daughter whom she had nurtured inside her for three brief months.

The doctor explained all the details to her and Andrew, how this was often nature's way to correct her mistakes. Nan didn't like to think of the child she had carried in that light. He assured her that she could have more babies, that most women have at least one miscarriage in their lives—clinical, crisp, encouraging counsel. But she still was empty inside, and her arms were empty, and her heart was a burning pain in her chest.

Nan thought it was as hard, perhaps even harder, for Andrew. He had his own disappointment to struggle with, and then the agony of seeing her suffer. She went home; the first day he hovered near her. The next morning she ordered him out of the house. She knew if he had work at hand—things he must think about, decisions to make—he would heal faster. But once he was gone her own spirits sank lower and lower.

She was dozing when Janet knocked lightly on the door. "May I come in?" Nan looked up and nodded. Janet entered and sat on the edge of the bed.

"I'm sorry to bother you, Nan, but we're being bombarded. I have a list here. You won't believe this. We have downstairs three cakes, two pies, two salads, five casseroles, and a huge batch of homemade rolls—which are simply delicious."

"Where did they come from?"

"Members of the ward have sent them. And I've had three calls this morning from ladies who said they'll come over at a minute's notice if you need help."

The two young women smiled at each other. "It's incredible, Janet. I remember that's how Grant said it was. We're brothers and sisters, he used to tell me, we take care of each other."

"What shall we do with it all?"

Nan shook her head. "Freeze it—have a party. Invite Neil over; he and Andrew between them could make quite a dent."

They laughed together and Nan was suddenly grateful that Janet was there; she didn't want her to go. She didn't want to be left alone with her own heavy thoughts and feelings. She didn't quite have the courage to say, "Will you stay with me, Janet?" So she asked the question that had been in her mind since she went to the hospital, hoping Janet would be willing to answer it for her.

"How is Jessie? What is she doing, Janet? I haven't seen her since—"

"Yes, I know, I know." Janet rose and paced a few steps. "I'm not sure how to explain it. You certainly know I've never understood my mother myself."

A small frown creased Nan's brow. Janet sounded angry—angry and resentful.

"I'm sure Andrew told you how Mother is—how she used to be. I'll admit she's been better since you arrived, since Andrew came back to her safe and sound. But she used to throw pretty wild tantrums around here. She was accustomed to—well, Father always gave her her way, spoiled her—"

Nan listened, surprised. This had little to do with her question. But Janet went on, her voice small and tense.

"Remember, while Father was in America she lost her first child, a little girl. It did something to her. She's carried the pain of it all these years; she won't let go. I think when this happened to you, when the baby turned out . . . to be a girl . . . I don't know, I'm just guessing."

Nan nodded slowly. "I think you've hit on it, Janet. Though exactly what she's feeling we don't know. She just can't handle being around the situation."

"I'm sorry. I apologize for her."

"Oh Janet, don't. I've been *concerned* about her, that's why I asked."

"She should be concerned about you right now—"

"She is."

Janet made a soft sound under her breath. "Don't count on it, Hannah." There was more pain in Janet's voice than anger now. Nan thought suddenly of all the times Janet must have suffered, longing for a mother's comfort when none was there.

"I don't claim to understand her," she said very softly. "Nor to excuse the things she's done, and hasn't done—the ways she's failed you, Janet."

Janet looked up, her eyes veiled, defensive now.

"The fact that she hasn't been able to . . . to love you as she wants to has caused her as much suffering as it has you."

"You have no way of judging that," Janet protested. "I don't believe you."

"I've seen it so many times in her eyes. When she looks at you and thinks no one is watching. When Andrew happens to talk about you, to praise you for something. I can see the pain and the hunger in her eyes."

Janet turned from the bed and walked to the window. "So, what if you're right? What good does it do? It's never helped me, and it never will, Nan. It's never made me feel loved and secure—

cherished, the way Andrew is cherished. I'm sorry—I don't really want her to suffer. But she's brought it on herself; you have to admit that, Nan."

Nan held her breath. "That makes it so much worse. In her darkest moments she blames herself bitterly, I'm sure. The biggest mistake people make with each other is that they think it's too late to change things. It's never too late."

"You think I could try now and it would make a difference with her? Prostrate myself before her, beg for her love?"

"No, no, that's not what I mean. You could *love her.* Offer her something she's never had."

Janet walked to the door. "I've got to feed Yankee now. I'll come back later."

Nan leaned forward. "Could I come with you? It's so lovely outside. I don't think it would hurt if I take it slowly. I love to watch the two of you play together."

The eagerness in Nan's voice touched Janet. She walked back to the bed. "Here, let me help you. The fresh air might be good for you after all."

The two walked out of the room and down the long stairs together. From a high, lone window Jessie watched until long after the dark head and the light head disappeared from her view, until long after the sweet young sound of their voices had faded into the silence that closed around her like the smothering walls of a prison.

Nan's call came while Julie was at the pool. She was a champion swimmer, and she'd worked the past three summers as a lifeguard. Grandma told her when she came home. The news upset her. She knew how much this baby had meant to Nan, how bitter would be her disappointment. Knowing her sister as she did, she could guess there would be feelings of failure, too. Nan was like that; she took everything personally, on its most intense and serious level. Her sense of responsibility was too highly developed. It had been confining to live with that influence when they were girls, to chafe under the subtle pressure. But now. Now she could appreciate the sincerity behind it, the gentle insecurity that pushed people like Nan to overcome and achieve until eventually they grew into their own cherished images. She thought, with not a little disappointment, of the passport Nan had urged her to get. "I'd like you to come when the baby is born," Nan had written. Julie hated to admit how excited she'd been at the prospect. Now the passport would sit useless—like everything else about her life.

She would give anything to talk to Nan now. If she had been here, would she have asked the question? Probably not. The timing couldn't be more wrong. She hadn't heard from Edwin once since he left. Perhaps Nan had seen him. Perhaps she might have volunteered information about him.

Julie shuddered. This was a dangerous line of thought. She ran upstairs to take a shower. This lifeguard job didn't help; it gave her too much time to just sit and think. She was sewing a vest for Edwin, a Stewart tartan, or the closest she could find to one in the fabric stores here. It was silly, but it made her feel closer to him. She tucked it away in the bottom drawer with her sweaters. *I won't touch it all weekend,* she promised herself. She was going out on a double date this evening with Tom's brother, Fred, and her best friend, Cathy, who had dated all through high school. She would be matched with Timothy Weston. Tim was all right; she had dated him on and off before Edwin came. It struck her suddenly how much her life had changed then, how every aspect of it had centered around him.

It seemed impossible now to go back. Those brief months had changed her. It wasn't that she disdained boys like Tim. It was just that everything about them seemed dull and empty. No one could be like Edwin; he was one of a kind. Even now when she thought of him she went weak inside and the pain could still eat through her heart like acid.

Time—would time make a difference? She didn't think so. She was graduated from high school now. She had a scholarship to Bradley University in Peoria. It was what she had wanted all her life. She supposed she would go, but there was no zest left in her, no excitement, no sense of purpose. She ran a brush through her hair and decided she ought to blow-dry it. Where was Edwin right now? What was he doing? Had he forgotten about her?

She slipped on her blouse. This was hard, every bit as hard as she had expected. What had he said? *I'd spoil you, Julie, I'd taint you.* She thought grimly, *You've done that already, Edwin. You've spoiled me for anything else but you for the rest of my life.*

15

The day shall not be up as
soon as I,
To try the fair adventure
of tommorrow.
KING JOHN

Edwin had been home nearly two weeks and nothing had happened. *Nothing.* It was July; there were only five weeks till the court date. His solicitor assured him he had the case well in hand, told him not to worry. But he had to take some action himself, had to *do* something. He thought of his various contacts, his possibilities. Then it came into his mind with perfect clarity: Janet. Why hadn't he thought of her before?

Finding a way to see her alone was another matter. He didn't want to risk going to Bieldmor House. Nor did he have the time or inclination to lie hidden in wait for her along some lonely country road. He'd played enough of that game already to last him a lifetime.

So he took the risk, which he considered small, of contacting Gordon MacGregor. Although his brother, Donald, had been Andrew's best man, Gordon wouldn't betray Edwin. He called Janet and told her there were some club matters that needed conferring on, and set an evening for her to come over. When she arrived the housekeeper let her in and escorted her to the game room where Edwin was waiting.

He turned in time to see the surprise wash over her face, a shocked surprise that turned her white skin whiter still.

"Where's Gordie?"

"He won't be here. I asked him to call you. You look beautiful, Janet. What's been going on?"

"With me, or with Nan and Andrew?" She took a cautious step forward. He met her more than halfway and took her hand.

"With *you.* You're glowing, lass. I can see it. You've never had that look about you before."

"You're too canny where women are concerned, Edwin," she complained. "It's not fair." But she told him about Neil and he listened with that particular warmth he reserved for her.

"It was bound to happen," he commented, "sooner or later. I hope the lad knows what a prize you are. Of course, he could never be worthy of you—"

"Now, stop it, Edwin. You were always hard on my boyfriends, I remember—"

"Of course. What did you expect me to be? I was jealous that I couldn't be in the running, that fate had made that impossible."

He had said the same thing to her often in jesting, but this time his voice had a different note. She tried to laugh it off. "I refuse to feel sorry for you, Edwin. I would have been just one more girl on your list, and you know it."

He laughed, too. "Don't be so certain, Janet. I'd have gladly thrown away my little black book for you."

The moment passed, and she was anxious to leave it. "So you want the news? I don't know where to begin. You know about Nan's miscarriage?"

His eyes grew instantly concerned.

"I thought you would know . . . perhaps from her sister . . ."

"I haven't been in touch. What happened?"

She told him the scanty details. "How is she?" he asked.

"Not bouncing back. It was a hard blow—for both of them."

The eyes watching hers grew guarded. "Don't try that, Janet. Don't make me feel sorry for Andrew; that isn't fair play."

"By whose standards?" Her voice had grown saucy. "I'd call it a very mild tactic compared to some I've seen—or heard of—"

"All right, all right. You know I can't argue with *you,* I've no heart for it." His eyes were anxious still, and pensive. "Janet. If I write a little note for Nan, would you give it to her?"

She was surprised, but she tried not to show it. "I suppose I could."

"Good. Thank you." He appeared to dismiss the matter and their talk turned to other, less vital things, and she warmed toward him enough to say, "There's one thing you might like to know. Nan lost the journal."

"What journal? What do you mean?" He was all attention.

She told him what had happened, how Tybalt had toppled the old book into the pond, how upset she had been, how devastated Nan was. "That will be good for your case, won't it?" she asked.

"I should think so." His voice sounded normal, almost reflective, but his eyes showed his excitement. "Thank you, lass. I won't ask you for anything further. I know how pressing divided allegiance can be."

But before she left he sat down at the desk and wrote his letter to Nan, and sealed it.

"If I give this to Nan," she warned him, "she'll know I've seen you."

He nodded. "There's nothing incriminating in it, and nothing improper. It's time to come out of the woodwork now, anyway."

So although she had misgivings she delivered it for him, handing it to Nan herself the next morning when Andrew had gone. She could see the warmth creep into Nan's eyes.

"From Edwin? You've seen him, then? How is he?"

"Do you mean, what's he up to?" she started to answer, then was sorry she'd said it. "How is he? Changed, I think. Little things I can't quite put my finger on. But it's hard to tell—who can tell with Edwin?"

Nan took her letter into her room and closed the door. Janet felt vaguely excluded, but convinced herself it was only curiosity that made her want to see what her cousin had written.

When Julie picked up the phone receiver and heard his voice it was as though her heart turned somersaults within her. *Be careful,* she warned herself. *Go carefully, Julie.*

Edwin got right to the point; he told her he'd talked with Janet, and filled her in on some of the details concerning Nan. He was kind, very kind. She relaxed a little. She asked him tentatively about the court case, so he confided the story of the lost journal. "Perhaps Lady Luck will smile on me a little," he said.

She swallowed hard. She hated to tell him, but she must. "Edwin, you'd better know this. Nan copied the pages from the journal, the ones that dealt with Charles Buchanan."

"Are you sure?"

"I'm sure. She was paranoid about it. She even had them notarized."

He threw it off as nothing important, treated it lightly. But she could feel the strain in his voice and her heart ached for him. She answered his questions about Tom and the business, and they talked a while longer. She told him about her scholarship. He said, "That's good. Is that what you want?"

She hesitated, then replied, "It's what I *wanted.*"

He made no answering comment. He didn't say he missed her, but he did say, "Take care, Julie."

When she hung up the phone she was miserable. But when Edwin hung up the phone he was frightened. He'd been telling himself all along that the American's case was flimsy. There was no real evidence of his parentage, nothing substantial. It was his responsibility, making claim, to bring *proof* to bearing. His solicitor had assured him—but the pages were there. *And the ring.* That was their one largest piece of evidence, the companion ring the old man had made for his lost son: two identical rings, one in Andrew's possession, and one in the hands of Brad Richards. Edwin convinced himself, as he sat in his lonely darkness, that the ring was his greatest enemy.

"So Andrew's American is arriving tomorrow. You don't have to look so glum, Janet."

She scowled at Neil. "You don't understand. It's not just that he's a 'Utah Mormon'; I can't abide him."

"He's a very nice person, Janet. You refuse to see that."

"I *can* see that. I don't care how nice he is. He has no right here, he has no right to the money." She paused. She didn't know how far to go. "I love Edwin, I've always loved Edwin, he's just like my brother. The money by right is his, no matter what crazy ideas the old man had."

"You still blame Andrew for finding Brad Richards, don't you?"

She ran her fingers through her fair hair. "I guess I do, Neil. But more than that, I can't forgive what he did to Edwin."

"You can't judge that, honey. You weren't there; you're not Andrew."

She made an impatient sound. "There are certain things you just don't do to people who love you." She rose from the chair where she was sitting and walked to the window. Before her eyes stretched the green, vast Bieldmor acres. "I don't want to talk about it," she said. Neil came up behind her and placed his hands on her shoulders. "You can come stay with me when the usurper arrives. Wouldn't you like that?"

She turned to him with a smile in her eyes. "I just might take you up on the offer. What would your mother say?"

"She'd put you in the farthest guest room she could find and lock the door."

"Doesn't she trust you?" Janet laughed. She liked Neil's mother. In fact, she liked both his parents. She often wondered how it would be to have a regular family. His father was a quiet man, somewhat like Neil—very capable, very successful. His mother was dainty, with a sparkle in her eye, and she'd kept her figure even though she had borne five children. They seemed so *normal.* Andrew often had said that real money set people apart from their neighbors, that wealth was a lonely stewardship to keep. But Neil's parents were very far from poor. His father held a top-flight engineering position at Chrysler and was here in the Scottish plant for two years. Two years that were due to end next April. What he would do after that Janet hadn't asked. Neil was doing graduate work at the University of Glasgow. Even his plans were something they hadn't discussed much.

"Come now, Janet, you're brooding on something. Go get that mutt of yours and we'll take a ride."

She leaned over and kissed his cheek. "I love you, I love you," she whispered, then turned away, fearing how much he might see in her eyes.

Once Andrew had made up his mind he let nothing stop him. "It's your summer vacation," he told Brad. "You're not teaching now. You'd be doing me a favor. I need you. Besides, you'll have to be here for the court date as it is. A few extra weeks—it would make a great difference to me."

In the end it was concern for Nan that won him. He agreed to come, but with Jennie only. "It's a big house," Andrew reminded him, "there's room for the children." But no argument touched him. Brad carried too vivid an image of Jessie's face. He knew he couldn't invade her realm with a passel of children.

Andrew sent tickets for the two of them. He planned to spend a few days with Brad, walking him through the various tasks he'd be doing, making sure he had a grasp on things, introducing him to the managers he'd be working under, except when he was handling some of the personal correspondence Andrew had delegated to him. Then he'd turn his back on it all and take Nan to the Highlands. He was a little worried about her. She was busier than she'd ever been. She served in several Church callings and wrote articles now for two local papers, as well as for her old editor in Illinois. It wasn't that she was depressed, or unhappy, really—just so subdued, as though the fine, shining edge of her spirit had been rubbed off, or covered over with layers of pain to dull it. They needed some time alone together. And the Highlands—the Highlands with Nan at this time of year!

Nan made preparations for the trip with mixed feelings. She wasn't comfortable leaving Brad and Jennie, whom she considered guests, alone in the house. She was concerned about Jessie and how she would manage. Even Janet, as much as she'd changed these past months, still harbored ill will against Brad, and well Nan knew it.

"They're all adults," Andrew assured her, "they can work it out for themselves. In some ways Brad and Jennie will feel more freedom without worrying about pleasing us, Nan. They can do their own thing, feel their own way."

Nan still hadn't spoken much to Jessie since the loss of the baby. She felt a need to approach her, although she trembled to do so, and found small reasons day after day to postpone the encounter.

Early Monday evening she was alone in her rooms; Andrew and Brad had not yet returned from Glasgow. She didn't hear Jessie's approach through the sitting room doorway, and so was startled when she spoke.

"Hannah."

She turned and smiled. "Oh, Jessie, it's good to see you. I was going to come to your rooms myself—"

"I know. I've seen you watching me, but your eyes were fearful. So I thought I'd do it for you."

Nan stared. "I didn't realize . . . you could read me so well," she said lamely.

Jessie laughed. The sound was delicate, but not unkind. "Women come to know such things, Hannah. And I've been a woman for a long time."

"I know all this has been difficult for you," Nan said, "us leaving and—"

"Andrew's American, as Janet calls him, coming? Difficult isn't the word, my dear. But that's neither here nor there. I suppose I'll survive it. If life teaches a person one thing, it teaches patience. Even I have come to develop a small, precious store."

Nan smiled, but before she could respond Jessie continued.

"However, there are other things I still sorely lack. I don't have a great tolerance for pain, Hannah, and the loss of your baby threw me back to another time—"

"I know, Jessie, I know—you don't have to say it."

"There is much I *can't* say, that cannot be put into words. But I indulged my own pain, and I apologize for that, Nan. I left you to fight yours alone, without me. That was an inexcusable thing to do."

"Inexcusable? I don't think so. Ever since Andrew first told me about you back in Nauvoo I've admired you, Jessie. I found more to admire about you when I came here. And I'm grateful for the way you accepted me—"

"You were easy to accept, Hannah."

"No, no, I was everything you had come to hate: an American, and a nobody at that, a Mormon sympathizer, a stranger—"

"You were the woman Andrew loved."

The way she said it made Nan draw in her breath. "You see," Jessie continued, "I know my Andrew. I knew he would never love more than one woman in his life. I used to pray through all those years that he would find her."

She put her arms lightly around Nan's shoulders. "You *are* the girl. I could see it in your eyes the first time I met you. The wrong kind of woman could have ruined him, Nan. I can trust him to you, and I'm very grateful."

Nan's eyes filled with tears. "I love him, Jessie. You know how dearly I love him."

The answer came whisper soft. "I know." In the stillness no other word was spoken. But between the two women was understanding, and words would never really be needed again.

They drove north-northeast from Glasgow to Stirling, with the breath of the morning new on their cheeks and the silver-blue Healey humming beneath them. This was Bruce and Wallace country, Nan knew, with Dunfermline, the ancient capital, a few miles to the east and the Trossachs only a few miles to the west, with the Lake of Menteith a few miles distant and, of course, Stirling Castle itself right there—ranking with Edinburgh as the most romantic castle in Scotland.

Their first pilgrimage was to the Wallace Monument. They climbed the steps of the great stone tower carefully, for Nan's sake. And although it was July and the sun shone warmly, there was a chill to the air that blew in through the arrow slits.

They didn't stay long at the Hall of Heroes, but lingered by the Wallace Sword, and came to stand at last on the top of the windy tower, looking down through a blue haze to Stirling below.

"It is magnificent," Nan whispered. From the height they saw clearly the barrier of the Grampian Mountains to the northwest and five separate battlefields: Bannockburn, the only one Nan knew anything of; and just beyond it Sauchieburn; Falkirk at the foot of the ridge of Pentlands; Sheriffmuir on the high, sloped land by the Black Hill; and below, on the fringe of Stirling, the spot where, from this very height where they stood, Wallace himself had swept down to smite the wicked Cressingham.

"There's more history in this one view," Andrew mused, "than perhaps any other in Britain."

He refused to think in terms of days; they would be gone, he said, as long as they wanted. They would traverse the whole of the Highlands, then cross to Skye, where age and magic, mystery and heroism blended in a music no human voice could sing, in a music that only the pipes could echo from the tall and terrible turrets of Dunvegan Castle.

Nan was enchanted. She had never had Andrew to herself quite like this before. And here, in his natural element, he flourished, and the strength and beauty and poetry around them laid healing fingers upon both their hearts.

16

What! I love! I sue! I seek a wife!
LOVE'S LABOUR'S LOST

Once it came to him Edwin could not forsake it, couldn't shake the idea out of his mind—couldn't drown it, argue it, bluster it away. He took careful preliminary steps, laid his groundwork, and everything fell so easily into place that he came to wonder if this was in truth the direction fate itself had ordained.

The first step was by far the easiest; he still had his own key. He drove a rented, unknown car to Bieldmor—late, but not too late, for his time would be marked. He parked in a close but secluded spot he knew of, then walked the remaining distance on shoes that were padded to muffle sound. He unlocked the door and stood a moment in the entrance, with nothing but the barely audible rhythm of his own breathing.

There were no lights in the silent house. The summer moonlight filtered through tall, leaded windows into pools on the stairs and dancing, fairylike patterns that spattered along the walls and ceilings to disappear into cracks and hollows, shadow-filled. He climbed the stairs. He knew the wing where the guest rooms were; he opened doors and glided through empty hallways, never once needing to hesitate. He picked the room that was farthest away, guessing that this was where Jessie would place the unwanted American. Here he froze for a moment. Now came the test.

He tried the handle; it turned for him noiselessly. He opened the door with one swift movement; there was still no sound. He forced himself to stand still till his eyes grew accustomed to the absence of light in the curtained room. Then he moved to the tall man's bureau in the corner. The two figures in the bed didn't stir. He felt over the surface. Nothing. He moved to the long lowboy. There were items scattered here. His hand felt for them.

There was a soft sound from behind him. He froze, then turned his head very slowly toward the sound. Jennie had moved in her sleep and sighed a little. Edwin felt again. There was a ring here, two rings—maybe more. He switched on the tiny penlight he held in the curve of his hand. Two seconds, three, his hand closed around the circle of metal and the light winked out like an errant star. He disciplined himself to remain standing: three seconds, four seconds, five—till his eyes had adjusted again.

The ring was deep in his pocket now. He moved to the doorway. The heavy door fit noiselessly into place. He retraced his steps, counting his way, growing confident as he cleared the stairway, ecstatic as he pulled the door and felt the kiss of the cool evening air sink into his pores. He went directly to the car and started the engine. The dash clock read 1:11. He grinned. One, one, one—first step successful.

It took ten minutes to drive to his rendezvous. The shop was nothing more than an underground room, ill lit and dirty. Edwin parked the car and let himself in with a key. For a moment he stood alone in the empty darkness. Then from somewhere a hand reached out and snapped on a small, overhead light.

The thick yellow beam nearly blinded Edwin. He groped in his pocket and held forth the ring, cradled in his palm. A short, stooped little man moved out from the shadows. His fingers were short and thick. Edwin noticed, as he reached for the ring, that his nails were dirty and that one or two were broken or torn. The back of his hand crawled with long white hairs. He picked up the ring and laid it gently in a box lined with rich dark velvet.

Edwin watched as he drew out a small jeweler's glass and carefully louped the ring. Long minutes passed while he continued his examination. Edwin's hand on the edge of the high wooden ledge was clenched so that it ached. He flexed his fingers. The small man raised one eye.

"Dis is de ring, all right. It is not easy—not easy to copy such work as dis." The man's eye, a glowing orb in the stream of trembling yellow light, blinked and narrowed. "Eet vill cost half again as much as I told you. The quality of dees stones is rare, Edvin, and dey are cut with the old cut. I shall need to use a cubic zirconia and take great care."

Edwin nodded. "All right, go ahead. But hurry."

The old goldsmith bent his head again to his task. "No hurry, no hurry in dis, Edvin."

Edwin watched the hands on the small cuckoo clock on the wall; they seemed frozen. He watched the slow, sure movements of the man's hands as he photographed the ring from several directions, carefully weighed it and, with a micrometer, measured each stone. Edwin glanced back at the clock: 1:47. He walked to the window and watched the moon come out from the clouds. They boiled around it, brittle wafers of white with inky black edges. The man beside him was pushing the ring into a raw rubber mold that he would vulcanize to create a deep, crisp impression.

Two-thirty and still not done. The moon was hidden again by the jealous clouds. Edwin thought fleetingly of the money this was costing, how it would deplete his precious hoard. What kind of chances, what odds were there that the ring would repay his investment—once, ten times, ten thousand times over?

The old man's fingers were deft and efficient; he was a master at his craft. Edwin stared at the torch, at the miniature jeweler's saws and files, until they swam in his tired gaze. The minutes ticked. At last the man reached over and handed the ring to Edwin. The watch on his wrist read 3:14.

"I vill call you," the little man said.

"When?" Edwin demanded.

"Vhen we arranged. Fourteen days, twenty days—vhenever."

Edwin nodded.

"You vill be careful?" the old man cautioned.

"I will be careful," Edwin assured him. A moment later he was turning the engine on his car, the ring in his pocket, retracing the route he had come step by step.

It was easier the second time. He knew what he was doing down to the smallest detail. He set the ring back in the identical place and position. He didn't need to use the small pocket light. Seconds later he was outside, heading for the car. A minute more, two minutes, in three he had reached the main road.

Success. Complete success. That exultant feeling, as heady as wine, surged through him. Near four o'clock. There was nothing to do, no one to share this elation with. The pub windows were closed and shuttered. He'd go home and try to sleep it off. Tomorrow was another day, and tomorrow for Edwin looked much brighter than it had for a long time now.

The third morning following Andrew and Nan's departure Janet gave in and called Neil for help. "Please come out," she asked him, "and teach Brad's wife how to drive a right-hand drive stick shift car! We've got to do something with her. She can't just sit around here day after day while her husband's at work. Mother doesn't even come out of her rooms. It's all on my shoulders, and you know how *I* feel—"

"All right, honey, all right," he laughed, "take a breath—and take it easy. I'll be there as soon as my next class is over."

The moment she saw his car pull into the drive she felt better. They walked for a while with the dog. "Your problem," he said, "is that deep down inside you're afraid of people."

She smiled winsomely. "My problem—singular? Haven't I any others?"

"None." He winked and grinned. "None that I've discovered. But seriously, Janet," he pressed, "have compassion on Jennie. None of this is her fault; she didn't ask for it to happen. For that matter, neither did Brad, really."

"So it's all right if I keep blaming Andrew, then?"

He laughed out loud. "You're hopeless, Janet."

"One fault, and that makes me hopeless?"

Neil laughed again and kissed her lightly. How she loved being with him! He had a way of bringing out the best in her—in everything he touched, in all around him. It was a gift, Janet felt, and she basked in it gratefully.

The first driving lesson was not as painful as Janet had expected. She sat in the back seat and watched Neil instruct the young woman. Jennie was actually very quick to learn. Janet felt better knowing her guest would be mobile. Jennie could take the Magnetta now and do what she liked, and Janet wouldn't feel so responsible for her. She didn't like this, she wished Nan and Andrew were here, she wished Edwin—*Edwin!* She hadn't thought of him for some days now. Edwin spoiled her, even more than Andrew. He had always seemed to sense when something was difficult for her and take care of it just like that, ever since they were children. Sometimes she sorely missed him.

She looked at the woman bent over the wheel. She was here, she was real; Janet couldn't change that. What she had thought would endure forever was already past. She was learning that life was a series of surprises—capricious, hard to predict or control. Just then Neil turned his head and grinned at her. "Now, this girl in the back seat there," he was saying, "could teach you more about driving than any ten men."

Jennie inclined her head and smiled. She was really quite pretty: small, nicely molded features, honey-brown hair. Janet leaned back against the cool leather seat and tried to relax. Neil was here; Neil was good at handling surprises, good to have around in emergencies.

"Your problem," she said, leaning up close to him, "is that you're too happy—*contagiously* happy."

"You're right, it's a dangerous condition," he agreed.

"It would be easy to get addicted to your kind of happiness," she murmured.

He touched her fingers where they rested on the top edge of the seat. "I'll let you in on a little secret," he said. 'This kind of happiness needs constant renewal, and there's only one source I've found that can do it. So, you see, it's not self-sufficient at all. Without the power source, what would become of it?"

She smiled and he thought how deep her eyes were, warm with her smile like the blue summer sky was warm with the sun. "I'll remember that," she whispered.

"I'd appreciate it. I'd be beholden to you, lass, if you would."

They reached a corner and Neil turned to help Jennie. Janet felt ridiculously light and happy inside. How could any of life's surprises seriously matter as long as she could look into Neil's eyes and see the beauty and strength and love that burned there?

He'd been depressed before; he was given to moods and tempers. But Edwin knew himself well, and this was different. And now, with the letdown following his night's adventure, in the cold, searching light of day he was forced to face it. Did he have courage enough to lay himself on the line? He doubted it. He had every chance of making a royal fool of himself.

He could look back now and see the imprudent pattern. It was a pitfall he'd dug for himself, and he knew it. Oh well, if he failed very few would know. He could slink off to some miserable hole and bury his shame. He checked his bank account and blanched at the sadly depleted figure. He was playing out his hand; when the cards were gone he had no ace in the hole to fall back on. The only thing that gave him courage was the knowledge that this was what he wanted —that and the fact that the timing was right. It was a sure case of now or never. He made his plans.

It was just as Brad had feared. He told Jennie, "I've never been happier at what I'm doing in all my life." She could see it in his face. He worked long hours—much longer than teaching could ever require. Yet when he came home there was a glow in his eyes, a lilt to his step, a sense of excitement that seemed like a whole new dimension. In spite of the pressures and demands, the work seemed to relax him, renew him in some inexplicable way.

The first few days in Scotland Jennie had thought she would die of homesickness and sheer boredom. But now, after Neil and the driving lessons, after Janet's show of friendship—however tentative —things had changed. She had gone out alone several times exploring. This in itself was different for her: the freedom, the solitude of her own company, no suspended responsibilities to cause her to feel guilty or neglectful. At first she had been very nervous, ill at ease. But with each day that passed she could feel her attitude changing.

Her sense of awareness expanded, too. She and Brad were left very much to their own devices. She began shopping the small local markets, cooking the food that was new and foreign to her. Brad loved it. She found herself talking to people, asking questions, listening patiently to their stories, enjoying it all. She began to develop an intensely personal sense of possession: this Scotland was virgin territory to them—hers and Brad's alone. It wasn't crowded with relatives, habits, rules, and customs—there was no one and nothing to dictate to them, to confine them here. It was removed from all the old struggles and pressures and expectations. Their relationship took on new color, new meaning. Jennie found herself sometimes holding her breath, fearing the day when the newfound dream would end.

He gave her not even the slightest warning. She went to answer the door and found him there.

"Aren't you going to let me in?" He leaned on the door frame, his manner casual and noncommittal, a barely concealed spark of mischief in his eyes.

"Edwin?" Julie spoke his name with a question. Her eyes were deep and troubled; she didn't move. He walked past her into the room. "Are you alone, lass?"

This was too much like what had happened before. "What are you doing here?" Her voice was devoid of emotion.

"I've come to check on my investment." His tone was light. But there was something tense, even nervous in his manner.

"Tom's out of town. He won't be back till Monday."

"I didn't come to see Tom," he replied, and he turned to face her. She was taken aback by the naked openness in his face. "I've come for you."

She moved her hand nervously, helplessly. "What do you mean?"

"I've missed you."

"I've missed you, too. Why didn't you write?"

"I didn't *want* to write—I didn't want to miss you! I didn't want to feel this way!"

"I remember," she said.

"Sometimes things happen, and once they happen they can't be ignored or wished away. But Edwin Bain! the unassailable, the invulnerable! I didn't think it would ever happen to me; surely not at the hands of a child like yourself."

Her heart was beating against her throat; she could barely speak. "You're talking in riddles, Edwin. What are you saying?"

He cocked his head and his mouth grew thin and twitched at the corners. "Are you going to make me ask, Julie? Go the whole distance?"

"Yes."

For the longest moment he didn't move or speak. Then he came over to where she stood and took her hands. "I love you, Miss Martin. Yes, I love you. Impossible, but you can believe it, my dear. If I say it, you can believe it!"

"You don't want to say it, you don't want to feel it—still."

He stared at her. "Julie, you're a hard one for all your youth and your gentle ways. I love you! If I hadn't come to grips with that I wouldn't be standing here. Four thousand miles—that smacks of commitment, doesn't it, Julie?"

She trembled; she couldn't resist him much longer. He took a deep breath and started again. "I want you with me. Come to Scotland, Julie."

"That would be crazy!"

"No! It's the only way. I want you to marry me, Julie. But you must do it with your eyes wide open. I am what I am, and I'm not a great catch for any woman."

He paused. His eyes were sincere and gentle. "I have so little to offer—I would have waited. But I couldn't! Once the court case is decided I would look suspect either way. If I win I would seem insincere and presumptuous: the playboy out to impress you. If I lose—" he winced unconsciously at the thought—"I would come a beggar, asking sympathy, wanting a shoulder to cry on. Do you see?"

She nodded wordlessly.

"I've come now, so you'd never wonder, Julie. So no matter what else happens you'll always know that I love you—no strings attached, no conditions."

His voice had grown soft. She no longer fought him. Her green eyes were emerald jewels in a pool of tears. Very gently he put his arms around her. She clung to him. "Edwin, I love you," she cried. "I love you."

She said it against his ear, against his hair, against the smooth skin of his cheek, against his mouth that closed hard and possessive over her own. She repeated it in her heart over and over, knowing its meaning, knowing its burden, embracing the whole as only a woman can embrace love, asking no questions—willing to give her all.

17

O Scotland, Scotland! . . .

MACBETH

The days merged into each other; there were no days, just one long stretch of discovery and pleasure. Andrew had never been so in love before. Their honeymoon hadn't been like this; their love had been too new then. It was cemented now by shared joy and sacrifice, by the heavy hand of grief that had sanctified them, united their spirits with cords that were stronger than death. Nan was lovely, gentle, captivating—spontaneous as a young child would be. It seemed each day he discovered some new aspect of her, like the facets of a fine-cut jewel, endless and gleaming.

For Nan the adventure was all-consuming. Her romantic soul, never properly fed, ate ravenously. It was pure delight, pure untamed sensation, to stand in the haunted solitudes of the Western Highlands, looking off through a lacework of lochs to the wild Atlantic, hearing sea-sounds and bird-sounds she never had known, smelling the ocean spray and the vague fragrance of heather, looking off through shadowy glens to mist-shrouded peaks.

They went from Elgin through Nairn to Inverness, hurrying past the loch and its monster, clogged now with tourists. More than one highland loch boasted its own monster, or water sprite, or haunted ghastie. They spent time in Fort William, taking the Ballachulish ferry over Loch Leven, dipping down to visit Inverary where it sits on the edge of Loch Fyne, an ancient relic, a royal seat of the Campbell clan, with its castle—a magnificent bulk crowned by four graceful turrets—flying the proud and fearsome standard of Argyll. The next leg of their journey would take them seaward, out to Portree and the Isle of Skye where the magnificent mass of Dunvegan brooded over the relics of MacCrimmon and Rory Mor, and the fairy flag with its strange, mystical powers guarded the secrets of the Clan MacLeod.

Jennie had thought she could be complete here, but she was mistaken. Perhaps once it would have been so, but now there were four extensions of Brad and herself—what union she found with Brad was regrettably marred by their absence. It had been good for her to exist for a while without them, without the sap on her energies and her spirit which children exert upon all conscientious mothers. She didn't mope; she didn't complain about it. But her thoughts began to dwell more and more upon them, and her new exuberance seemed to wane and fade. Brad noticed, of course, but he too avoided the subject. There was nothing he could do to remedy things now. Perhaps when Andrew returned he'd approach him about it. If worse came to worst—he'd send Jennie home then.

There was someone else who noticed. Her deep sense of fair play rankled, and *she* took action. She called Neil and asked him to come to her. He came, cautious and rather mystified. He entered the extensive, lavish apartments he'd only heard of. He noted her regal bearing, her fine yet gracious sense of control.

"I've sent for you, young man," she informed him, "because I've been told you're the kind of person who gets things done. I need you to handle just one small task for me."

She *was* charming. "It would be my pleasure," he replied.

Just the hint of a smile touched her mouth. "I believe you mean that. In fact, isn't that one of your fine points my daughter praises?"

"Your daughter is very generous." Neil smiled.

She allowed her own mouth to curve in a smile: delicate, controlled, like all else about her. "Come over here. I'll explain what I want you to do." He sat down in the chair she indicated. It was a very simple thing, but the last thing on earth he'd expected from her.

Goes to show how wrong you can be, he chided himself, *when you make up your mind to judge a person you don't even know. Besides, after all, she is Janet's mother. She'd have to be special for that one reason alone.*

It was a small apartment, very different from her home in Nauvoo, with different names for everything: a flat with her own room and a water closet. Julie laughed at the idea. She couldn't believe she was here, it had happened so quickly. She had not been with Edwin when he first spoke to her father, but she remembered the look on his face when he told her, "If I couldn't hold Nan, I can't expect to hold you." She probably felt less guilty than Nan had felt; she was not his favorite. If he could live without Nan, he could live without her. She wished she could explain it to him, but she knew she couldn't. If she wanted Edwin it had to be now; he would not ask twice.

She'd never been on a plane before and the trip was a long one. But it was an adventure, and with Edwin beside her she was both happy and entertained. Now and then a small panic would rise inside her: *What am I doing here? What will Nan say?*

The day they arrived Edwin himself called Bieldmor House and asked for Hannah. She was on holiday in the Highlands, he was told. Who else might help him? he had asked, and the woman told him either Miss Janet or the American woman, Mrs. Richards. Julie could hardly stay at Bieldmor with Nan gone and Andrew's American there. Besides, Edwin wasn't too sure he wanted anyone to know of her presence, at least not yet.

So he prevailed on a friend of his to put her up for a while. The friend, Margaret, was a pleasant girl in her mid-twenties who did nothing more glamorous than work all day in a bank, but spent her weekends singing in a pub not far from her place. She was cheery and very kind to Julie.

"So you've caught the fish by the tail? Well, good for you, he's a slippery one, Edwin. Many a girl's tried before, lass, you can believe it."

Her blithe words didn't increase Julie's sense of security. She wondered how "caught" Edwin was. She felt it was more a matter of his swimming into shallow waters of his own accord. If he chose to stay there, then he chose to stay there. There was no hook that could hold him against his will.

It was only weeks until the court date and his solicitor warned Edwin that they'd best not do anything official till then. Marriage, even engagement, would be unwise until this thing in the courts was settled. It might be construed as being done for the wrong reasons and do him more harm than good.

So they marked time. Edwin took her everywhere with him. He seemed content to be in her company. Early, very early one morning he drove her to Bieldmor. Nan had described it for her; she had even seen pictures. But they hadn't prepared her for the sight before her now.

"No one lives in a place like this," she breathed.

Edwin chuckled under his breath. "Lots of people do. And your sister's one of the few who deserves to."

Julie nodded. "Nan would fit in, wouldn't she? It's just what she always dreamed of."

"Dreams do come true, you see." Edwin's voice was soft.

"I never believed that."

"Do you believe it now?"

She looked into his eyes, those beautiful eyes that were smiling at her. "I'll never doubt it again," she said.

"Where is Nan's room?" she asked. "It's like a hotel."

"I'll explain it for you," he offered, and he showed her the wing where Jessie kept court, where he'd sat beside her long into the afternoon and then discovered the will no one knew existed that bore his name, that carried the instructions of Andrew's own grandfather to give Charles's hoarded fortune to Sarah's son. He showed her the wing where Nan lived, her bedroom window, and the wing where the American guests would be.

"It's like several huge houses connected together," she marveled. "I felt a little sorry for Nan living with her mother-in-law. But it isn't anything like that, is it?"

"Great houses, they were called, and their day is over. The way everything that is beautiful dies."

Julie stared at him. When he said things like that it disturbed her a little. He lifted his eyebrows at her but didn't smile. "Let's go get a bite to eat, shall we? Good Scots-fried tatties and trout, how does that sound? I've had enough American hamburgers to last me the rest of my life!"

Jessie herself hand-delivered the plane tickets for their four children to Brad and Jennie. "They're all in order," she explained, "Neil took care of it for me."

Brad protested emphatically, but Jessie stood firm. "You've had a vacation of sorts without them, but it's time they were here."

There were tears in Jennie's eyes; perhaps that was what moved Jessie. She put her hand briefly over the young woman's. "My dear, a mother should never be forced away from her children. I understand that particular suffering well enough not to wish to see it imposed on you."

She swept gracefully from the room, pausing at the doorway. "If you have time this afternoon, Jennie, you and I can go over arrangements for their coming. Helen's airing additional bedrooms right now. We'll make plans—"

With one small, bright smile she vanished. Jennie looked at her husband. "Brad," she whispered, "I've been praying that this might happen. But I never dreamed my prayers would be answered through *her.*"

Brad shook his head. "I'm ashamed of myself," he responded. "I've been so selfish. I've prayed for Nan and Andrew and us, even Janet. But I've never thought to pray for Jessie."

"That's all right, Brad." Jennie took his hand. "There's always tomorrow. Thank heaven we're given the chance to make it better than today."

He drew her into his arms and kissed her. "Ah, Jennie, Jennie, I love you," he said. "How lucky I was to happen upon you! You're so good to me, Jennie, so patient, so kind."

She put her head against his shoulder. "It wasn't luck, Bradley," she whispered. "I'd been praying for you to come, you just didn't know it."

He stood holding her, remembering suddenly what his father had told him—not once, but many times when he was a boy. "A good wife is more than a man's 'better half.' She's the spirit behind everything he does. If you want to succeed, Brad, first take care of the woman who loves you, then everything else will work out for your good."

He had sometimes failed in that stewardship. But Jennie, God bless her, had stood beside him. He felt strengthened by the thought. No matter what happened on that day in court she would be there to see him through, to love him.

18

By cruel fate, and giddy
Fortune's furious, fickle wheel . . .
HENRY V

The bay of Portree lies in a natural basin surrounded by cliffs and low, broken hills. The town has not much in the way of fine buildings or statues, except the window in the Episcopal church of St. Columba dedicated to the memory of Skye's heroine, Flora Macdonald. Around the harbor sweeps a picturesque crescent of houses; above these spreads the upper town in a small stretch of forest that has made way reluctantly here and there for the marks of man. There is the town square, but the larger, lovelier homes have been constructed on the outskirts of Portree where the moor begins, open and lonely, with hills rising from it.

Nan needed only one long, sweet sight of it to love it. They arrived in the early evening and, after securing their room, walked together along the shore, arms about each other. "There are mountains to climb here," Andrew told her, "with hidden lochs."

"Lochs up there?" she asked, pointing upward to the brooding gray masses.

"No part of the island," Andrew explained, "lies more than four miles from the sea. The lochs wind in among the moors and skirt the upper reaches of rock and mountain pasture. Wait till you see."

"And Dunvegan?"

"Oh, we'll go to Dunvegan," Andrew promised. "We'll steep ourselves in Skye before we're through."

Nan slept better that night than she had for a long time. A small breeze blew in through her window with the sea in its breath, and she woke to the cry of the gulls and curlews. It was a lazy morning, and they both felt the need to relax. They washed the car, had an early lunch, wrote postcards, wandered the shops along the shore-line. In the late afternoon they took a long, slow ride out over the moorland, dotted now with bog myrtle and purple heather, soft saffron moor grasses and green mosses, and a variety of small wild-flowers Nan didn't recognize. The fragrance assailed her senses like some pure elixir, rising to mingle with the lonely piping of hidden birds, the warm humming of bees, laced now and then with the bright, clear call of the lark. It was a world of soft and persuasive power and Nan relented, giving herself up entirely to its spell.

That evening they ate a light supper in Portree and went to bed early in the waterfront room they had rented. Near midnight Andrew was awakened by a strange tapping sound that seemed to be coming from directly under their window. He tried to ignore it, but it grew louder and more insistent so that Nan, turning and tossing, woke too.

"I'll go see what it is," Andrew said, pulling on his trousers. "I'm sure there's some simple explanation."

Nan cuddled sleepily down under the covers; the night air was cold. "Hurry, Andrew," she called as she pulled the door closed behind him. Andrew stood on the small porch step and peered uncertainly around him. The noise seemed to have stopped. He couldn't see much in the thick darkness.

Suddenly a hand closed over his mouth and at the same moment a heavy object came down with a thud on his skull. He slumped, unconscious, but strong arms were there to support him, slip his body back into the room and onto the bed.

Nan, slipping back into sleep, never knew what hit her. The blow given her was much lighter, more carefully delivered. Someone wrapped her in a blanket and carried her out the door—lightly, over his shoulder. A few seconds later she was in the back seat of a car that sped out of Portree, across the darkened, boggy moorland toward the mountains looming like black, ominous giants against the night sky.

Back in the room deft hands bound the unconscious man lest he should awaken too quickly for their purposes. The place grew still; the small disturbance, a scratch on the surface, was swallowed by the heavy lethargy of the night.

Andrew didn't know what time it was when he awakened. He felt like a drunken man with limbs of lead crawling up through dark water. He could see faint light sifting through the thin slits of the shuttered window. He had a fierce headache, like a large hammer pounding inside his skull. He tried to lift himself onto his elbows, but a weak dizziness spun him around and around, at cross purposes with the room, which whirled dizzily with him. He fell back and swallowed painfully, his throat constricted and dry. There was a feeling of sickness in the pit of his stomach. For a moment or two all these physical symptoms held his attention. His wrists, bound with tight cords, throbbed painfully. His ankles were bound as well and the ropes were twisted around and around the old black bedposts and tied in place. He was trussed, as the saying went, and helpless.

Then suddenly his consciousness widened with instant pain. *Nan!* He turned his head, though the movement caused him great agony, knowing as he turned that she was not in bed beside him, she was gone. *Gone!* What chasms of fear that brief word held open to his recoiling gaze!

He twisted and strained but the effort was futile; he made no headway. He forced his mind to examine painstakingly the details of the last night: There was nothing in them, no clue whatsoever. *What happened—what happened, and why?* His mind reeled and strained, striving to come to some understanding. Nothing could be worse than this nightmare of helplessness and dark ignorance. Night closed around him, the heavy, smothering night, like a hand on the brain—something to struggle against, something dank and evil. But the darkness tightened down, snuffing out his pathetic struggles, bringing him a weighty, unwanted, uneasy peace.

Hours later the maid found him. Then it was only a matter of minutes till Andrew was free. There was much fuss and bother, a doctor was called, there were questions following questions—the note was brought forward: words typewritten on a plain piece of paper. Andrew held it in his hand with a sense of horror and loathing. The words typed out on the paper said:

> Nan safe. 200,000 pound ransom. Four days. Bring money to place indicated on map at midnight of fourth day. Do not contact authorities or SHE DIES.

The last words were capitalized and underlined in red pen. Andrew turned the note over—on the back a rough map was penciled. His mind had gone cold at the very first word: *Nan.* This was not a freakish, unexplained occurrence. These people knew him; this thing had been carefully calculated and planned. *But why?* Who resented him? Who had a grudge against him?

There was no time to waste. He thanked the doctor and paid him. He calmed the girl who had found him and the older couple who ran the inn.

"I've a friend on the Glasgow police force," he told them. "I'll contact him and he'll know what's best to do. It's vitally important that you don't contact your local police force. I've no idea where they're holding her. If they see anything that looks to them the least bit suspicious, her life will be in danger. Do you understand that?"

They seemed to. He packed their belongings; his hands shook a little as he folded Nan's things, but his mind seemed cushioned, insulated against the full weight of what was happening. It was true. He did have a friend on the Glasgow police force. He drove the Healey to the ferry and waited his turn, looking just like any other tourist on a fair summer's morning. He hadn't decided yet if he would go to his friend. That might not be the best way to handle this thing.

Once on the mainland he found a phone and rang up Brad Richards at his own main Paisley extension. He was there. It seemed ridiculous when he told it to Brad, when he actually tried to put words to it all. He told him what steps to take to start getting the money together.

"Have you any ideas at all?" Brad asked him.

"Nothing substantial. I've been thinking about it all morning. Has to be some malcontent—but if so, what connection with me? Perhaps someone who works for me? Edwin has friends on Skye—a rough bunch, some political activists among them. That just might be a clue . . ."

He was suddenly tired, exhausted in a way that frightened him. Brad could feel it. "Andrew, why don't you stay right there? I'll drive out and get you. Or take the train—I don't think you ought to hazard the drive alone."

"I want you there! I want that money! Besides, mother and Janet—it will be better for everyone if you're there."

Brad couldn't move him. At last they rang off. Andrew drove the blue Healey as fast as he could toward Bieldmor. Before his eyes was the image of Nan's face, her auburn hair tossled loosely about it, her eyes warm and sleepy and smiling at him . . . the last time he saw her.

Brad followed Andrew's instructions carefully, to the letter, then drove to Bieldmor to tell them, as Andrew had asked. He thought Jessie would faint; her eyes grew wide, almost sightless. She walked to her room as though in a stupor. Janet, though shaken, was angry. "You shouldn't have told her! You had no business. I don't know what it will do to her. How I wish Edwin were here!"

Brad had been praying for some kind of direction ever since Andrew's call. *Edwin.* Only Edwin could help with Jessie. *Edwin.* Edwin had friends on Skye. It came suddenly into his mind that Edwin could help them. Why, he didn't know. He recoiled from the thought. But that name wouldn't leave his mind. He went up to his bedroom and prayed about what he was feeling. When he arose he went off in search of Janet.

"Excuse me," he began, "but do you know if Edwin's in Glasgow? He has a flat there, doesn't he? Is he in Glasgow now?"

She stared at him. "Yes, I believe he is."

"Could you get in touch with him? Could you give me his number—or, better still, his address?"

She continued to stare. "I don't know what you have in mind, but you don't know Edwin. It wouldn't be wise for *you* to approach him."

Brad swallowed, feeling his throat grow dry. "Do you have the address, anyway?"

Janet gave it to him. He drove straight to Glasgow, not giving himself time to back out. He stood before the door that loomed like a barrier and knocked lightly. Nothing happened; he heard no movement. He knocked again. Noiselessly the door swung open.

Edwin stood behind it looking so much like Andrew that Brad had to bite his lip to keep from exclaiming. The dark penciled eyebrows shot upward, the blue eyes darkened.

"To what do I owe this pleasure?" Edwin's voice mocked. There was something uneasy within him as he looked at the American, standing awkward and uncertain at his door. He had never seen him this close before, the weasely culprit. *So it is you who stands between me and my happiness,* Edwin thought. But some signal inside him warned that whatever reason would bring his enemy to him could not be good.

"May I come in? This is very important or I wouldn't have come here."

Edwin demurred, biting back the cutting reply. "Tell me instantly then, man. What is it? What is it?"

Brad told as dispassionately as he could what had happened. He watched the shades of reaction and emotion play over the face of the man who hated him. Edwin said no word until the tale had woven itself out. Then, without moving a hair, with his eyes fixed on Brad's, he demanded, "Why have you come to tell me this? Why you? You want something from me."

The last words were a statement, not a question. Brad felt his mind was on pins and needles. "Yes," he acknowledged. "Andrew said something over the phone." Brad repeated for him the statement Andrew had made: "Has to be some malcontent—but, if so, what connection with me? Perhaps someone who works for me?

Edwin has friends on Skye—a rough bunch, some political activists among them. That just might be a clue . . ."

His voice wound down. Edwin turned from him, a cold sickness growing inside him. An old conversation came to him suddenly, clear as a bell. "We've got a little deal going," Jamie had said, calling from Portree. "Thought you might like to throw in. It's of special interest to you . . . special interest to you . . . to you . . ." The words echoed, bouncing like blows against the inside of his skull. *Dear heaven, it couldn't be! It couldn't!*

"What do you want me to do?" he asked, still not turning to face Brad.

"I don't know what you *could* do, I just wondered—I just had this feeling that you might be able to find her . . . might at least know where to start looking." It sounded lame put into words.

"You have no idea what you ask." Edwin turned and his eyes were cold and angry. "You've got a lot of gall asking me to go to bat for Andrew. I ought to throw you out on your ear."

"You can still do that. I just had a feeling, don't ask me why, that you'd want to help."

"*Help!* Lovely sentiment. But in this case hardly applicable." His voice was as cold as his eyes; it demoralized Brad; each word struck him like a small blow. "But then, no one's more dispensable than Edwin, right?"

He moved a step or two toward Brad. Brad felt himself cower, and struggled to conceal his inner reaction.

"Get out of here." Edwin walked to the door and opened it wide. "You heard me. Get out—and feel lucky we leave it at that."

Brad forced his eyes to hold the gaze of the burning blue coals. Then he walked past Edwin. The door shut so close behind him that he fancied he could feel the pressure of it against his legs. He stood facing the empty door a moment, feeling totally drained and disappointed. At last he turned and retraced his footsteps out of the building and back to the car.

Edwin poured himself a tall, stiff whiskey. "It's none of my business. Let Andrew stew," he said out loud. *The lad could use a little humbling, heaven knows.* "Two hundred thousand pounds." He whispered the sum and whistled. "That's stiff. But that will be good for Andrew, too." He downed the whiskey and poured another. "It's none of my business. They want the money, they won't hurt Nan."

The mere word, the name, created an image of her. He shook his head. Her face wouldn't go away. He checked his watch. It was an hour before noon. Julie was shopping with her roommate; it was Margaret's day off. They'd have lunch together and Margaret would drag her around for another two hours or more; Edwin knew the pattern.

Jamie and Ian ought to know better. If they'd told me about it, I would have discouraged them, Edwin seethed. "But I didn't let them tell me about it." He said the words slowly, remembering. "If I had, this might never have happened . . ."

He thought of the men and pictured their faces in his mind. He could guess at several who would be involved in such a venture; acquaintances of his, not actually friends, men whose activities he knew of but didn't countenance. He couldn't understand political fanaticism, and had never been involved in activist squabbles as some of these men had. He had to admit there were one or two who could get quite nasty, whose hatred for the system Andrew represented bordered on the fanatical. What did they call it? *Martyr mentality:* the words sent a chill through him. They'd be happy to risk their lives for the cause—they'd be more than happy to sacrifice Nan for the cause, to sacrifice Andrew. If Andrew took the money in himself he might never get out alive. And he was stubborn enough to do just that. *And Nan?* There were so many ways they could hurt her. He could feel cold sweat at the base of his neck and along his backbone. What could he hope to do? If he went, what would happen to Julie?

He rose slowly, he took a shower, he packed lightly. Twelve twenty-five. He sat at his desk: *Dear Julie.* He tore up half a dozen pages. What could he say? He could close his eyes and picture her face, hear her laughter, see in her eyes the wonder and love that *he* had created—he, Edwin! Why should he throw it away? Why was life determined to deal him one losing hand after another?

He had no choice, no real choice; he knew that. He'd have to play out the hand with what grace he could muster. He thought fleetingly, *The ring will be ready Monday. But where in the world I'll be Monday is anyone's guess.* "I go to my fate," he said through clenched teeth and laughed out loud. His mouth formed the unconscious grimace that Julie loved.

He propped the note on the front table where Julie would see it when she stopped by to find him, turned out the desk light, picked up his bag, and walked out the door, turning the small iron key in the lock behind him. In six hours or less he would be in Portree; this time tomorrow he would know what fate had in store for him.

19

Do not you fear; upon mine honour,
I will stand betwixt you and danger.
THE WINTER'S TALE

The road from Portree that leads to Sligachan is nine miles long. It runs through a lonely moorland beside a river with a name that smacks of old Nordic legends: Varragill. The moor gradually rises through tablelands seamed with torrents. This is the road the old Morris Minor, with Nan in the back seat, traveled, with an intermittent moon lighting the moor, casting shadows the length of a giant across the low hummocks, shadows that trembled in the low, moist peat bogs like something alive. The mighty Cuillins rose before it, growing closer and closer. The car took a turn and was suddenly swallowed by the mountains, rising up through the clefts in the rock to a mist-filled glen, blocked at the further end by a dented ridge, at the entrance protected by shoulders of serrated pinnacles, rising silent, dark, and unassailable in the still night.

Nan slept. The car pulled to a stop by a squat, thatch-roofed cottage. She was unaware when strong arms lifted her out of the car and in through the low cottage door. "She's a pretty one, ain't she? I'd set great store by her mysel'." The short man with the warts on his nose backed away so the other could carry her to the bed.

"You watch her, Harry, the others 'ill be here any time now. I'm going out back to check things over."

Harry nodded and Rab, his brother, turned and left. When he walked around, the collie set up a wild barking, but then recognized who it was and fell silent again. The cottage, lit only by the glow of a small peat fire, was silent, too, and shadowed; Harry dozed a little. When the door opened he jumped to his feet, upsetting the stool on which he'd been sitting. It clattered noisily, then rolled to a stop.

David Ross moved a foot and kicked it disdainfully. "That's what *you* deserve, Harry, you clod. You're supposed to watch her. Where's Rab?"

Harry rubbed at one large wart on his nose, his eyes on the ground. "Out back, where else 'id 'ee be?"

"Don't get smart, Harry," Ian warned. "You wanta light Davie's temper, do ye? We've got a long stretch ahead, remember. We don't need no fireworks 'tween the two of you."

Harry mumbled under his breath and Davie said, "Scum!" and spat once.

"When will she wake up?" Jamie asked, walking over by Nan.

"Soon enough," his brother answered him, "soon enough."

When Andrew arrived home there had been much to do and much to discuss. Brad didn't conceal it; he sincerely forgot his encounter with Edwin in the face of everything else. It was late when it came into his mind, and he went directly in search of Andrew. He found him sitting outside on the low stone wall by the pond.

"You must sleep—somehow," he said gently. "You're running on empty as it is. What about tomorrow?"

Andrew turned wide, anguished eyes upon him. "What of tomorrow? That's all I think about, Brad, with each breath I take."

Brad took a deep breath himself. This wouldn't be easy. "Listen, Andrew, today before you arrived I went to see Edwin."

"You what?" Andrew rose and stood with his hands clasped behind him. "Whatever possessed you?"

Brad had never seen him like this before. "I had a *feeling*. I asked Janet for his address—"

"What did Janet say?"

"That I'd better not see him alone—"

"Then, in the name of heaven, why did you?"

Andrew was breathing hard; Brad's own mouth had turned dry. "I prayed about it; I felt it was what I should do."

Andrew made a sound, but no other response. "Tell me what happened."

Brad did so as quickly as he could. When he reached the conclusion—the part where Edwin ordered him from the apartment—Andrew went white. "You meddling idiot, have you any idea what you've done?" Andrew was shouting. Brad had never heard him raise his voice. "You've sealed her fate, that's what you've done, Bradley."

The words sent a flash, like an electric shock, through Brad's system.

"There's a good chance Edwin will throw in with them," Andrew continued, "or if he doesn't, he'll try something foolhardy like attempting to rescue her. Either way—" Andrew's voice broke, hoarse with fatigue and emotion—"either way, you've endangered her life and his. If he tries to help her his own life's not worth a farthing. If he doesn't—"

He slumped back to the wall, sitting hunched and desolate. Brad shuddered. "You don't know for sure that he's gone," he attempted. "I had the feeling—"

"You and your feelings! I'd bet the next ten years of my life that he's gone—I know Edwin."

Silence fell between them—a forlorn, weighty silence that seemed to sink into their very bones. "Go to bed." Andrew's voice was barely discernible. "Go to bed, Bradley. Forgive me—I know you were doing your best. I'm just . . . I'm just so frightened for her."

Brad clapped his arms around Andrew's shoulders and squeezed him tightly, then turned and walked back to the house. Andrew sat on the wall till the morning spread fingers of light on the far horizon, and the night clouds parted, and behind the gray mountains the red sun rose, harbinger of the day he dreaded, warm and lush and butter-yellow in the blue dish of the sky.

Julie rushed eagerly up the stairs to Edwin's flat. She was anxious to show him the things she had bought and to tell of her day. She rapped on the door with staccato fingers. When there was no answer she knocked harder and called to him. Where could he be?

She searched for the key in her crowded purse. He'd insisted she have one. It turned easily in the lock. She opened the door. The place seemed strangely withdrawn and still without Edwin in it. She glanced about her. It looked the same as it always did, yet something was different. She could feel it.

In the small entrance hall stood a French commode with a mirror above it. She caught sight of the note in the mirror: her name scrawled across it. With hesitant fingers she picked it up, as though it might bite. She went to the desk for Edwin's letter opener, then carefully slit the envelope. She pulled out the paper and read the few words in a whisper, out loud:

Julie, my love—Brad Richards was here (can you believe that?) Nan's been kidnapped from Portree, and some of my lads are suspected. I must help her. As fate would have it, there's no one to do it but me. Take courage—try not to worry about her. I shall return, Julie. Please believe that.
Edwin

She sat down slowly, the note in her hand. There was no feeling. *No feeling.* She folded the note, tucked it away in her purse, and left the flat, carefully locking the door behind her. She would go back to her own apartment and Margaret's company. She felt nothing: no curiosity, no fears, no anger. There was nothing but a great, gaping emptiness inside.

Andrew arranged everything carefully, to his own satisfaction. By midday he would leave and return to Portree alone. When the money was ready Brad would bring it and meet him. When he returned to Bieldmor following a long, tense morning in Glasgow, he noticed the little white MGA parked back by the garages. Once out of the car he could see Neil leaning against a post, apparently waiting. When he saw Andrew he came quickly forward. Andrew paused, somewhat annoyed.

"Please, Andrew," Neil said, his eyes revealing his deep concern. "I'm here to help. There must be something I can do—"

Andrew began to wave him aside.

"I know Brad will be meeting you on Skye. Let me handle things here—whatever you'd like." He smiled his slow, almost shy, boyish smile. "I've taken care of all my own commitments; I'm at your disposal."

Andrew couldn't resist smiling back. "Thank you, Neil. There *is* something you can do." He had thought of it while the boy was talking. "Janet and Mother and Jennie will be here alone. Would you consider looking after them—perhaps staying at Bieldmor while we're gone? I'd feel much better, come to think of it, with you here."

Neil grinned. "So far you've done nothing but accommodate *me.* What about *you?*"

"Well, there are a few other things you might see to. Come with me."

They walked together in through the house to Andrew's office. Janet found them there nearly an hour later. "I see Neil persuaded you to let him join the home team," she said softly. Andrew smiled—the first smile she had seen since he came back from Skye.

"Join the team? I've appointed him manager, Janet!"

She and Neil exchanged a brief, happy look. Andrew saw it. His own face unconsciously sagged, more haggard and drawn than before.

Janet took him by the arm. "I've a lunch ready, Andrew. I won't let you go until you've eaten." He didn't resist. But at the door she paused as a thought came to her.

"Did Neil tell you the ward was fasting?" she asked. Andrew's eyes grew wide; he shook his head mutely. Janet squeezed his hand. "They're fasting and praying for you and Nan. I thought you should know that."

Neil, watching, could see Andrew's gratitude, the recognizable response of someone who believed in the power of such an action. *But Janet?* He thought he could read the same shining emotion in her eyes. That was what he had been praying for. He smiled to himself. He would keep on praying.

When Nan awoke the first thing she saw was the blackened wood beam that stretched across the cottage ceiling above her head. An old set of pipes was propped in the crevice, a shepherd's horn, strings of onion and what looked like dried fish, a rusty old rifle slung by a raveled cord. She called faintly for Andrew. Was she in their room? Was this the same inn? Something told her *no.* She turned to look and a sharp pain pierced her forehead. She closed her eyes. When she opened them again she saw a man standing right at the foot of her bed. She screamed—or tried to scream, but the sound was a frightened whimper. The man moved, shifting the gun cradled in his arms.

"Now, lassie, won' do ye no good tae make a fuss. You be good to Harry an' ole Harry be good tae ye." He moved slowly toward her, a grin on his face. Nan shrunk back against the thin blankets. From behind a hand gripped Harry by the nape of the neck and swung him, feet dangling above the floor.

"Keep yer hands off the lass!" a voice growled. The hand dropped him. Harry sprawled in a heap on the floor. The rifle, dislodged from his hands, scudded across the wide boards and came to rest several yards from its owner.

"You can't trust this one with a gun—you can't trust 'im with nothin!" Davie scowled at the giant, Rab, from across the room.

"I know that. But he's me brother, and he's in wi' us."

Davie spat at his feet with disgust. "This brother business gets a bit old," he muttered. He glanced at the girl. Her eyes were watching them, wide with terror. She was as pretty as he remembered. He strolled across the room to stand beside her.

"Ye ain't so perky as ye were the last time I saw you. Why's that, lass?" He grinned and the others laughed.

Nan took a deep breath. "I know who you are," she told him. "I even remember your name: you're Davie Ross, a friend of Edwin's. You were rude to Andrew—"

"I'll be more'n *rude* to him 'fore I'm through!" The venom in his voice made Nan want to shudder. With all her energy she strove to control herself.

"What am I doing here? Where is Andrew? Have you hurt him?"

"None o' your blinkin' business, miss. Less you know, the better." Nan strove to make her expression as disdainful as she could, though inside she was aching. Two more men entered the house carrying sacks of groceries. The older of the two, who had long fair hair, turned toward her.

"As long as the lass is here she may as well earn her keep. Come cook a meal for us, *Mrs. Buchanan.*"

Nan shrank at the thought of moving and working beneath their eyes. Slowly she raised herself to a sitting position, then swung her feet over the edge of the bed until they were touching the floor. Her head was dizzy. She felt weak, as she had when she lost the baby.

"Get a move on it, woman, we're starving," the other man said.

Shakily Nan stood on her feet. The blonde man pulled her forward. "Unpack these things, Jamie. I'll get her started." He was surprisingly gentle. Grateful, Nan moved to the long wooden table to see what she had to do, what food there was to work with. From a corner, crouched in cobwebs and evening shadows, Harry watched her. His gaze made her skin crawl. She dropped her own eyes and concentrated on the meat and carrots and onions she had found.

Edwin had made one small error, or it might better be said he had chosen unwisely. The lads would be at one of two places only. The first one he tried—the MacGlaughlin farm on the lee side of Sgurr-nan-Gillean—was the wrong choice; no one had been near the old place for months. That cost him one, maybe all of two hours. But time wasn't all-important, not at this point. It was the trouble of it that stuck in his craw: the driving and climbing, the huffing and puffing, the stubbing his toe and scraping his arm. What *was* important he took great care over, choosing meticulously the people into whose hands he would place his life. He planned every step, then reviewed it carefully—then left instructions, down to the smallest detail, the slightest discrepancy or extenuation that might arise.

At last he headed south from Portree toward Sligachan. His mind was itching, tense, on fire. The moment was here. Any one of a number of unforeseen things might foul it. This had to be the most brilliant, convincing performance of his life. He had worked himself up to a frenzy of readiness, but he was frightened. More was at stake, much more was at stake here than ever before.

He took the turn that led into the shadow-choked glen. The road fell before him. He drove through the shadows and the silence. Small pockets of ground mist floated wraithlike before his headlamps. He rounded a corner and the squat, rude cottage rose from the low ground like a lichen-covered stone. But from the dark mass a glimmer of light shone like a beacon, solid and golden against the gray night. Edwin slowed the car and cut the lights and pulled off into the short weeds and grasses.

Nan stood at the small back window of the cottage, low and recessed and deeply cut. She had seen the last show of the sun on the mountain flowers: tints of blue and pink and white and deep yellow—milkworts, stitchworts, pimpernels and honeysuckle, and the glorious purple majesty of the heather. She had watched the pink light fade until the soft peaks gleamed indigo, then went black, outlined against the sky that still held a warm glow, not a harsh silvery light, but a deep, soft essence.

The food she had prepared and eaten with the men had restored her strength. She no longer felt so faint, but she was still frightened, and she dreaded the coming night in this room full of men. She drank in the beauty and peace outside her narrow window and uttered a silent prayer.

The key twisting in the lock caused no alarm, caught no one's attention. So when the door flew suddenly open, letting in a rush of night air, all eyes turned to watch Edwin walk in, as dark as the night he came from and twice as stormy.

"I'll be hanged," Davie said out loud. "What ill wind blew you here?"

Edwin disdained reply. He stood in the middle of the room, casually removing his driving gloves. His eyes moved deliberately from face to face.

"You're not only a bunch of blackguards, you're a bunch of fools."

"Fools are we? How's that?" Davie challenged.

"Aye, several times over," Edwin said, with disdain in his voice.

"You had your chance," Jamie chimed peevishly. "I asked you to throw in with us—"

"But you never *explained.* If you had I'd have laughed at you, Jamie. What's this—all in the name of Scottish rights? I suppose you're going to turn every last bit of the money over to the party?"

Rab rose to his feet and stretched his large frame. "Ye make no sense, Edwin. We have causes, we have rights—we have places for the money to go."

"We've as much right to the money as he down yonder." Harry whined a little as he spoke, and licked his dry lips.

"Why Andrew? Why not someone unknown?" Edwin asked the question generally and Davie responded first.

"He deserves it—he deserves whatever he gets out of this. He's insulted the party in more than one way. Puts himself above—always above—"

"We could follow his movements. We *knew* he could handle the sum," Ian added, softening Davie's venom.

"We knew he set great store by the lass," Rab added.

"An innocent little exchange of funds from one hand to another?" Edwin arched an eyebrow. "Did you ask for a fortnight's vacation, Davie, is that what you did? And after this is all over, then what?"

Nan watched the men's faces. From the moment Edwin had entered she had stood frozen, startled and confused. Edwin here! For what purpose? How should she act toward him?

"I have more at stake here than the lot of you together," Edwin said.

Jamie nodded. "That's true. We all know that. Are you willing to go as far as it might take? What have ye in mind?"

Edwin took a deep breath and glanced for the first time directly at Nan. "Patience, Jamie, in time, in time. First matters first."

He walked slowly across the room. Nan raised her eyes to meet him—questioning, confused, but guarded. His eyes, deeply blue, were devoid of expression; they held no clue for her. What stance should she take? Was he friend, or foe? How best could she help, or perhaps prevent him?

"So, fair Nan, we meet again. But how different the meeting!" He grinned over his shoulder at the watching men. "I told you once that one man's good fortune is another man's misery. Do you remember?"

She nodded slowly.

"Good. I thought you might. Now I stand in your shoes and you in mine, lass. How does it feel?"

Nan went suddenly weak inside; she could feel herself trembling. She couldn't bear this. She began to brush past him. He grabbed her wrist, wrenching it tightly, pulling her back.

"I asked you a question. You will answer it," Edwin demanded.

"Leave me alone. Don't touch me," she cried.

His hand shot forward and slapped her roughly across the mouth. She cried out and put her fingers up to her lip. Tears filled her eyes and she tried vainly to blink them back.

Edwin's mouth turned down at the corner, hard, unrelenting. "This one's been spoiled, wouldn't you agree, lads?" he said to the men. Then he turned his attention back to Nan. Her wrist where his fingers pressed it was throbbing. "I'll not treat you as soft as Andrew, remember that. The party's over, as they say in your country."

He dragged her with him and threw her across the low bed. "Cry, lass, if you want to. Just don't disturb us, we've things to attend to.'' He pulled the curtain that separated the one large room into rough divisions, then strode to the table and pulled back a chair.

''Have you anything to drink?''

Jamie grabbed for a pot from the stove, but Edwin grimaced. ''Nothing stronger than coffee? All right, lad, I'll take a cup. But that's the first thing about this operation I plan to remedy.''

Nan smothered her mouth against the harsh blanket and sobbed. She knew she ought to try to listen to what the men were saying. She struggled to control her crying. She took a deep breath. But the curtain was an excellent insulator; it muffled the voices so that only a word or two filtered through. She heard Edwin laugh and the sound sent shivers through her. Her head was throbbing. At last she dropped it against the pillow and, after a moment or two of tossing and turning, slept.

In the next room the five men gathered around Edwin and listened to him far into the night. He cajoled them, he insulted them, he amused them—he bullied them, he fed their greed. He bought time, he bought their allegiance—all the while planning what he would have to do to save his own life and the life of the sleeping girl.

20

She has that ring of yours.—
I think she has . . .
ALL'S WELL THAT ENDS WELL

The old German came directly to Julie's apartment. It was late and she was afraid to open the door since Margaret was performing that night and she was alone. But the heavily accented voice called, "Ees a friend of Edvin. Important to let me in." So she said a prayer and opened the door to the stranger.

Through a sense of caution she didn't tell him where Edwin was. When she realized what he was giving her she went cold inside. He watched her expression as she gazed at the ring. "You like eet? Perfect copy. No one, no one who seez my ring can tell. Not efen the American when he puts eet on his finger."

He laughed, and the sound was raspy and low. "I vill go now. Edvin vill call me, no?"

"He will call you," Julie assured him. "And thank you. Is this all paid for?"

The old man nodded. "Oh yes, all taken care of een advance. Good efening, young lady."

She locked the door behind the man. Her hands were trembling. The understanding of what Edwin had done sunk into her like a weight. She walked the floor and stared at the ring. It blinked back at her, seeming to glow with a life of its own. She didn't want it here.

What should she do with it? Edwin was gone, and when he got back it might be too late.

She poured herself a drink and paced again. The trembling inside was worse, not better. She knew what she had to do, but it terrified her. Everything inside her shrank from the very thought.

She paced for ten, perhaps fifteen minutes longer. Then she said out loud, "This is ridiculous. If I'm going to do it I may as well get it over with now, and stop torturing myself."

She picked up the ring and put it carefully into her purse, left the apartment, locking the door behind her, then walked the short distance to the pub where Margaret performed. She stood in the dim, smoky room till her number was finished, then hurried around backstage.

When Margaret saw Julie her face lit up. "Whatcha doin', luv? Gettin' lonely? Want me to fix you up with a nice fellow? There are two or three—" She winked as Julie protested.

"I need your car. Could I borrow your car?" she blurted.

Margaret looked at her very carefully. "Well, I guess. Sure, luv. Just you be careful with it."

"I'll bring it straight back here," Julie promised as she grabbed for the keys. She turned quickly, afraid that with Margaret's eyes on her she might weaken, abandon the whole idea—or, worse, much worse, confide in her friend. She must not do that, not under any condition.

She felt better once she was safely behind the wheel; driving the street with other cars she felt sane and normal. She had driven Edwin's car all over Glasgow. She was comfortable with both the traffic and the right-hand drive. She drove first to Edwin's apartment and let herself in. She knew the secret drawer where he kept, among other things, his keys. She pulled it open: three keys—four keys stared innocently back at her. She thrust them all into her pocket and left quickly, pushing herself to keep going, refusing to think, to feel, to weaken.

She had a good mind for directions, perhaps because she'd been raised in the country. She knew she could find her way to Bieldmor House. She turned on the overhead car light and looked at her watch. Ten minutes to one. It would be late enough when she got there. She drove quickly, but surely, and when she pulled in the drive she forced all thoughts of Nan from her mind. *This has nothing to do with Nan,* she told herself vehemently. *Edwin. This is for Edwin,* she said to herself over and over. She shut off the noisy engine, closed the car door and began walking toward the house, locating the wing Edwin had pointed out where the guests would be staying. She drew the shutter over all the clamoring thoughts in her head and concentrated on one thing: the ring. There was nothing right now but herself and the ring.

She had to try two of the four keys in her pocket before the door opened. It was a heavy door but it made no sound as she pushed it before her. There were no lights on in the house. She flicked on the small penlight she held in her hand and with it's warm pool of light to aid her, climbed the long stairs, her stockinged feet barely touching the floor, creating no sound. She took the hall that led off from the stairs to the left and walked all the way down it. The silence around her was heavy with stillness and sleep. She turned left again when another corridor dissected the first one. If she was correct, she was now in the guest wing. She passed all the doors until she came to the last one. She almost paused there. But she knew if she did she would never go in. Carefully she turned the handle and moved into the room as though she were part of the door.

It was eerie. She not only felt like an intruder, she felt like a pervert, some kind of a Peeping Tom to be gazing down on the innocent couple in the bed who slept on, oblivious, unaware of her presence, unaware of any danger or threat. She walked with slow, careful steps to the dresser. The ring was there! It seemed to blink at her, just as the other had done. She had taken the old man's ring from its case and slipped it inside her pocket. She reached for it now and, with it still safe in her hand, picked the other one up with her fingertips.

Just as she touched it Brad moved in his sleep and snored. The sound may as well have been a gun shot. Julie jumped, and the rings went clattering to the floor. She stood a moment with her hand to her throat, frozen.

There was no further noise from the bed. She dropped to her knees and, scanning the floor with her hands, found one ring, then the other. She held them both out on her palm, like two poisonous spiders. They winked back at her. Which was the copy, and which the original?

Julie thought she would perish inside. *All this anguish, for nothing!* She picked one up, then set it back and chose the other. *Which, oh which?* She felt sick inside. Suddenly fear washed over her skin like the feel of cold water, like the first tingling, almost painful sensation when she jumped into the pool and it was early and the morning sun hadn't warmed the water. She had to get out of here—now! Just as fast as she could!

Eenie, meenie, miney, moe—she put one ring back on the dresser and one in her pocket. Somehow she found her way out and back down the stairs. With trembling fingers she locked the big door behind her. She didn't bother to pick her steps slowly, with care. She fled. The stars winked down at her, seeming to mock her as the rings had mocked her. She had risked everything to help Edwin, but she had failed him—ridiculously, clumsily, childishly so!

21

Come, come, we fear the worst;
All shall be well.
RICHARD III

The six-hour drive from Glasgow to Portree became four and a half under the hands of Andrew and the Healey. He reached the coast and caught the ferry at Kyle. Ten minutes later he drove the car down the slope and onto Skye soil. A uniformed officer waving his arms approached him. Andrew slowed the car and leaned his head out the window.

"Mr. Andrew Buchanan, is it?" the man asked politely.

"I'm Andrew Buchanan," Andrew responded, "what do you want?"

"If you'd follow me, sir, please, I'd be glad to explain."

Andrew tapped the wheel with nervous fingers. "I've important plans, I—"

"This won't take a moment, sir."

"All right, all right, if I must."

The officer smiled, a wide, toothy grin. Andrew followed him slowly, the Healey in second gear. There was a small public building of some kind. They walked in together.

"Sit down," the man said, not unkindly.

"No thank you. What is it, then?" Andrew demanded. A slight concern was building inside him; he wasn't sure why.

"You really should sit, sir, but suit yourself."

"Thank you." Andrew felt himself growing angry. "My wife is—you don't understand—"

"Aye, but we do. We've been in touch with your cousin, Edwin. We're acting on instructions from him. He's with her this moment."

Andrew sat down; he felt that his legs might give out beneath him. "Might I ask what right you have to act upon Edwin's instructions?"

The man smiled again. "Calm yourself, sir. I've known Edwin Bain for the past nine years. He knows what he's doing."

"What *is* he doing? Are you the police? Have you authorized Edwin to act?"

"Aye to the second two, sir. He has a very good plan; I'd trust him sooner than I would most of my own fellows. He's certainly got more of a chance than you'd have walking in there with a satchel full of money. Doubt if you'd come out in one piece, or your missus either." A small chill ran along Andrew's spine. "Have a drink, sir. We'll go over the plan if you'd like."

"Am I being detained here? Is that part of the plan?"

"That's right, sir. Sorry, but we can't have you fouling things up."

Andrew leaned his head down into his hands. He felt suddenly tired. And with the fatigue came the fear which he'd battered and bullied down. Another man began walking into the room but the officer held up a hand to stop him and motioned for him to go back out and to shut the door. After a few moments he said very softly, "Buck up, lad. I know this thing's beastly hard."

Andrew looked up, his eyes bloodshot and haggard. How could he tell this kind man who was fussing over him, how could he say, *I'm not at all certain that I trust Edwin the way you trust him. I'm not at all certain that he doesn't hate me enough to do just the opposite of what he told you.*

The man touched his shoulder. "Let me show you the plan. That might help a little." He brought out a map marked with roads and mountains and other landmarks. He drew a pencil out of his pocket and stuck the point in a spot nearly in the middle. "This is the cottage where they're keeping your wife. See here—that's the main road. Over here—do you see that faint line?'' Andrew nodded. ''That's a small footpath leading a back way out of the glen. We'll have men posted here—'' he pointed with his pencil—''and here—all along this narrow stretch. There's a rendezvous point. We'll have a car waiting.''

''Edwin's coming out that way, I take it—with Nan.''

''That's right. Either tonight or tomorrow night. We can't be certain.''

''And if he doesn't—if he doesn't come out, what then?''

The man hesitated a moment while his eyes searched Andrew's face. ''Then we move in, sir. That's the last day; they'll be expecting you. We'll have to move in.''

''That plan *does not* meet with my approval! I have the money. My man's bringing it to me tomorrow—''

''I'm sorry, sir, in our opinion—''

''I don't give a hang about your opinion! They want the money. If I give it to them—''

The man leaned closer. His voice was stern, but still very gentle. ''The money assures you no guarantee that they'll return your wife, sir—no guarantee.''

Andrew sank back into his chair. ''For one thing, she can identify them,'' the officer continued. ''A couple of these lads are high-strung radicals—crazy, you know.''

Andrew shook his head. ''How can Edwin possibly do it?''

The man brightened a little. ''Well, you see, he's contrived a deal. Convinced them—we hope—that they need him to get through to you. And he's upped the sum—twice the amount.''

Andrew sat up a little—interested, wary. ''Can he convince them that I'd pay that?''

''I think he can. Said something about a will and a stolen inheritance. Told me both you and the fellows up there would understand.''

Andrew smiled bitterly and nodded. ''Go on—what's your name?''

''Angus MacDonald, sir.''

''Go on, please, Mr. MacDonald.''

"He's also provided them with an escape plan. Has an American contact, a place to lay low for a while, let things cool off some, spend a little of their money." Angus grinned, his white teeth showing. Andrew couldn't smile. A sick feeling had settled low in his stomach.

"So Edwin convinces them of his sincerity, then what? What's his plan for getting out of there?"

"That part's simple enough. We've prepared bottles of drugged whiskey for him to take along with him Chloral hydrate—it's harmless enough, but it works splendidly. Takes only half an hour, forty-five minutes to take effect."

"That sounds too easy. What about Edwin? He'll have to drink with the others."

"Some bottles aren't drugged. He'll just have to be sure to pour his glass out of those. And he won't really drink much. I believe Mr. Bain could fake being drunk quite well, don't you?"

Andrew nodded. Angus stood. "Listen, Mr. Buchanan, you can barely keep your eyes open. You get some rest—"

Andrew shook his head. "No, I want to be there."

"It will be hours yet," Angus urged. "I promise I'll wake you. Come on now, there's a bed in the back room, through here. You'll be right close by."

Andrew hesitated, but he really was exhausted. He knew he couldn't last much longer. He rose to his feet and followed Angus to the back room. Once his head hit the pillow the lights went out altogether and he was at peace in the healing oblivion of sleep.

The long hours of the day went slowly for Nan. The task of preparing meals was a blessed relief from the otherwise watchful boredom. She avoided Edwin and he seemed to avoid her. The men talked and argued and played cards together. She had gathered that Andrew was to arrive with ransom money by the fourth day. This was the second day. She tried to be patient. She tried not to think about what might happen to her when they had the money. Every now and then she stole a long look at Edwin. But he never seemed aware; he never happened to look back. She strove resolutely to control her fears, but the cottage was like a swamp where they bred and hatched and thrived and swarmed around her.

Day gave way slowly, reluctantly, to the dim shades of night. Nan was washing the rude plates and cups from their dinner when she heard Edwin say, "What the lot of us needs is, as they say in America, a good bash. This sitting around strings my nerves like piano wire. I've a case of the finest, unblended Scotch in the boot—"

Just then, at the window, there came a tapping, more like a scratching sound. The men looked up, eyed each other. Rab rose to his feet and walked slowly toward the window. Halfway there he stopped and swore softly under his breath. "It's old Duffy, the shepherd from down the hill. He's got his wife with 'im."

"Well, get rid of him," Davie growled.

"I don't think we ought to. He's a funny sort; he'd consider that strange, unfriendly behavior—and mark it."

"That's right," Jamie agreed, rising to his feet. "He'd remember it afterward. But if we let him in and entertain him awhile he'll think nothing of it."

"We could crack out your whiskey—"

"I'll not waste good whiskey on the likes o' him," Edwin protested. "I don't want a blubbering old drunk on our hands."

Jamie agreed. Rab, who knew the couple, went to the door and ushered them in. Nan turned to observe them. They looked like a picture from an old history book. The woman had a tartan shawl thrown over her head and shoulders. She hobbled across to Nan with a wide, toothless grin. "Who be the lass?"

Suddenly Edwin was there with his hand on her elbow. "My wife, Lizzie. She's new to the Highlands; she's a city girl." Nan smiled kindly at the woman, then turned her eyes up to Edwin. She thought she saw a brief flicker of anguished appeal flash into his gaze.

"She's as bonnie a girl as I've seen in a long time. Yer a lucky young man."

Edwin gave the old woman a wink and his most charming smile. "Aye, and well do I ken it." He bent to kiss her, his lips to her cheek. But they closed suddenly over her mouth, still bruised and tender. Nan stared, shocked, into blue eyes as gentle as the lips. The watching men cheered, and the moment broke up in levity. Edwin turned and left her. But Nan felt a rush of confused emotions pour through her. The old lady was talking, asking her something—she must pay attention! She forced herself to give her attention to the moment before her, to ignore the demands of her confused and overwrought mind.

The old people were starved for human company. This was a treat. They laughed appreciatively at Davie's jokes and Ian's stories. They started a game of cards that drew on and on, then became uproarious. Nan sat with the old lady on the outskirts of the circle for a long, long while, then, growing sleepy, crept off to bed.

The game continued. The men, after all, were enjoying themselves. They, too, were in desperate need of diversion. Only Edwin sat straight as a ramrod, his hand in a fist at his side. His eyes burned like two brittle blue stones in a still, white pond, devoid of all warmth, all color.

Angus woke Andrew as he had promised. The patrols had been set. They waited with the dark, unmarked car at the rendezvous point. The minutes ticked. The first dozen were slow and painful. But as the minutes passed into hours the tightly wound spring within Andrew threatened to snap. As dawn broke the gray sky above the mountain peaks into chipped fragments, as the pale pinks and golds and lavenders stained the sky, the weary men gathered their equipment and their weapons together. "Not tonight." They were too tired to be discouraged.

But Andrew stood with red-rimmed, burning eyes staring up the mountain, past the jagged points and projections of rock that obscured his view. *How is Nan? Is she hurt? Is she frightened?* An image of his cousin's face rose before his eyes. *Oh, Edwin,* he thought, *take care of my Nan. Bring her back to me, Edwin . . . please . . .*

It had been arranged that Andrew would not call home until he had some word to give them. It would be a useless exercise in pain to do otherwise. But the hours stretched empty and listless before them.

Janet could never have made it without Neil's help; none of them could. After Brad left for Portree a pall seemed to settle over the household. Jennie's children had arrived from the States a few days before. She didn't feel it was proper for them to run around sight-seeing and celebrating. She didn't feel like it, anyway. She was terribly worried. But what does one do with four suppressed children through long summer days?

Neil came to the rescue: he provided activities for them, quiet games they could play on the grounds of Bieldmor. He assigned to each certain jobs to be done, and he paid them. They were delighted by the sense of camaraderie he established, and the feeling of being needed in a time of crisis. Janet watched Neil maneuver things into order, and her respect for him grew. There seemed no challenge he couldn't handle—except perhaps one: Jessie hadn't come out of her rooms since Andrew left.

Neil was aware of it. After dinner that evening he said to Janet, "I think I'll go up and try to talk to your mother."

She didn't encourage him. "I don't think she'll let you in. Helen brings her meals and attends to her wants—"

"Have *you* tried to see her?"

Faced with the direct, almost too-blunt question, Janet drew inward, a little resentful that he had asked it. She had avoided thoughts of her mother on purpose; now Neil made it awkward for her to demur. Seeing her reaction he dropped the subject for the time being, but he had planted an irritant seed, and she could not dislodge it.

As the long evening wore into night her irritation grew, until resentment overcame guilt and she'd nearly decided to do nothing about the whole unpleasant mess. But she had occasion to go into Nan's rooms. There was a vase of wilted flowers that needed removing; she had noticed it earlier in the day. She stood in the still room with the vase in her hands. The rank and dying flowers seemed an ill omen. The room *was* Nan. There were touches of her everywhere: her books, the bust of Shakespeare, her American paintings, one a Mississippi river scene. Little memories of Nan flashed into her mind and suddenly she could hear her sister-in-law saying: *The biggest mistake people make with each other is that they think it's too late to change . . . you could offer her something she's never had; you could love her . . . love her . . .*

Janet set the flowers back down on the table and walked from the room and along the halls to her mother's apartments. The closed door stopped her. She stood for a moment undecided. Then a sound came to her ears. She couldn't quite place it. She strained to hear and suddenly it registered: someone was weeping. The sound tore through her as though the sob were her own. It was her mother, crying as if her heart was broken. She had never in her life heard her mother cry.

She thought suddenly, illogically of Neil. *What if Neil were in danger? What if I feared for his life? What if I lost him?* The pain, even imagined, even feigned, made her insides tremble, gave her an aching sense of urgency.

"Mother!" she called. "Mother, it's Janet. Please let me in. Please, Mother."

The sound ceased. Janet waited long, agonized moments. Then slowly the door handle turned and the heavy door opened. Her mother stood there, her eyes pools of misery, her pale cheeks tear-stained.

"Oh, Mother, I'm sorry I've let you suffer," Janet cried—far beyond thought, far beyond self-protection. "Please forgive me. I . . . love you . . . Mother, *I love you!*"

Jessie gasped, and her hand fluttered briefly against her throat. Then slowly she opened up her arms to her daughter. And with a little choking sob Janet went to her.

22

But such a night as this,
Till now, I ne'er endured.
PERICLES

Day Three. Brad Richards left Glasgow for Portree. The six-hour drive that the Healey had devoured in less than five took Brad nearly seven. When the ferry from the mainland drew up on the Skye shore Andrew was waiting. He wasn't alone, Brad noted; an officer of some kind was with him. He was shocked at how haggard and drawn Andrew looked. The brave smile he put on to receive him wrung Brad's heart. Andrew introduced the two men to each other, then took Brad by the arm and with a wry, almost bitter, expression explained, "Officer MacDonald has our itinerary kindly planned for us."

"How thoughtful." Brad smiled, not at all sure what was going on.

"I'm glad you're here," Andrew said, and Brad knew he meant it. "We've got a long day ahead—and an even longer night."

"Mr. Buchanan's been through the mill, that's certain," the officer added. "Heaven knows how he's stood it so well. But tonight is the night. I can feel it in me bones." Angus grinned his wide, toothy grin. "Mr. Bain will pull this thing off tonight. You wait and see, sir."

Andrew gazed up at the blazing white sun in the summer sky. Bright and blue and friendly and sane—just another day. He shuddered, dreading the night and its shadows, and the sinister nightmare of darkness it might contain.

Andrew had said that first night they arrived in Portree, "We'll steep ourselves in Skye before we're through." Nan woke up her third morning in the cottage to the sound of bagpipes. To her weary, saddened heart it sounded like fairies were piping a morning welcome through the sun-flooded glen. She dressed in the one set of clothes she had with her and slipped out the back door of the cottage.

She saw no one there, but Skye had on her fairest summer's gown to greet her. Resplendent in strings of pearl, in gems of amethyst and ruby, draped in cloth of gold and gossamer, land and sky held out a hand of beauty in modest offering. Nan ached inside. Beauty always made her ache with a nameless longing. She ought to loathe this place of her misery. But she felt instead a strange comradeship with it. There must have been other strangers, other wayfarers who found sanctuary here. The untamed, uncivilized, ageless spirit was too strong to ignore, too strong to resist. She had longed to come to Skye. She was here now. She might never go anywhere else again.

Through dappled leaves and a web of green branches the piper came walking with his pipes cradled in his arm. It was Rab. When he saw her he stopped dead in his tracks.

"Ye go on inside, lass. What be ye doing out here alone?" He came a few steps nearer, still watching her closely. He shook his head. "Five men to watch you and I come down the mountain to find you alone in the glen, like a young deer startled in the meadow."

"Well, I won't bolt and run. I've got nowhere to go," Nan said softly.

"Go on inside now." Rab's voice was gruff. Nan hesitated.

"Would you—will you play me just one more tune? Please."

He stared at her and his eyes were as deep and slow and deliberate as his actions. "I suppose it won't do much harm. Are there any you know?"

"Not many. I know 'Speed Bonnie Boat.' "

"I'll do that," Rab said. Nan found a tree where she could lean back and listen. He played "Speed Bonnie Boat," but he didn't stop. She closed her eyes and Rab played one tune after another until Ian came out and stopped him, and the music and its spell fell apart, like pieces of broken glass at Nan's feet, and she saw Edwin at the window and she went inside. But all the beauty of Skye seemed to stop at the door. The cottage was musky and dim and tense; she could feel the tension—like thick dust it clogged her throat and choked her breath.

Twice during the day scouts were sent down the mountain to reconnoiter, look for signs of danger of entrapment. Both times they returned with nothing of note to report. But the men were restless. *One more day,* they kept saying, *just one more day.*

When the evening meal was done Davie brought out the cards and Edwin went to the boot of his car to get out his whiskey. He came through the back entrance, the small kitchen area where Nan, drying dishes, failed to see him—they bumped into each other back to back. He seemed to push her as their bodies met, then he half-turned to help her, with his hand on her waist and his head close to hers.

"Tonight." He said the word softly against her hair, but it surged like a shock of electric current through her system. There was no time to question, to meet his eyes. He had already stumbled, laughing and cursing, to where the others waited. Tonight! What did he mean, tonight?

The men downed three of the half-dozen bottles and Edwin drank with them. There was much friendly bantering between them. Nan sat on the bed with a shawl around her shoulders. She tried to read from a small volume of old poems she had found in the kitchen cupboard. But she couldn't concentrate; the tension was in her, too. She pulled the old plaid up about her shoulders. She felt chilly, the way she did when coming down with a cold, her skin prickly and close to shivering. Edwin sent Jamie out for the last few bottles. When he didn't return quickly enough Edwin rose grudgingly and said he'd go hurry the lad along. They were out there a long time together. She could hear them laughing, perhaps telling jokes in the friendly darkness, sharing long swigs of the whiskey.

When Edwin came back in Jamie didn't come with him. But nobody noticed. Harry had been snoring in his dirty corner for hours. Rab was asleep with his cheek smashed against the rough, stained hide of his pipe bag. Ian sat with his knees up, his elbows propped on them, his chin in his hands. "Powerful stuff, packs quite a whallop, Edwin," he slurred, then hiccuped, and his elbow slid and his face fell, smashing against the table. He lay quite still.

Edwin and Davie slapped their thighs in uproarious laughter. Nan crept further into the shadows, but kept her eyes on their every move. Edwin poured two tall glasses as full as he could, but they both spilled over. Davie took his with an unsteady hand. "Bottoms up, lad. I could always outdrink ye, Edwin."

Edwin grinned, raised his glass to his lips and turned, preparing to down it. Davie, with one manly slurp, drained his glass, except for the ounce or two that had spilled down his shirt front. He smacked his lips with a satisfied sigh. "Nectar of the gods, eh, Edwin?" He slumped back against the sofa and Edwin turned, like a mountain lion unsheathing its claws, exposing its teeth.

"I could bury you ten feet under and still be standing, Davie," he muttered, then doubled up his fist and hit his friend square in the jaw. "But you're taking too long for me this time, laddie." He turned to Nan. "It's time," he said. In three long strides he reached her and grabbed for her hand. She scrambled off the bed to her feet.

"The moment is ours," he breathed, "let us take it, fair Hannah."

Before she realized what was happening they were out the door, the night air a kiss on her cheek, "Edwin?"

"I'm rescuing you. I'm sorry there's no white steed, no trumpet's blare, no golden sword with a tongue of lightning. Don't let go of my hand, Nan." They had reached the edge of the clearing and plunged now into a dark, shadowed tunnel. She slipped on a stone, but righted herself. "That's the girl. You'll be all right. We've a long way to go yet."

Nan wanted to stop and laugh out loud. Her knees, weak with shock, threatened to crumble beneath her. She wished she could fall in a heap on the ground and sob. She wished she could throw her arms around Edwin's neck and thank him. Instead she clung to his hand and kept walking.

Twenty minutes later they were still going. Her shoes had worn blisters that burned at each step and her breath was ragged. She was wondering how much longer she could keep walking when Edwin stopped—so suddenly that she stumbled into him. He encircled her with his arm and she leaned gratefully against him. "I'm not sure of the way. We used to hunt here. It's been a while."

He removed himself gently from her and she sank to the ground. "Stand up, Nan! You'll never get back on your feet if you don't." He walked a careful circle, examining the three paths that broke off, each in a different direction. He made up his mind, though she didn't know how; it was so very dark here! How could he tell landmark or direction? She groped for his hand.

"How much further, Edwin?" she whispered.

"Still a little way, Nan. But closer with every step, lass, closer!"

They walked on in silence through sodden leaves, over roots and old stumps. Her legs ached, her whole body cried out for rest. It seemed the trees were thinning ahead, she thought numbly. Perhaps they would reach the open moor; perhaps they could rest.

Edwin knew they were within minutes now, mere minutes. He was tempted to tell her, to turn and encourage her with the words. But they might affect her the opposite way and he couldn't risk that, couldn't have her collapse on him in the final stretch. One last narrow pass, then the tight curve, and the road would drop and the men would be posted, and a car would be waiting, and Nan would be safe. Beyond that he refused to think.

They reached the narrow defile. He felt Nan shudder. Perhaps he ought to stop and let her catch her breath for a moment. The air under the dark trees felt cold and uninviting. Nan hesitated again. He slowed and drew her closer.

The sudden light seemed to hypnotize them, freeze them. For

one brief instant Edwin thought, *They're here! They've come up further than we planned. We're safe now!* Then he knew, and the cold hand of fear gripped his insides.

"Edwin, lad, it's Ian here. I know you can't see me. But I can see you!"

Nan turned to Edwin. The fear in his eyes made her want to scream. She bit her lip hard and forced back the sound. Ian came closer; they could hear him through the brush. The beam from the flashlight in his hand swerved and reeled like a drunken man. He stopped, and they stood in the searchlight like two snared rabbits.

"Clever, Edwin. You always were clever." Edwin acknowledged the praise with a small, graceful nod of his head. Ian was still forty, perhaps forty-five yards from them. Without turning his head Edwin whispered to Nan, "You keep behind me and to the left. When I start moving, you move with me, like a shadow. If you hear a shot, drop straight to the ground. Do you understand?"

"Yes, Edwin." She tightened her grip on his hand. They stood in the silence waiting for Ian's next move. That disturbed him; he had expected a more dramatic reaction.

"You didn't think I'd figure out what you were doing, did you, Edwin?"

"No, I didn't," Edwin admitted. "I thought Jamie might, but I underestimated you. I apologize for that."

"Cut out the games, Edwin! What do you think you're doing?"

"I'm taking her down the mountain to Andrew. Would you like to join us? There will be a nice substantial reward, I'm sure. Much cleaner that way, much—"

"You're a turncoat, Edwin! You louse, you're a hypocrite and a turncoat! The lads believed you, they *trusted* you, Edwin, an' you betrayed them!"

Edwin moved, almost imperceptibly; Nan moved with him. "It was a scheme doomed to failure from the first, Ian, that's what I told you."

"It was none of your business!"

"I chose to *make* it my business!"

"Well, 'twas the poorest choice of your life, lad, and mebbe the last. I'm not letting you down this mountain, Edwin."

Edwin kept moving; Nan moved with him. The spotlight wavered. Ian was coming closer. "All right, Edwin, I can see you're moving. Stop!"

"Nan!" Edwin hissed under his breath, "keep moving. When I let go of your hand, run as fast as you can!"

"Edwin!"

"Do it! It's your only chance. There are men just over that ridge. They'll see you."

Edwin knew if he could get Ian close enough he'd have a good chance to disarm him. He could hold his own, he felt, if it came to hand-to-hand combat. The beam froze again. "I'm warning you," Ian called, "for the last time, Edwin."

"Come out of the shadows and fight like a man, Ian." Edwin dropped Nan's hand and turned full face to the light. Nan moved outside the reach of the fingers of light and was swallowed in shadow. For the moment, in Ian's mind, she had ceased to exist.

"You're going to shoot me, Ian?" Edwin called back. "That's serious business. The least you can do when you shoot your own friend is to show your face."

Ian growled in frustrated protest. Edwin heard him. He was emboldened by the sound. "Come on, face me, Ian," he cried. "Do this thing like a man."

Ian came closer, out of the trees and shadows that hid him. He was carrying a sporting arm, a double-barrel Greener. "You don't want to shoot me, Ian, and you know it. Be reasonable, man. What will happen to you if you shoot me?"

Nan had made only a few yards in the dark. She stumbled over a fallen trunk. Ian heard the sound. "Edwin, you black-hearted fool, she's getting away!"

With sudden rage Ian swung the weapon in Nan's direction. Edwin moved with catlike swiftness. The rifle barked. *He's really going to shoot, then!* Edwin thought as he ran. Just as Ian had the girl in his line of vision a black smudge moved into his sight. He squeezed the trigger. From twenty-five yards away the shot tore into Edwin's middle. He bent double, then slowly straightened again. He staggered forward, away from the light, away from the rifle. Another shot rang out in the stillness, and then another. Slowly Edwin dropped to the ground and lay still.

Nan, crying softly, crawled to his side. "Edwin, Edwin," she sobbed. The uniformed man who had heard the first shot, who had scrambled up the mountain, sighted and then dropped the man with the rifle. He shouted to his friend who was just coming into sight, "Get an ambulance, Mac. And get the car up here for the lady."

He bent down by Nan and tried to pry her away. She threw her arms over the body; he couldn't persuade her, he couldn't move her. At last he stood back. The car rounded the curve and pulled into view. Angus MacDonald got out of the car and the two conferred. The young man in the back seat got out. Angus tried to dissuade him. But the officer on the scene merely shook his head. "She won't budge for me. You'd best let him go to her, sir."

Nan heard nothing, saw nothing until suddenly, in the darkness, there were hands on her face. The feel of those fingers, the warmth, the gentleness! *Andrew?* She hardly dared think it, she hardly dared hope. Out of the swirls of darkness and pain she felt him lift her. She struggled. "Edwin—Edwin—"

"Yes, darling, I know. There are men to take care of him now. Come to me, Nan—"

"Andrew!"

His arms were there. They kept the pain and the darkness at bay. "Andrew! I didn't know if you'd ever hold me again."

"Hush, darling. It's over, it's over now." They stood outside the circle of light; they stood in the darkness while the stretcher carried Edwin's body away, while the men with their sirens and loudspeakers did their business. Nan thought it would never end. At last Angus came. "There's a car you can use," he said. "You can take her down now. Heaven knows how long I'll be stuck up here. Can you handle the drive? I can send an officer."

"I'll decline the offer, if you don't mind, Mr. MacDonald." Andrew smiled faintly.

"I thought so." Angus flashed his wide, boyish grin. "You take care of this little lady." He winked at Andrew. Nan looked up at the sky full of stars stretched above her head. She heard strains, echoed strains of the fairy music. The pain came rushing back. There was part of the pain Andrew could never touch or understand. The gentle giant playing "Speed Bonnie Boat" in the glen . . . the shepherd couple laughing and dealing cards . . . Ian peeling potatoes and cutting the meat . . . Edwin—*Edwin!*

She closed her eyes. She couldn't face it. She had no strength left inside to face it. She laid her head in the warm circle of Andrew's shoulder and wept.

They flew Edwin to a Glasgow hospital. Andrew and Nan flew with them. She couldn't have slept not knowing how Edwin was. The doctor said it was lucky the gun had been loaded with quail shot or Edwin would be a dead man. They would operate and do an abdominal exploration, but he was now in stable condition. One of the other shots had grazed his arm, but the injury was minor.

Andrew went quietly, almost reluctantly, into his cousin's room. He hadn't seen Edwin since the night of his wedding. He bent over the unconscious man. What a puzzle, what a complicated puzzle Edwin was!

Suddenly Edwin's eyes flickered, then opened, and their gazes met. "Is Nan all right?"

"Yes, Edwin, she's going to be fine."

Edwin nodded. His eyes were pale blue and weary, and dulled by pain. "I brought her back to you, cousin. Does that even the score a little?"

"More than a little."

Edwin grinned. "You can bet I was scared for a minute or two there. I thought we'd both had it." He paused. "Is Ian—"

Andrew shook his head. "He didn't make it," he said softly.

Edwin nodded. He muttered a word under his breath.

"The others were taken by Officer MacDonald and his men. But I imagine you know that."

A nurse stuck her head inside the door and said softly, "You'll have to leave now."

Andrew motioned to her. "Just a moment more, please," he said. He turned to Edwin. The blue eyes were watching him closely. He'd never done anything so difficult in all his life. "I want to thank you for saving Nan the way you did, Edwin."

Edwin seemed disturbed. The blue eyes blazed weakly. "I don't want your thanks. I don't want—"

"I know, I know. But please, Edwin. Please don't make it any harder for me."

Edwin had never heard Andrew talk like this before—in this voice, in this manner. He raised his head on the pillows a little. "Am I going to die? Is that it, and they haven't told me?"

Andrew laughed a little. "Heavens, no."

"Why else the true confession? The baring of your soul?"

"You *are* going to make it hard for me. All right, Edwin. You were always a brother to me, you are still. I want you to forgive me for all that I've done to hurt you—"

"Why? Would you do things differently if you had it all to do over again?"

"Oh, yes," Andrew's voice was soft. "Yes, I would, Edwin. Many things . . . I've learned a lot in the last little while."

"Well, if forgiving means forgetting, Andrew, I can't accommodate you. I still plan to fight, I still want the inheritance—"

"That has nothing to do with what I'm asking you. Nothing at all. I just want you to know I still love you, Edwin, and I'm wretchedly sorry for all the things I did to abuse and destroy that love."

He rose and turned away for a minute. He didn't like getting emotional, especially here with the appraising blue eyes upon him. There was a movement at the door; the nurse was returning. Andrew looked up to see Nan enter; he met her eyes.

"I'm sorry if I'm interrupting you two," she said, sensing the atmosphere. "But the doctor wants you, Andrew."

"I'll go." He turned back to the bed. "You don't make it easy on a man, Edwin, you don't make it easy. But by heaven, I'd miss you—miss every miserable thing about you if you were gone." His voice was rough. He turned and, without even a glance at Nan, left the room.

"What was all that about?" Nan asked softly. Edwin blinked the moisture out of his eyes. "That was Andrew's nonsense. I think his conscience is hurting a little; it will pass."

Nan sat down on the chair by the bed and took his hand where it lay white and still on the covers. "I don't think so. Not this time, Edwin, not this time." She smoothed back the thick black hair from his forehead.

"You need to go home to bed," he said. "I'll be all right." She didn't reply. "Listen, Nan," he said heavily, "I'm sorry I hit you. I had to do it, they had to believe—"

"I know." She put a finger against his lips. "I understand, Edwin." She continued to stroke his hair. "Though I really don't—I don't understand why you'd risk your own life to save me."

He laughed briefly. "My life against yours? It's not even a contest."

"Edwin, Edwin." She bent down and kissed his cheek. "When will you stop playing hide and seek and come out in the open?" She was trembling. There were tears in her eyes.

"You're tired, Nan. Go home." His voice was gentle.

She nodded. "You're right. I believe I shall. *Go home.* Doesn't that sound nice?"

She rose, still holding his hand. "But there's one more thing— I nearly forgot—" She was smiling. "There's someone to see you." He searched her face, he looked into her eyes. "She loves you, Edwin," Nan whispered, "she truly loves you. And I'm happy—for both your sakes."

She turned and left him. In a moment the door opened softly and Julie was there. She walked slowly toward the bed; she hesitated.

"Edwin?" She moved close, bent over him. He was crying. She buried her head in his neck.

"Julie, hold me," he whispered fiercely. "My love, my love!"

23

And so success of mischief
shall be born.
HENRY IV, PART 2

The morning of the court date came. It was anticlimactic; it couldn't help but be. How many years had this day been in the making? Andrew and Nan had been married for over half a year. Nearly nine months had passed since that day in Salt Lake City when the Scottish stranger had knocked on Brad Richards's door and calmly, unalterably changed the course of his life. It was close to two years since Andrew's father had died, over fifty since his grandfather had amended the trust, more than a century since the original Andrew Buchanan had conceived his outrageous idea.

Both parties were there, represented by their barristers. This was a public courtroom hearing, but few people were present outside the immediate, interested parties. Edwin still lay in a hospital bed. Perhaps that was poetic justice. It would be far less colorful, far less flamboyant without him here. Julie sat alone, a little removed from the others. Nan had urged her to sit beside her, but she had refused.

The petitioning party presented the opening argument. It was nothing new; they had all heard it, gone over it time and time again. The barrister outlined the case, reviewing the clauses and conditions of the original will, explaining carefully Andrew's grandfather's instructions that, if the missing heirs were not found during Andrew's search, it was his wish—it was his most *firm desire,* that the accumulated monies pass to his sister's issue. And his sister had but one living grandson, and that was Edwin Bain. Those facts were firmly established. He expressed concern that the opposing party prove their claim that the true and legitimate heir could be otherwise ascertained.

Andrew's barrister, as respondent, went over the facts of Andrew's search and investigation. He called Nan to the stand and she told of finding the old tombstones. Edwin's lawyer cross-examined her. Yes, she admitted, there was only partial lettering on the stones, no full names. She just assumed, he asked—filled in the names as she wanted? And where were the grave markers now?

Nan, answering the questions as patiently as she could, sighed. It seemed suddenly silly, tedious, unimportant. "They are missing, sir," she said, "they no longer exist." He thanked her. He changed his line of questioning. When he asked her about the journal she stirred with new life. It was her great-great-grandfather's journal; she knew it was true. She presented the copied sheets which her American neighbor had notarized. The barrister smiled frostily. This was feeble, thirdhand, personal hearsay, not proof. A man's journal written nearly one hundred and fifty years ago?

Had she copies of legal certificates or records? Nan shook her head. No birth, baptism, or death records? There were many early converts to the Mormon church from Scotland, were there not? Even many with the name of Buchanan? Nan agreed. This infant, this Richards infant—was there not a blessing certificate for him on record? Was he not blessed with the Richards name? Were not the Mormons sticklers for record keeping, for genealogy, for *family lines?* Why, then, would they not keep the child's name if it were Buchanan? Was it not possible there was a Richards son? Was it not possible this Buchanan infant had perished—*if* he had ever existed at all?

Nan was exhausted when at last they released her. They called Brad to the witness stand, but he could provide no proof. Testimony, sincerity, family stories handed down from each generation. And the ring. He drew the ring off his finger. It was the one solid, vital piece of evidence.

Julie, watching the proceedings, felt her head grow warm with embarrassment, with humiliation. She glanced around. No one knew. It didn't show. Andrew's lawyer, or barrister, was speaking, describing the rings, comparing Andrew's and Brad's, explaining the unusual design of the ring with the large diamond in the center which represented the old man, the family, the mills, the fortune—and the rubies, one on each side, representing the sons. What coincidence could bring such a rare and unusual ring into Brad's possession *along with* the continuing story of the adopted son, the unknown original ancestor?

Julie sighed. She felt hot all over, miserable, wretched. She had one ring in her possession, at home in her drawer. What if one of the rings on the stand—blinking and sparkling under the lights when the lawyer turned it—what if one of the rings wasn't real at all? What if—

Edwin's barrister rose, he cleared his throat, he requested—as his client had instructed he should—he respectfully requested that the court examine the evidence.

Someone gasped; everyone stared, amazed. The judge consented. A licensed goldsmith was called as an expert witness. He presented his credentials; he answered basic questions to establish his own qualifications, his validity. He drew a loupe from a small velvet case and examined the ring. The courtroom held its breath. Julie's heart was beating, her pulse pounding against her temples. Oh, what had she done? Edwin had planned this thing through to the end. She had not only spoiled it, she was about to discredit him in everyone's eyes.

The jeweler looked up. All eyes were on him. He knit his brow and bent over the ring again. Slowly he shook his head and raised his eyes to the judge. "This ring is a superb and masterful . . . imitation," he said.

Julie looked down at her hands clenched white in her lap. She had done it! Good heavens, *what* had she done?

Brad's face was drained of color. He looked at Andrew. They were helpless before this monstrosity. This must be Edwin's doing, but when? and how? What could they do? What defense did they have? They could very well make things worse by protesting too much, by overreacting.

The parties collected themselves; the proceedings continued. The appeals wound themselves out and the barristers delivered their summations, their finely couched last appeals.

The judge rose. He would retire and make his decision. But due to the unusual circumstances of this case he requested that the court reconvene in two hours. He would deliver his opinion then.

Julie hurried out; she had no desire to face Nan. Nan saw her retreating figure but didn't pursue. She was worried right now about Brad. He was devastated, heartbroken at the loss of his ring.

"Nothing else matters," he said to Andrew. "*Nothing* else matters. I wish to heaven I'd never come here at all. It's not right—I was sick in there, Andrew, I hated every minute of it. You couldn't drag me back into something like this again if my life depended on it."

Andrew tried to calm him. Inside he felt much the same way. He hadn't known it would be like this; he hadn't imagined. He saw Edwin lying in the blood-stained heather with Nan's arms around him. He blinked his eyes to dislodge the vision. It was Edwin's fault they were here today. Yet it wasn't solely because of Edwin.

Julie found a phone and called him in the hospital. He was terse, but gentle with her. She didn't tell him about the ring; it would be too hard to explain now. He had conferred with his lawyer only briefly the day before. He must have forgotten to amend his instructions about the ring. He had been ill, in pain still; he hadn't been thinking. But she would have to tell him sometime what she had done. She dreaded the confrontation. Today was enough. Today was wringing her emotions from her unmercifully.

She walked from the phone booth and saw Nan's group all huddled together. If only the date could have been postponed and Edwin be here beside her! She watched Nan. She was so gracious, so in control, so lovely. She thought of the night she came to the hospital and found Nan there. How shocked they both had been, how overwhelmed, after everything else that had happened! But even then—even after all she had been through—Nan had stood firm, had accepted Julie, helped her, loved her.

She turned and walked in the opposite direction. She'd get a bite to eat. It would give her something to do; it would help pass the time.

Four o'clock. They all filed back into the courtroom, found their places, settled into their seats. It was here. No matter what happened, in a few moments it would all be over. To everyone in the room that thought brought a sense of relief. To Edwin, alone in his hospital room, watching the clock, this moment spelled either defeat or a chance to go on.

They stood while the judge entered the room; they remained standing. He delivered the opinion of the court: "The court is persuaded from the preponderance of the evidence that a decision should be rendered in favor of the petitioner—Edwin Bain."

That was all. Andrew looked at Nan and lifted his eyebrows. Brad put his head down into his hands and remained very still. Nan looked around, but Julie had already left the courtroom. She felt tired, but not as drained as she had expected. She reached for Andrew's hand. "Let's go home," she said.

"That sounds good to me." He smiled and they turned together. Brad smiled weakly at Andrew. "I'm sorry," he said. "You must be regretting the fact that you ever met me."

Andrew was startled and showed it. "Not at all, not at all," he replied. "You're just tired, Brad. Get Jennie and let's go home."

Jennie was ready. The four walked out together. Brad felt nothing, he couldn't think, he was weary and numb. Jennie thought, as they drove toward Bieldmor, *This really has become home. I don't mind too much not getting the money. We never had it. I never believed it could really come true. In many ways I'll be glad to get back to Utah. But Bieldmor . . . it will be very hard to leave Scotland and Bieldmor behind.*

Julie took a cab directly to the hospital. Edwin knew as soon as she walked into the room and he saw her face. But he asked her anyway.

"Yes, it's true. The court ruled in your favor," she told him. She watched him carefully, wary of his reaction. She remembered something Nan had said to her early that morning: "You must take good care of Edwin, Julie, and not just if he loses. It might be harder for him if he wins."

"What do you mean?" she had asked.

"It's hard to explain," Nan had replied. "But he's always fashioned himself a loser. That's what he's hung his hat on, that's what's kept him going on. He has little faith in fate or life, or whatever you want to call it. If he wins, if fate comes through for him, he'll have some problems adjusting, Julie. So go easily with him." She had bent and kissed Julie's cheek, then gone back to Andrew.

Julie thought of that now as she waited for Edwin's reaction. He sunk back against the pillows. "It can't be true. There'll be some loophole, they'll find some error, they'll reopen the case—"

"Stop it, Edwin. It's true and you must accept it. But not all at once—" She sat down on the edge of his bed. "I have a story to tell you first. Do you want to listen?"

He smiled gently back at her. "Yes, nurse, by all means, go on. Calm me, divert me—" he winked lightly—"you're very good at it."

She told him the story about the ring and what she had done. This time she caught him off guard; he couldn't believe it. "You brave little soul," he said, "you poor little thing." He looked suddenly into her eyes, his gaze deep and probing. He thought to himself, *In the name of heaven, what have I done—that this beautiful, innocent child would steal to protect me—would hazard herself so completely—for me?* It made him feel small inside and ugly; it frightened him deeply. "That's the first thing we shall remedy, princess," he said.

"What do you mean, Edwin?" Julie asked.

"Never you mind," he replied, lost in his own thoughts, "never you mind. Have you any kisses to spare for an old wastrel?"

"You always put me off that way, Edwin," she smiled. "I shouldn't allow it."

He pulled her close to him and said softly, against her hair, "I intend to take good care of you, Julie. I don't mean for you to be embarrassed or frightened or ashamed because of me ever again."

She found his lips and kissed them. "I love you, Edwin." He stroked her hair, like silk in his fingers, and thought fiercely, *I shall earn your love!*

It was his first promise to himself.

24

So stand thou forth; The time is
fair again . . .
I intend to thrive in this new world.

ALL'S WELL THAT ENDS WELL

Brad paid his last respects, said his last farewell to Charles Buchanan. He had argued long hours with Jennie, and long hours with Andrew; they were both persuasive. He wanted desperately to weaken, to do what they asked. But some stubbornness deeply imbedded within him refused and held firm. After all, his prayers had been answered. What had he gained?

He looked up at the handsome young man in the portrait. *Life has dealt more justly with me than with you,* he thought. *I'm not complaining. I have a wonderful wife, four beautiful, healthy children.* He smiled at the picture. *Yes, and now I know who I am—in spite of Edwin.* Then why did he feel so empty, so unhappy inside?

He turned around; Andrew stood in the darkened doorway. "Have you come to make your apologies, Brad?"

"What do you mean?"

"I believe you know what I'm saying." Andrew walked through the long, narrow room until he stood close to Brad, until Brad was forced to meet his eyes. "The Lord works in his own ways, Brad. You know that. He's worked very hard to bring you here. Why do you deny it? I want you here, true; you could be of great use to me. Jennie wants you to stay—she loves it, she's at home here. But none of those things is reason enough. There's something more."

"How do you know that?"

Andrew smiled. "I don't. I just have this feeling . . ."

Brad's eyes filled with tears; he shook his head slowly. "You're hard to fight, Andrew."

"You're not fighting me, Brad, you're fighting yourself. Some weakness, some pride, some fear within you."

He put his hands behind his back and gazed up at the portrait before them. "Charles here, with his mild, kind face and his gentle eyes, had more courage than you. You've admired him, Brad. Have you stopped to wonder if perhaps you're not failing both yourself and Charles—and someone else."

He turned and began to walk out of the room, then paused, as though remembering something. "Have you prayed about this, Brad? I think you'd better. Long and hard, until you're completely sure. If you do that, I promise I won't oppose you. No matter what your decision. Good night, Brad."

Brad stood alone in the silent room. Evening was falling. This room was seldom if ever used, and the door had a lock. He knew what he had to do; he could no longer run away or avoid it. He turned the lock on the door, then dropped down on his knees.

Brad wasn't the only one who'd been praying. Morning broke above Ben Lomond, lighting the sky with the splendor of sunrise. Nan saw it and thought of that other mountain, that other sky, and shuddered, and went in search of Andrew, just for assurance, just to see the warmth in his eyes, feel the warmth of his touch.

"Do you remember our first day in Salt Lake?" she asked him. "I've been thinking about it, with all that's happened."

He nodded. "It seems so long ago."

"Do you remember how we stood by the temple," Nan went on, "and you said, 'The power comes from within those walls, Nan. Rachel knew that power could unite her with Charles'—how did you put it?"

"Past doubt, past death—forever," Andrew whispered. *Love and truth together,* Nan remembered. *There's nothing those two powers united cannot achieve.*

"I'm not really sorry that any of this has happened," she said. "It's helped me remember the things that are most important—get my perspective back into place."

"I know," Andrew agreed, "we've been blessed, my Hannah, just as Grant promised."

They walked together out through the gardens. The hour was early. Jennie was already out with the children, but Brad was just rising. He left his room and hurried down the front hall in search of Andrew. When he found him in the garden with Nan he hesitated. But Nan ran up and took his arm.

"Come, Brad. Why do you suppose I have Andrew out walking? He can't hold still with wondering what you've decided." She smiled warmly. "I'll leave you two alone for a while."

She slipped off. Andrew watched her go, lovingly. "She's quite a woman," Brad said softly.

Andrew nodded, and Brad went on. "It's a big responsibility I'm taking upon my shoulders, walking into a family where every person is extraordinary, where outstanding accomplishments are daily fare."

Andrew looked up; a slow smile spread over his features. Brad's voice was thick with emotion as he continued.

"I was afraid, Andrew. You were right, I was running away. If I didn't stay, I couldn't fall short, I couldn't fail . . ." He paused. "It was such a selfish outlook. I think I'll be all right, Andrew, now that I've faced it. I think I can do what I'm supposed to do—"

Wordlessly Andrew grasped his arm; there were tears in his eyes. "I wanted this, Andrew, you don't know how badly. For some perverse reason, through my doubts and my fears, I denied myself—"

There was the sound of footsteps behind them; they turned together. Janet was running down the brick path. "Andrew!" she called. Brad moved a little aside as she approached them, but she drew him back with a smile. "Stay and hear my news. I'm going to be baptized, it's all arranged. Neil's baptizing me Saturday."

She danced close and put her arms around Andrew, kissing him softly on the cheek. "I'm so happy," she whispered. She turned to

Brad. "I hope you're not planning to leave. I'd like you and Jennie to be here for my baptism."

Brad cleared his throat. "Do you mean that, Janet?"

"Yes," she cried. "I've grown very fond of Jennie and the children. They're part of the family. It would be wrong of you to take them away." She walked closer and put out her hand in a shy, gentle manner. "I've come to respect you these last few weeks," she told him. "I'd like to apologize; I'd like to be friends."

He took the small, warm hand in his own. "Thank you, Janet. It would be an honor to be your friend."

She smiled. "I must go now and tell Nan and Jennie. You're the first ones I've told."

She whisked away from them, like a bright sprite of the morning. Andrew smiled a long, warm smile. "Welcome home, Brad," he said.

There was one last thing remaining to be done and Brad knew it. Perhaps no one else may be aware, but he knew. He drove Friday morning into Glasgow, to Edwin's flat. It was very early; he hoped he might find him there. When Edwin answered the door and saw who it was he cocked his head and the old roguish smile tugged at the corner of his mouth.

"Mine old enemy at my door," he cried. "To what do I owe this honor? If you've come to send me on another difficult quest, please spare me. I am not yet fully recovered from the last . . ." He paused. Brad was uncomfortable, and he could tell it. "Do come in," he said, standing back.

Brad entered. He took the seat Edwin offered. "What can I do to help you?" Edwin began. "You *are* here for a reason."

"I'm glad you said it that way," Brad replied, "because I do need your help."

Edwin raised an inquisitive eyebrow.

"I've accepted Andrew's offer to stay in Scotland and work in the business." Edwin felt a rush of conflicting emotions: a little stab of jealous pain—this man working with Andrew, part of the mills, part of Bieldmor as *he* used to be—and also a warm sense of relief.

He'd been carrying a nasty burden of guilt around since the trial. He was happy how things had turned out; he would not change them. But the American had been left rather high and dry.

"You're a fortunate man, then," Edwin responded.

"I know that. There's no greater family on the earth than your family, Edwin."

"Here, here, I don't claim them—or, I should say, they don't claim me."

"That's the very reason I'm here," Brad said. "And I'm not clever, and I don't know how to put it nicely. There's a big dinner at Bieldmor Saturday—a celebration of sorts—"

"Celebration?" Edwin was a little taken aback at the idea. Brad smiled, almost apologetically.

"Janet's being baptized into the Church. And then there's my working with Andrew—my staying." He took a deep breath. "I want you to come. I want you and Julie to be there."

"Out of the question, my boy." Edwin rose in a nervous manner. "I appreciate the sentiment—"

"You don't understand. It's your right to be there, Edwin. It's also your duty."

That stopped Edwin, at least for the moment. Brad took a deep breath and went on. "Let's be open. You have what you want; so do I. On my part there are no hard feelings. I wanted to know who I was; I wanted desperately to find my family, to fit in somewhere. I have that and more, much more." He paused and a smile flickered playfully at his lips. He twisted the large diamond ring on his finger. "I even have this."

"Whatever do you mean?" Edwin asked, but his eyes had grown wary and his face a little pale.

"You know what I mean. The day of the trial—that ring they examined—that wasn't my ring! As soon as I looked at it closely myself, I knew. I don't know what you did, or when, or how you did it—"

Edwin inclined his head. "That's right, lad, you never will."

Brad nodded. "I'm sure you're right. But that doesn't matter. I have my own ring back now." He touched it lovingly. "There are little things: small nicks and scratches and worn spots—I can tell the difference."

"That's good. A man ought to be able to identify his own property."

Brad smiled. "You're an amazing character, Edwin. Don't you see, all that went before doesn't matter now. It's as though the trunk of a great old tree has been rent in two. That's not good. It destroys both the strength and the beauty."

Edwin nodded slowly. "I know what you're saying . . . I know. . . . Such a rift—do you think it can ever be mended?"

"Oh, yes. When the tree is still strong and living, yes."

Edwin walked the space of the room and then back again. Brad held his breath. At last he stopped and fixed his blue eyes on Brad's face. There was something in the gaze that drew Brad, something he'd never seen there before.

"Saturday. What time?" Edwin asked.

"Seven."

"Seven." He seemed to be mulling something very slowly in his mind. "I have more to think about than myself now," he said slowly. "I promised . . ." He smiled very slightly. "All right. I'll be there. Julie and I will be there by seven."

Brad rose. He didn't know what to do or say. He walked to the door. As he reached it Edwin held out his hand. "Thank you, Brad Richards." Brad took his hand and shook it warmly.

The blue gaze held him still. "You're a better man, a far better man than I."

Brad walked down the stairs. He remembered the last time he left here, the empty, hopeless feeling he'd brought away. So much that seemed bitter and tragic had happened. But was it, really? Who would have thought that out of such darkness and suffering could come this day?

At ten minutes to seven Saturday evening the doorbell rang. Andrew went to answer it; Brad trailed a few yards behind. When Andrew saw Edwin he was speechless. Brad, coming up beside him, winked and smiled.